He'd bec ...
that one awful moment.

Someone Laura would run from if she had met
him on a dark street. The image bothered her.
During the past few weeks, she had allowed
herself to forget what Connor was trained to
do—Connor the cop had been replaced in her
mind by Connor the man, a man she respected.

A man she could easily love.

But was the real Connor gentle or violent,
compassionate or ruthless, tender or cruel?

Dear Reader,

Hot weather, hot books. What could be better?
This month, Intimate Moments starts off with an
American Hero to remember in Kathleen Korbel's
Simple Gifts. This award-winning author has—as
usual!—created a book that you won't be able to put
down. You also might have noticed that the cover of
this particular book looks a little bit different from our
usual. We'll be doing some different things with some
of our covers from time to time, and I hope you'll keep
your eye out for that. Whenever you see one of our out-
of-the-ordinary covers, you can bet the book will be out
of the ordinary, too.

The month keeps going in fine form, with *Flynn*,
the next installment of Linda Turner's tremendously
popular miniseries, "The Wild West." Then check out
Knight's Corner, by Sibylle Garrett, and *Jake's Touch*,
by Mary Anne Wilson, two authors whose appearances
in the line are always greeted with acclaim. Finally, look
for two authors new to the line. Suzanne Brockmann
offers *Hero Under Cover*, while Kate Stevenson gives
you *A Piece of Tomorrow*.

I'd also like to take this chance to thank those of you
who've written to me, sharing your opinions of the line.
Your letters are one of my best resources as I plan for
the future, so please feel free to keep letting me know
what you think about the line and what you'd like to
see more of in the months to come.

As always—enjoy!

Leslie Wainger
Senior Editor and Editorial Coordinator

Please address questions and book requests to:
Reader Service
U.S.: P.O. Box 1325, Buffalo, NY 14269
Canadian: P.O. Box 1050, Niagara Falls, Ont. L2E 7G7

A PIECE OF TOMORROW

Kate Stevenson

Silhouette®

INTIMATE MOMENTS®

Published by Silhouette Books

America's Publisher of Contemporary Romance

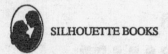 SILHOUETTE BOOKS

ISBN 0-373-07576-6

A PIECE OF TOMORROW

Copyright © 1994 by Kathleen F. Williams

This edition published by arrangement with Harlequin Enterprises B. V.

® and TM are trademarks of Harlequin Enterprises B. V., used under license. Trademarks indicated with ® are registered in the United States Patent and Trademark Office, the Canadian Trade Marks Office and in other countries.

Printed in U.S.A.

KATE STEVENSON

got hooked on romance novels after reading *Gone with the Wind* to fulfill a high school history requirement, but it wasn't until her two children started school that she began writing her own. Kate lives at the foot of the Colorado Rockies with her husband and two unruly cats, and keeps busy teaching and writing about "what makes the world go round—romance."

For those who supported me—Colorado Romance
Writers, my family and friends—and for my
husband, Rick, who believed.
With special thanks to Rob Bresciani, Boulder
Juvenile Probation, and Tim Perkins, Longmont
Police Force.

Chapter 1

It was the break he'd been waiting for.

Eyes fixed on the television screen, Connor McCormack watched a dark-haired youth slip from the shadows, glance right and left, then saunter to a late-model sedan at the edge of the motel parking lot. The camera zoomed in on the license plate and held for a moment before the car glided away.

The screen went gray. Connor absently smoothed the report on his desk and waited for the picture to resume. The tape held no surprises; he'd played it so many times that he could recite the unfolding sequence of events without looking. No, its fascination lay in the actors—or more exactly, one actor.

The static cleared, revealing the same dark-haired teenager at a picnic table outside a Mexican fast-food restaurant. Connor's finger tensed over the remote control as the camera lens moved to the youth's companion.

Hitting the Pause button, Connor leaned back in his chair and examined the slightly blurred face on the screen—blond, smooth cheeked, deceptively youthful.

The key.

It was a gut feeling, intuition. The same feeling that ferreted out lies, cautioned him of danger and ultimately told him when to go for it. No self-respecting cop ignored gut feelings, and Connor was nothing if not a good cop. Instinct told him he was right; the report in front of him confirmed it.

Approaching footsteps echoed in the hall, and he swung to greet the thin bearded man who entered the office.

"Paydirt," Joe announced as he opened a metal wall cabinet and deposited cameras and a briefcase on an empty shelf. He relocked the door and tossed Connor a small plastic bag. "Nearly an eight ball."

Connor weighed the cocaine in one hand, agreeing that it felt like eight ounces. "Any problems?"

Joe pulled a paper headed Colorado Bureau of Investigation from a cubbyhole and began filling it out. "Nah. My snitch was a little nervous about wearing a wire, but everything went down like clockwork. Soon as we get the report back from CBI we should be able to move." Rounding his desk, Joe scooped up the bag and deposited it in an envelope with the completed form. He looked at the television screen and paused. "That your boy, Mac?"

"That's him—Ben Westing."

"Rather young."

"Old enough. Sixteen." Connor knew his tone was defensive. As a matter of general policy, narcs avoided using minors as informants, but this time he had no choice. It was Ben Westing or nothing. Opening a drawer, Connor dropped in the report. "I'm headed over to meet his probation officer."

"Too bad he's already in the system. Harder to cut a deal." Joe studied the teen's face. "Who's the P.O.?"

"A woman named Laura Douglass."

"Oh, geez."

With a punch of a finger, Connor ejected the tape and shut off the machine. "What's that mean? She some kind of dragon?"

"No..." Joe appeared to choose his words carefully. "Just...elusive. Very professional. A couple of the guys have tried to put the move on her, but she wouldn't bite."

Connor pictured a cool, icy blonde. "Good-looking?"

Joe grinned. "Let's just say that if I weren't a happily married man, I'd give her a tumble myself."

"If she's so hot, how come I haven't noticed her?"

"Not your type, Mac. Definitely not your type."

As he shoved the tape into its sleeve, Connor considered the sparse information and decided it didn't matter what Laura Douglass was like. "I can handle her."

"Good luck, Mac. You're going to need it."

Half an hour later, as he stood in the doorway to Laura Douglass's office, Connor tried to imagine what had sparked Joe's admiration of the woman. Bent over a file folder on her desk, she was as yet unaware of his presence, and he took the opportunity to catalog her assets: light hair—more brown than blond—that curved softly into a slender neck, high cheekbones, firm chin and a small nose that tilted slightly at the tip.

Interesting, but definitely not the stuff of which legends were made.

"Laura Douglass?"

Turning from her notes, she took off heavy-rimmed reading glasses. "Yes?"

Her lips parted around the word and her eyebrows arched in query above dark brown eyes, as liquid as melted chocolate. Connor felt as if he'd been slammed in the gut. From far off, he heard an echo of Joe's mocking laughter.

"Detective Connor McCormack, Boulder Police Department. I'd like to talk to you."

Laura wondered how he'd managed to get past the front desk. The receptionist rarely sent someone back without checking first, but then again, she was notoriously susceptible to good-looking males. And Detective McCormack was certainly that—if you went for rugged and muscular.

Her gaze slipped over his broad chest, his curly black hair and settled on his face. She blinked in surprise when she met his eyes—eyes that made her think of a windswept Colorado sky. Mesmerized, she realized only after a moment that he hadn't moved.

Heat rose in her cheeks as she recovered herself. She motioned him in, suddenly sensitive to the office's chaotic condition. Normally, she gave little thought to the disorder since she could lay a hand on any piece of information she needed within seconds, but now she wished she'd taken time to straighten things a bit. Shoving a strand of hair behind one ear, she covered her embarrassment by transferring folders from a plastic chair to the floor. "Here, sit down."

He eased himself gingerly into the seat, as though fearful it might collapse beneath his weight.

Not that he was heavy, she noted as he settled one foot on the opposite knee, causing the faded denim of his jeans to strain at the seams. Just . . . solid. There didn't appear to be an ounce of excess fat anywhere. She pictured him working out at a gym, sweat rolling off his straining muscles—

Filled with horror at the direction of her thoughts, Laura slammed the door on them. She'd always hated the way some men mentally undressed every woman they met, and here she was doing the same thing to McCormack. It was little consolation that such a thing had never happened before.

Hoping her voice wouldn't betray her discomfort, she asked, "What can I do for you?"

"I'm with Special Enforcement."

Special Enforcement? Alarm skittered through her. The Special Enforcement division dealt primarily with drugs. Surely, none of her clients... Telling herself not to jump to conclusions, she crossed her legs and spoke with practiced unconcern. "Is one of my kids in trouble, Detective McCormack?"

His gaze moved from the swell of her calf to her face. "Not as far as I know."

"Then what, exactly—"

"I need your help." He smiled in an obvious attempt to set her at ease.

The smile was disarming, and for the span of a heartbeat, Laura fell prey to its seductive spell before reason gained the upper hand.

"*My* help?" She straightened in her chair. The probation department rarely worked with the police; her job took over when the police and court system were through. "Surely, Detective McCormack, you're aware that probation files are confidential. If you want information—" Interrupted by an emphatic shake of his head, she regarded him with confusion.

Connor eyed her speculatively, then seemed to come to a decision. He leaned forward. "You have a kid—Ben Westing—on your files, right?"

She nodded, distrustful of the direction he was taking.

"On probation for breaking and entering?"

She was instantly alarmed. What did Special Enforcement want with Ben?

One of her newest probation cases, Ben had managed to touch a responsive chord in her from the start in spite of his wary, flippant attitude. She wasn't green enough to believe he was falsely convicted, but she'd known instinctively that he was salvageable. In Ben, Laura saw her brother, Jared, and she was determined to give Ben the chance Jared never had.

"You've obviously done your homework."

The stiffness of her reply didn't seem to faze McCormack a bit. Indeed, he continued as though she hadn't spoken. "What do you know about his family situation?"

Laura bristled. He said he wasn't after information, but his questions suggested otherwise. "Detective McCormack, until I know why you're here, I can't—"

"Drug trafficking."

If he expected her to be startled, he was in for a big disappointment. With supreme confidence she said, "Ben is not mixed up in drugs."

"How can you be so sure?"

"Nothing in his records indicates use, and his urine analyses show no trace of substance abuse."

He nodded. "That fits with my information."

"Then, I don't understand . . ."

"Ben Westing could be useful in a case I'm investigating."

"Absolutely not!"

A sound of annoyance escaped Connor's lips. "You haven't even heard what I have to say."

"I said no, detective. You are *not* going to involve one of my kids in some harebrained scheme. Now, if that's all, I have a client waiting."

From the set of his jaw, Laura deduced that her response didn't sit well, but instead of arguing further, he merely glanced at the clock over the desk.

"Look," he said reasonably, "I understand your hesitation, but the least you can do is give me some time to explain. What if I take you to lunch after your appointment?"

"I already have plans."

"One hour. That's all I ask."

"I won't change my mind."

Under his brooding gaze, Laura prepared for an extended battle, but something in her manner must have convinced him she meant what she said. To her surprise, he shrugged and gave in.

"You can't blame me for trying."

This time, Laura refused to be taken in by his boyish grin, though a vague suspicion nagged at her as he said goodbye. He'd accepted defeat too quickly, too easily, and that didn't fit with the picture she'd formed of him during their brief encounter.

She stared at the empty doorway, her unease growing, along with the certainty that she hadn't seen the last of Connor McCormack.

The midday September sunlight fell warm on Connor's back, soaking through his T-shirt. Drops of sweat cooled his forehead as he jogged, his legs and arms pumping steadily.

After the aborted attempt to win the probation officer's support this morning, he'd casually questioned several of his fellow officers and found out that when the weather was nice, she ate lunch down by Boulder Creek.

Fate was with him, he decided. Weather permitting, he ran the creek path every day at lunchtime. It was a way of relieving the stress of his job, giving him time to think. But today his run served an additional purpose—Laura Douglass.

His approach had been wrong, he realized. She'd become defensive and obstinate. But he wouldn't make the same mistake again.

Patience was the key to winning her cooperation.

He wasn't normally a patient man, but years with the force had taught him the value of a calm exterior. The kind of assignments he worked on were not conducive to quick, easy solutions; if you didn't learn to consciously relax once in a while, you invariably ended up with ulcers or worse. He'd learned the lesson well. When the need arose, he could be as patient as the proverbial cat stalking a mouse.

His steady pace carried him under the bridge at Ninth Street, and he checked his watch. Twelve fifty-five. Another couple of minutes would bring him back to the Justice Center. There, if the luck of the Irish was with him, he'd find Laura at one of the picnic tables.

He pictured her in his mind. Her body curved softly in all the right places, and he'd liked the way her soft, dark honey hair framed the oval of her face. But, surprisingly, it was the sharp intelligence in her deep brown eyes that had drawn his attention. No, she wasn't at all what he'd expected.

In Connor's experience, probation officers fell into two categories—the young, idealistic ones who were going to "save the children," and the older, more hardened group, made cynical by countless failures. This woman didn't seem to slip neatly into either slot. Though she appeared to be not much older than some of the kids she worked with, she had an aura of determination and self-confidence that usually came with maturity.

Emotions flashed across her face like news bulletins, and he hadn't missed her reaction to the mention of Ben Westing. Apparently, the boy meant more to her than just another wayward juvenile. Connor knew that most probation officers, despite their attempts to remain objective, at one time or another were drawn to special clients. Hell, everyone got too close to a case once in a while, even cops. In this instance, it was going to make his job a little tougher. But Laura Douglass was not the only person with determination. Connor possessed it in abundance.

This time, he was determined to turn on all the charm at his disposal. After all, he was Irish, albeit two generations removed from the Old Country. Hadn't his grandmother always told him he could have been born under the Blarney Stone, such was his gift of flattery. A smile tugged the corners of his mouth as he recalled how the indignation on her face used to melt into laughter before he was halfway through with an elaborate excuse for one of his teenage pranks.

He sobered, thinking of the case. This was not a game. It was deadly adult business, and the people involved weren't carefree teenagers. His jaw muscles knotted. He had worked too long to let anyone stand in his way, even Laura Douglass. Maybe Ben Westing was an innocent bystander, but it made no difference. Connor needed him. The risks for the boy were minimal, but Connor's gains could be immense. With the probation officer's help, Connor would reach Ben, and through him, break the drug ring wide open.

Shoes slapping purposefully against the pavement, Connor passed under Third Street. Ahead loomed the gray concrete building that was his destination. He smiled grimly. First things first. Round two was about to begin.

Laura, engrossed in her book, registered the sound of an approaching jogger on the nearby path without bothering to look up. She took another bite of her apple and flipped the page.

"Hello."

Raising her head, she made out the blurred figure of a man cutting across the slope. When she lowered her glasses, details sprang into sharp relief, and she recognized Connor McCormack striding toward her.

"Hi," she responded, hoping her unenthusiastic tone would discourage him.

No such luck. He flopped down across from her and leaned back against the table, arms stretched along the top, his legs thrust out before him. Shoulders rose and fell as he drew in ragged gulps of air. She stared at the black hair clinging wetly to the back of his neck, nearly touching his T-shirt. An almost tangible wave of male energy radiated from him.

Laura shivered and took another bite of apple. Pushing her glasses back up her nose, she returned her attention to her book. For some reason she had difficulty concentrating on the words. When the glasses took their inevitable slide downward, she risked another peek over them.

"Enjoying the sun?" he asked, slanting a look across one shoulder. Her breath caught in her throat when his sea blue gaze captured hers.

Nodding speechlessly, she returned his infectious grin.

"Good." He stood and peeled off his T-shirt, using it to wipe the moisture from his body. Her fascinated gaze followed the impromptu towel's path across his face and muscled chest, down to the elastic of his navy running shorts.

With a snap she closed her book and removed her glasses. She focused her attention on the creek, to no avail. Short of turning her back, she couldn't ignore him. All her nerve endings seemed to be on alert.

"Do you run often?"

"Almost every day." His muffled voice came from beneath the T-shirt he was now using to scrub vigorously at his hair. "When the weather's bad, I walk instead."

"Why haven't I seen you before?" she wondered aloud, a knife edge of suspicion wedging itself between her words.

The wadded shirt landed on the far end of the table. Lifting first one leg, then the other, over the wooden bench, Connor sat down and rested his elbows on the tabletop. He used his fingers to comb unruly hair back from his face.

"I don't know. Maybe because I usually run before lunch. Today, an appointment held me up." He met her penetrating look with an innocent expression. "But I'm glad it did. I may just start taking a later lunch hour on a regular basis." He smiled impishly.

Though Laura was almost certain this meeting had been arranged, she couldn't resist his banter. "I was just thinking about an *earlier* lunch," she countered, then laughed aloud at his exaggerated look of disappointment.

As she raised her soda to her lips, she caught a covetous look on Connor's face. Lifting her eyebrows questioningly, she offered it to him.

"Thanks," he said and took a deep swallow.

Laura waved him off when he tried to return the drink. "I've had enough."

"Sure?" The can halted partway to his mouth.

"Positive."

Throwing back his head, he drained it.

A squirrel chittered at them as it raced up a nearby evergreen. Laura followed its progress along a branch, grateful for the chance to focus on something besides the man across from her. In a matter of moments, a clump of pine cones fell to the ground and the rodent scurried back to claim his prize.

"Winter must be coming early," she announced as they watched the squirrel pack his cheeks and race into the underbrush.

"Oh, I doubt that squirrels and woolly bears are any more reliable predictors of weather than the National Weather Service."

"O ye of little faith."

Connor chuckled. The sound curled in the air and grazed her ears as she struggled unsuccessfully to keep a straight face.

"So, Laura Douglass," he questioned as her mirth subsided, "how long have you been in Boulder?"

Laura couldn't help but notice how his chiseled lips softened beneath the smile. "I grew up here—graduated from Boulder High and went directly to Colorado University."

"Where you graduated with honors in sociology and criminal justice," he guessed.

She laughed. "Not quite. My degree was in accounting."

"Then how did you end up in probation?"

"Two years of volunteer work and night classes. A long, boring story," she assured him.

"I doubt that anything about you is boring."

The ambiguity of his words unsettled her. So too, did the intensity of his glance. Laura shook her head. "There's not enough time." She busied her hands with the task of cleaning up the table, reminding herself that she had never been attracted to men such as Connor McCormack. He was too... She cast around without success for the right word.

The sound of his voice cut across her thoughts. "Guess I'd better get back to work." He rose, pulling his T-shirt over his head, then paused to regard her in a hesitant manner. Seeming to make up his mind about something, he asked, "Would you have dinner with me tonight?"

Again she was forced to shake her head. "I have a class right after work—pottery."

"Then how about coffee? After your class."

"It'll be late, and I have to get up early."

"Just one hour. Anyway, I owe you." At her puzzled look, he explained, "For the soda."

Laura couldn't suppress a smile in response to his guile-less expression. "Okay."

Agreeing to meet at nine in a small café near where her class was held, Connor left her to collect her things.

Just one hour. The same thing he'd said this morning. She narrowed her eyes and watched him jog away, suspicion dousing the warm glow in her chest.

Suddenly she felt duped.

Chapter 2

All through pottery class, while pounding and shaping and smoothing the bowl she was working on, Laura argued with herself. The more she thought about Connor's invitation, the less she trusted his motives.

She wasn't his type. She couldn't say how she knew this, but she did. Just as she could tell Connor was a beer-and-pretzel man, she knew his kind of woman would be blond and vivacious and just a little flamboyant, not tailored and—she cringed as her father's favorite word of praise sprang to mind—sensible. No, Connor wasn't attracted. He merely wanted to plead his case about Ben.

She wouldn't go.

Purposefully, she ignored a twinge of regret and managed to block the detective from her thoughts for the rest of the two-hour session. It wasn't until she left the building that she questioned her decision.

She knew her first appraisal of Connor was right—he was not a man to give up easily. She'd lived too many years under her father's thumb to not recognize the signs. Determined. Single-minded in pursuit of what he wanted. Riding roughshod over anyone in his way.

Keys in hand, she stopped beside her car and tried to ignore the sinking feeling in her stomach. Experience told her a confrontation with Connor was inevitable. If not tonight, then tomorrow or the next day.

Get it over with now.

For an instant longer, she hesitated before common sense won out. Slipping her keys into her pocket, she straightened her shoulders and headed downtown. She would make it clear to Connor she wouldn't budge from her position, and he would have to drop the matter.

She hurried along the Pearl Street Mall, her shoes whispering against the brick pavement. In the daytime the area rang with voices and laughter as people wound their way along its three-block length, skirting flowerbeds and wooden benches, kiosks and food wagons. At night the mall wore a different face—subdued and mysterious. Patches of light pooled beneath the street lamps, pushing ineffectually against the darkness. From the shadows came the muted conversation of an occasional group of street people. She checked the art deco clock high on the tower of the old courthouse. Fifteen minutes late.

Laura entered the café and scanned the dimly lighted room, half-hoping, yet half-afraid, that Connor had given up waiting. A hand movement drew her attention to a booth in the far corner, and her heart skittered. Nerves, she told herself. Nodding in acknowledgment, she threaded through the maze of tables and slid onto the red vinyl seat across from him.

"Sorry I'm late."

"I was afraid you'd changed your mind."

A slanted grin softened his words, but Laura felt another twinge of guilt, anyway. Did he read minds? "Of course not. I just ran late." She brushed an imaginary crumb from the checked tablecloth. "I hope you didn't have to wait too long."

"No problem," he replied. "Would you like coffee or something cold?"

"Coffee's fine."

Connor crossed the room and spoke to the girl behind the counter, who set about filling the order while chatting animatedly. Laura was too far away to hear what was being said, but it was evident the girl was flirting with him. Laura brushed aside a stab of irritation, assuring herself it was the blonde's fluttering eyelashes and loud laugh that set her teeth on edge and not Connor's indulgent attention. It certainly made no difference to Laura *who* he smiled at. To prove the point, she looked away, her gaze passing over a group of noisy college students and settling on a bearded man who crumbled crackers into a bowl of soup, his eyes never leaving the pages of his book.

Another inane giggle drifted from the direction of the cash register.

Laura's resolve wavered, and she glanced at the counter in time to see Connor turn, shoving change into the pocket of his skin-tight jeans. Her mouth went dry, and she hastily shifted her gaze upward.

Their eyes met.

A quiver raced along Laura's spine, settling in the pit of her stomach, as he made his way toward her, and for the space of a heartbeat she forgot why she was there and imagined they were two ordinary people attracted to each other.

Somewhere in the room, a fork clattered against a plate.

Startled from her reverie, Laura blinked and looked away. A small lump of wistfulness formed in her chest. If only they were meeting under different circumstances. If only his interest wasn't based on a desire to use Ben. If only...

With an effort of will, she focused on the tray Connor set on the table. Next to mugs of steaming coffee rested two gigantic wedges of hot apple pie, topped with generous scoops of ice cream. Connor positioned one of the plates under her nose. "I told the waitress you were a *big* eater," he confided, "so act starved."

In spite of herself, her mouth watered. Seizing the diversion, she managed to reply in near-normal tones, "That won't be difficult. I haven't eaten since lunch."

She cut into the pie and raised a steaming forkful to her lips, her eyelids closing in unfeigned ecstasy as her taste buds blossomed beneath the combination of cinnamon, apple and cream. Chewing slowly, then swallowing, she uttered a sigh of contentment.

"Good?"

Laura felt heat rise to her cheeks when she met his glance. "Sorry," she said. "I got carried away."

Connor nodded thoughtfully, though his lips twitched in amusement. "Grandma was right, after all. She always insisted that the way to a woman's heart was through her stomach."

"I believe it's the way to a *man's* heart," corrected Laura.

"Not according to Grandma."

Laura conceded defeat. "Your grandmother sounds very wise."

"That she was."

Laura's laughter rippled between them, and Connor felt a responding tug of attraction. Laura was a damned appealing woman. Too appealing. Without her spiky professional armor, she made him forget his reasons for being there. And that was dangerous. He had a job to do, and the last thing he needed was emotional interference. Like the moment when he'd caught her staring at him from across the room. Talk about sparks. No, sparks was too mild a term for the inferno she'd ignited in him. If he didn't watch himself... He took a deep swallow of coffee, then lifted his fork and motioned at her. "Go ahead. Enjoy."

Scarcely tasting the food, he cleaned his plate and shoved it away. He took a last gulp from his mug, though the strong brew did little to combat his fatigue. It had been a long day, and he didn't relish the task still before him.

Rubbing his stiff neck, he noted that Laura didn't appear to be the least bit tired. Beneath the scarf-draped lamp over their table, glints of gold and red danced in her pale brown hair and her face glowed. He suddenly wanted to run a finger along her cheek to see if the skin was as smooth as it looked.

Laura laid her fork across her plate. "Thank you. It was just what I needed."

Abruptly, Connor pulled his thoughts away from her up-tilted nose and generous mouth. It didn't matter what she looked like or how she made him feel. He was a cop, and it was time to come to the point of this meeting. "Can we talk about Ben now?"

Her smile faded. Her expression took on a closed, guarded quality.

Damn, he thought. But he was tired of pussyfooting around. Crenshaw was on his back—the D.A.'s office was getting tired of waiting. He needed results or he'd be pulled off the case, and he wasn't about to let someone else come in and wreck everything he'd built so carefully.

"Just listen. I'm not out to hurt your boy."

Studying his face intently, she finally gave a curt nod.

"I told you this morning I'm with narcotics and have a special interest in Ben Westing."

She was silent.

"Well, he has a cousin—Todd Billings—who lives with him and his father."

"Lived."

"Pardon me?"

"Todd had a disagreement with Ben's father and moved out a week ago." Her words were clipped, as though she was being careful not to reveal more than necessary.

The news came as a surprise, though Connor let none of it show on his face. Without adequate manpower, he couldn't be expected to know everything, but it rankled that he'd missed such an obvious point. He consoled himself with the thought that where Todd was living made little difference. The boys had been observed together just yesterday, so he doubted the move had severed relations between the cousins.

He nodded and continued as though she hadn't spoken. "We've been watching Todd for some time now—ever since he came to Boulder last summer, as a matter of fact."

Laura's expression remained neutral, but the mere fact that she betrayed no surprise told Connor that she knew, or at least suspected, what he was about to say.

"We believe he's mixed up in drug trafficking."

"If that's the case, then why don't you arrest him?"

Connor's reply was blunt. "Because he's small potatoes. Sure, we could arrest every two-bit dealer we run across, but that wouldn't solve the problem. We're after bigger game."

"And in the meantime, the sales go on and more kids die."

Startled by the bitterness in her voice, he regarded her grimly set mouth and the white knuckles wrapped around her coffee mug. Was Ben Westing using? No, Connor thought, answering his own question. Laura Douglass didn't seem the kind of person to look the other way if one of her kids violated probation.

"That's why I want Ben."

"I told you, Ben's clean. He's a good kid."

"Good kids aren't convicted of breaking and entering," Connor pointed out.

"But he—"

Interrupting, Connor laced his voice with sarcasm. "Oh, yeah. He was probably only serving as lookout—" he paused, giving emphasis to his next words "—*this* time."

Though her look was mutinous, she allowed him to go on without contradiction.

"The kid's running with a pretty fast crowd."

"Not anymore!"

"What makes you so sure of that?"

"He told me."

"And you believe him?"

A twinge of shame shot through him when she visibly flinched, but he refused to let it deter him. Marshmallows didn't make good narcs. "Has he named names?"

She reluctantly shook her head.

"What about Todd?"

"Todd's his cousin. Ben wouldn't—"

"I've yet to see blood make a difference when drugs are involved."

"You don't understand!" The harshness in her voice rivaled his. "He made a mistake, and he's willing to pay for it. But he's not a bad kid."

"Then let him prove it. If he's as determined as you say to make amends, he should be eager to cooperate."

Laura stared at him with exasperation.

Connor was not reassured by her lack of response. If anything, it made him nervous. Abruptly he decided to change tactics, sensing that he'd pushed her as far as he dared.

"Laura," he said gently, leaning forward. "Given the influence Todd has over him, it's only a matter of time before he gets into worse trouble."

Her stricken look told him he'd hit his mark and triggered her own secret fears for the boy.

"He wouldn't..."

Connor nodded, refuting her argument before the words were spoken. Laura blanched and stared into the mug clutched between her hands. Her distress was so poignant that for an instant Connor relaxed from his role and reached out to comfort her. Beneath his hand, he felt her fingers stiffen, then she pulled away.

Her rejection stung more than he cared to admit, especially since his gesture was well meant. But it was just as well, he told himself. He had no business going soft over her feelings. Only an idiot failed to learn from past mistakes, and he was no idiot. The job was all that counted. With renewed determination, he spoke. "Ben's headed for a fall."

Laura's jaw tightened. Drawing air deep into her lungs, she seemed to gather a cloak of calmness around her. When she raised her head, her eyes were bright with determination.

"You don't know him, Detective McCormack. I do." He opened his mouth, but she rushed on before he could speak. "Ben is not going to get into any more trouble—not his own, and definitely not yours."

Annoyance tightened his jaw. "I don't expect there to be any trouble, at least not for Ben. He'll merely be a source of information, a pipeline through which we can keep a closer eye on his cousin. No danger."

"You expect me to believe that? What if someone found out? How safe would Ben be then?"

"Nothing will go wrong." Connor spoke with confidence. "I guarantee it."

"There aren't any guarantees in life."

Her answer raised the hairs on his neck. The face of a man—Old Sam—rose unbidden in Connor's mind, together with the memory of Sam's lifeless body being hauled from an abandoned mine shaft. Connor shook himself mentally. There was no connection between Sam's death and the information he sometimes passed to Connor in exchange for a few bucks for booze. Just a stupid accident.

Masking his irritation with Laura behind lowered lids, Connor dropped his voice to a deceptive low. "I don't need your cooperation, Miss Douglass. I just thought you might want to make things easier for him."

Her eyes widened, then narrowed, piercing him with a look of utter contempt as the threat hit home. Pressing her lips together, she rose and reached into her hip pocket. "Thanks for the company." A five-dollar bill floated to the table.

Pigheaded woman, thought Connor, watching her march stiff backed from the café. He drained his mug. *You may have won the battle, Laura Douglass, but the war is not over yet.*

Sleep proved elusive. Perhaps it was the coffee or perhaps the dessert. Or just maybe it was the sound of a little voice that kept telling her she'd botched the meeting with McCormack. Whatever the cause, Laura spent the night fighting the covers and warding off her pillow.

The bathroom mirror revealed dark smudges beneath her eyes that makeup did little to conceal. Connor's words returned to haunt her. *"Only a matter of time…running with a fast crowd…"*

As much as she disliked the man's bluntness, his words had a ring of truth. She had already decided that Todd Billings was a poor influence on Ben. The younger boy's devotion to his cousin bordered on hero worship. Todd's faults were overlooked, his excesses excused. Where Todd was concerned, Ben turned a blind eye. Laura strongly suspected Todd was the reason for Ben's running afoul of the law. Who else could convince the basically clear-minded boy to participate in a robbery? As far as she could see, there was no other person Ben felt such loyalty for that he would remain silent and accept full blame.

Laura didn't trust Todd's actions or his motives. Face it, she didn't trust *Todd*.

Dragging a brush through her hair, she tried unsuccessfully to clear her mind for the day ahead.

What if Todd led Ben into a worse situation?

Her hand stilled. The sound of moist earth scattered across Jared's closed coffin rang in her ears. Four years ago she'd consoled herself with the thought that there was nothing the family could have done to prevent her brother's death. He'd chosen his own self-destructive path. But doubt remained.

Tears blurred her vision. They'd failed with Jared, and that sense of failure had propelled her from an established career as an accountant to the less lucrative field of probation work. Jared was dead. But there were others who deserved a chance—others like Ben.

Laura swiped the tears away from her eyes, then tried to concentrate on applying shadow and lip gloss. Memories of Jared only increased her uncertainty. Was she really doing what was best for Ben by refusing to let Connor talk with him? Or was she merely bullheaded?

Indecision continued to plague her as she entered her office at eight-thirty and checked the calendar. Juvenile Court

convened on Friday mornings, and she noted that she
needed to appear concerning the Simmons boy. With a
flicker of guilt for putting things off, she pushed her con-
cerns about Ben to the back of her mind and grabbed a
notepad before hurrying down the narrow hall to Courtroom E.

As usual, the room was packed. She eased into an empty
seat at the end of the back row and directed her attention to
the bench, where Judge Wycliff questioned a somber young
girl before sentencing her to probation for shoplifting.
While the next juvenile on the list made his way to the
bench, Laura surreptitiously watched a long-haired teenager and his parents across the way. The boy's face bore an
expression of indifference that she found disconcerting when
contrasted with his mother's worried look and his father's
barely concealed anger. Laura studied the teenager closely
and realized he wasn't as unconcerned as he appeared;
darting eyes and a clenched jaw gave him away.

Two auto thefts and a malicious mischief charge later,
Laura's case was called. She briefly explained her client's
history of drug abuse and stated her position. "Your Honor,
this boy has run away from home and the group shelter
where he was assigned. I feel it is imperative that he be
placed in a secure facility if rehabilitation is to prove effec-
tive."

Judge Wycliff conferred in undertones with one of the
social workers before turning back to the courtroom. Her
serious expression was eloquent. It took little imagination
to guess what the decision would be.

"I'm inclined to agree with your view, Ms. Douglass.
Unfortunately, I'm informed that there are no beds available at Cleo Wallace, so I'll have to rule that the boy be returned to the group home for the present." Seeming to sense
Laura's frustration, she added, "However, I will recom-

mend that he be transferred at the first opportunity. It's the best we can do right now."

In spite of her disappointment, Laura kept her expression impassive. She thanked the judge and returned to the probation department. The receptionist greeted her with a fresh pile of phone messages, at the same time apologizing for the added load she'd assigned Laura. "I'm sorry, but with so many people out with the flu, there's no help for it."

Connor McCormack's name leaped out from one of the pink message slips. Besides the name, phone number and time, there was only the terse message "Call me."

Laura tucked the paper behind two others and addressed the receptionist. "Give me fifteen minutes, and I'll start on the first intake."

Entering her office, Laura closed the door and plopped into her chair. She shuffled through the phone messages, then placed the pile in the exact center of her desk with Connor's on top. She glared at the offending paper.

When had black and white begun to blur, like an out-of-focus photo, into a muddy gray? The detective was wrong to want to use Ben against his cousin, but what if there was a grain of truth in his words? If Todd was as deeply involved in drug distribution and sales as the detective seemed to think, Ben's association with him could land him in jail or—a chill raised the hairs on the back of her neck—dead.

No matter what she decided, she was gambling with Ben's future.

Heaviness behind her eyes heralded an encroaching headache. Laura pressed fingertips against her lids, then massaged her temples in an attempt to blunt the dull pain forming there. A sudden thought stilled her hands. *The kid who refused to name names to save himself would never agree to play stoolie.* She pictured Ben's reaction to Connor's plan, and a small smile appeared on her face. The throbbing in her head eased.

Wetting her lips, she picked up the phone and dialed.

"Special Enforcement. Jones speaking."

"Detective McCormack, please."

"He's not in right now. Can I take a message?"

After all the agonizing she'd done, Laura didn't know whether to feel disappointed or relieved about not speaking directly to Connor. Relief won out. "Just tell him Laura Douglass called. I have an appointment with Ben at three o'clock and he can sit in on it."

Gently she replaced the receiver in its cradle. Connor could talk till he was blue in the face for all the good it would do him. Ben would refuse to cooperate, and Laura would back him up. Stalemate.

She stared at the blank wall before her. An image of Connor's ice blue eyes and hard mouth smiled grimly back at her. Abruptly she shook her head and hunched her shoulders to work out the crick in her neck. Then she glanced at the next slip in the pink pile. Repeating the number in her head, she pulled the phone closer and dialed.

Being a probation officer was good experience for telephone sales, she had once told her mother, only half jesting. The need for thorough information on every new probationer generated phone calls to schools, employers, relatives—anyone who could help flesh out the picture of the young offender—as well as calls to social services, counselors and community services. By a quarter to three, when Connor arrived, Laura's ear was numb and her head felt as if someone was tunneling through it with a pickax.

Connor responded to her crisp greeting with a disarming smile. "Thanks for letting me come."

"Did I have a choice?"

Last night should have prepared Connor for a cool reception, but for a brief span of time this afternoon, he'd allowed himself the hope that Laura had been swayed by his logic.

Apparently not. Whatever had changed her mind, it hadn't been his glib tongue. Well, it made no difference. He was here, and he planned to make the most of the opportunity.

"We all have choices," he replied, running a hand through his hair.

The skeptical twist of her lips and her raised eyebrows conveyed her disbelief louder than words and told him she didn't intend to give an inch. He admired her determination, however misguided. Too bad she didn't stand a chance of winning.

Leaning one shoulder against the door jamb, he looked around pointedly. "Where's the kid?"

"Before *Ben* gets here, I want to make a few things clear." Her gaze contained a challenge and something more—a veiled declaration of war. "First, no intimidation."

"Intimidation? As in big bad cop?"

"I'm serious." She glared at him, unamused by his attempt at levity. "If any threats are made, I'll terminate the discussion immediately."

He nodded, wondering from what TV show she'd gotten her ideas of police tactics. "Understood."

"And secondly," she continued, "any decision Ben makes will be final. You will not continue to badger him if he refuses to cooperate."

"Agreed. Is my word okay, or would you like it in writing?" He smiled pleasantly, knowing his easy capitulation would disconcert her.

Her eyes narrowed with suspicion, but the ringing phone forestalled any further comments. "Ben's here," she announced after a brief exchange. "I'll bring him back."

Connor nodded, allowing her to slip through the doorway. His gaze was drawn to the gentle sway of her hips as she disappeared down the corridor, leaving behind a light scent of citrus. Restless, he wandered across the room to scan the titles on the bookshelf, then moved to her desk where he studied a framed snapshot. A younger Laura and an adolescent boy laughed into the camera lens. Although the boy's hair was a much lighter shade than his sister's, Connor could see the family resemblance in their features and smiles. The photo made him think of his father at innumerable family gatherings, instructing his subjects to "Say cheese" while he recorded events for posterity.

Straightening, Connor moved to the doorway and peered down the empty hall. What was taking them so long? He swung around impatiently and recrossed the office. After months of useless contacts, leads that didn't pan out, he was sick of waiting. The kid *had* to be the key. His fingers found the reassuring presence of a small smooth stone in his hip pocket. Absently he turned it over and over as he paced a cramped circuit.

One teenage boy.

What could go wrong?

Anything.

Everything.

Footsteps echoed in the hall. Connor whirled, taut with anticipation. He forced himself to relax, willed the muscles of his rigid face to reflect a calmness he didn't feel.

Ben Westing was his second surprise in as many days. Irritation prickled beneath his skin as he observed the boy who dropped awkwardly into the seat beside the desk. In person, the kid bore little resemblance to the blurred tape image. Whatever he'd expected, it wasn't this lanky blond...child.

He looked like a damned choirboy.

Chapter 3

Surface. All a facade. Ben might fool Laura Douglass, but Connor knew better. Looks did not necessarily mirror the inner man. Shiny red apples sometimes harbored worms. He reminded himself that Billy the Kid and Ted Bundy had probably been beautiful children, too.

"I've explained to Ben who you are, Detective McCormack, and he's agreed to allow you to sit in on our appointment."

Somewhat smug, Laura's voice cut across Connor's musings. She was obviously determined to show that she was in charge. Well, he wouldn't burst her bubble just yet. He extended a hand. "Good to meet you, Ben."

Platinum hair fell across the teen's forehead as he mumbled a response. His fingers were limp within Connor's grasp.

"If you don't mind," Laura said in clipped tones, "we'll take care of the formalities first." Without waiting for a reply, she addressed Ben while Connor eased into the chair that gave him a clear view of the boy's face. "How're things at school?"

"Fine."

"No missed classes?"

"No."

"How about your community service? Did you bring your sheet with you?" Laura took the paper Ben handed her and made a notation in his file. For Connor's benefit, she explained, "Ben's working for Eco-Cycle on Saturdays."

Familiar with the county's restitution requirements for probationers, Connor nodded. But though he mentally filed each detail of the interview for further reference, a portion of his brain strayed to Laura—the soft curve of her cheek, the no-nonsense set of her chin and that damned elusive scent. He'd never smelled perfume like it before. Maybe it was her shampoo or bath soap. An image of her reclining in a tub caused him to fidget in his chair. With a harsh directive, he corralled his errant thoughts and focused on the conversation.

Laura referred to a note attached to Ben's folder. "Fred says you missed your counseling session this week."

"I didn't have a ride. Dad's out of town, and I'm not allowed to drive my car yet."

The excuse itself didn't surprise Connor, or the petulant tone in which it was uttered. Teenage boys always chafed at restrictions. But he did wonder how Laura would react.

"Ever heard of the bus?"

Not bad, Connor silently approved, stifling a grin at the quick comeback.

Ben squirmed. "I don't see why I have to see a shrink." Defiance crept into his voice. "It's a drag."

"Come on, Ben. You know it's one of the conditions laid down by the court. Not going could get your probation revoked." Her tone was casual, but Connor heard the scrape of steel beneath the statement. Apparently Ben did, too, because his lips thinned rebelliously.

"You *will* call Fred and reschedule?"

The boy met Laura's steady gaze, then looked away. After a moment, he nodded curtly.

Connor had to give her credit. She was good—understanding, sympathetic, but firm enough to assure an adolescent she meant business. He admired her ability to tread such a fine line. His guess was that she seldom allowed personal feelings to interfere with her job. Now, if she only accorded him the same courtesy...

"All right." Laura snapped the file shut. "Now it's Detective McCormack's turn." She smiled at Ben as if to reassure him. "Remember, he's here in an unofficial capacity. You don't have to agree to anything."

The battle lines were drawn—no holds barred. Connor narrowed his eyes, irritated that he'd let her lull him into thinking otherwise. She'd made her opinion clear from the beginning, and he'd been crazy to forget for even a moment.

No matter. He'd play it without her cooperation.

"Miss Douglass's right—you're not in any kind of trouble."

"I didn't think I was."

Ben's initial nervousness was gone, replaced by a calm detachment. Hazel eyes gazed with unconcern into Connor's. For a moment Connor caught a glimpse of what the arresting officers must have faced when they questioned the boy. Confronted by a narcotics officer, most teenagers would be scared spitless. Not Ben Westing. At sixteen, he had more sangfroid than many men twice his age.

The boy's composure told Connor all he needed to know. Frontal attacks and scare tactics were out. He didn't doubt for a second that Ben would react to them with disdain, if not amusement. No, another approach was needed. Connor squared one jeans-clad leg across the other, adopting an air of nonchalance. "Must be hard—people telling you what to do all the time."

"It's okay."

"Come on, get real," Connor scoffed. "I was a teenager. The last thing I would've wanted was someone in my face all the time."

Ben shrugged. "I manage."

"Yeah? Well, I guess I was different. Anything my parents wanted, I was dead set against. Figured they were out to spoil my fun, keep me a kid. Maybe yours aren't that way."

"Dad's okay."

"Must be nice. My old man was always yelling at me. Called me a smart-ass kid. Said I'd never amount to a hill of beans." Connor silently begged forgiveness for maligning Big Mac, who was known for controlling his temper under the most aggravating of circumstances, and there had been many.

"So..." Connor let the word hang in the air before casually dropping his next question. "If life's so good, how come you're on probation?"

A churlish expression settled over Ben's face. His eyes flickered toward Laura.

"Detective McCormack—"

Connor cut off Laura's warning. Without a glance in her direction, he continued to address Ben, his voice mocking. "Don't tell me—you got dumped on, huh?" He leaned forward, continuing in conspiratorial tones, "Don't worry. It happens to the best of us."

"No one dumped on me. It was *my* choice—"

"To take the fall?" Connor finished for him. "What'd you think—that you'd be some kind of hero?" He sneered in derision.

Ben's pinched lips gave evidence that Connor had struck a nerve. He glared at the detective, refusing to respond.

"Pretty stupid, if you ask me." Connor twisted the knife a little. "Your buddies are off scot-free while you're doing the time." Turning thoughtful, he fixed Ben with a bland look. "Of course, it makes sense if they're over eighteen. Why risk jail sentences when a minor will only get a slap on the wrist?"

"Probation is *not* a slap on the wrist." Laura was indignant. "It's a chance for a kid to make up for his mistakes and prove he wants to do better."

"Sure," Connor soothed, capitalizing on her swift defense of her profession. "And Ben here wants just that. Right, kid?"

Ben nodded warily, obviously uncertain where the conversation was leading.

Connor smiled to himself. It was going to be easier than he'd thought. Keep him off balance, throw out the bait and reel him in. A piece of cake, as long as Laura stayed out of things. "Don't worry," he assured the boy. "I'm not here to go over old ground. The burglary's history. I need your help on something else."

"My help?" Confusion flickered across Ben's face. "Laura said you were a narc."

"I am. That bother you?"

"No. I'm not into drugs."

"What? No experimenting with uppers? Never even smoked a little grass?"

"Now, just a minute!" snapped Laura. "I insist you stop this immediately. I did not give you permission to *interrogate* Ben."

Even knowing in advance that she wouldn't let him get by with it, Connor was irked at her interference. "Miss Douglass, a couple of innocuous questions can hardly be construed as an interrogation."

For several moments their gazes locked, hers flashing with displeasure, his carefully bland, as they battled for supremacy. Laura was the first to look away, her lips drawn into a thin line of annoyance.

"Just be careful how you phrase things," she warned.

"Right." He smiled, gracious in victory, and turned back to Ben, raising a questioning eyebrow. "Well?"

"No, sir."

"No, what?"

"I've never done drugs."

The kid was lying. "Good. Then you've got nothing to worry about." Connor paused just long enough to let Ben know he was aware of the lie before going on. "However . . . someone you know does."

"What do you mean? Who?"

"Todd."

At the mention of his cousin's name, Ben stiffened. "You're crazy, man."

"Afraid not. Todd's in over his head. He owes a lot of money, and they're pressing him."

"Who?"

"His suppliers."

White faced, Ben stared at Connor. "I don't believe you."

Hooked. Now all he had to do was reel him in. Connor shrugged, feigning disinterest. "No skin off my nose. Just thought you'd like to prevent a tragedy."

"Tragedy?" Ben echoed hoarsely.

"These guys don't take kindly to deadbeats. They play for keeps."

Ben's anxiety was almost a presence in the silent room. Gone was the cocky, self-confident mask. In its place was a frightened, unsure kid.

Connor refused to allow himself to feel remorse for his part in bringing about the change. It had to be done. Sometimes you had to play rough to win the game, and he was determined to win. Still, when Laura's hand crept out to cover Ben's in unspoken empathy, Connor avoided meeting her glance, knowing her eyes would be harsh and accusing.

Rising, Connor addressed Ben with nonchalance. "Well, I guess I have your answer. Let me know if you change your mind, kid."

"Detective McCormack."

Ben's voice halted him at the door.

"You're wrong." Ben scowled. "People like you think Todd's bad because he doesn't follow the rules. But he's not. I *know* him and he's not into drugs." His chin lifted in stubborn conviction.

Faced with arguments Ben might have continued to defend his cousin, but Connor remained mute, arms crossed over his chest as he leaned against the door jamb. Ben would have to learn the truth for himself—a truth Connor knew the boy already suspected, despite his denials.

In the face of the detective's steady look, Ben's assurance faltered, but only for a moment. When he spoke again, his voice was harsh with bitterness. "Yeah, I'll help. But not because you're right. Because you won't believe me till I prove you wrong."

Ben's reasons didn't matter in the least as long as he cooperated, but Connor knew better than to let his feeling of triumph show, especially with Laura watching. For some strange reason, her opinion mattered, to say nothing of the fact that she still had the power to throw a monkey wrench in the whole deal.

Raising his hands in protest, Connor said earnestly, "Hey, I'd like nothing better than to be proved wrong. I don't like to see kids in trouble."

Apparently unconvinced by that lofty statement, Ben merely repeated his earlier question. "What do I have to do, Detective?"

"Just a minute," Laura interrupted.

It was wishful thinking to hope she'd concede defeat. Connor was only surprised she hadn't jumped in sooner. Resigned, he looked at her questioningly.

"Ben can't make this decision alone. He's a minor—his father will have to give permission."

"Give me some credit, Miss Douglass. I'm as aware of the law as you are. I've already made an appointment to speak with Mr. Westing."

"Oh. Well, I insist on being present when you see him."

"Of course. I wouldn't have it any other way. Tomorrow at five. His office." Connor almost smiled when a look of chagrin crossed her face. Despite everything, she was still in there fighting.

"Dad won't care," Ben interjected bleakly. "He doesn't like Todd."

"Be that as it may, he *does* like you, and I think he needs to hear my opinion, too," Laura said.

It was time for a strategic withdrawal, Connor decided. "I'll be in touch, Ben, after I see your dad." He inclined his head toward Laura and smiled politely before slipping through the doorway. "Tomorrow."

Laura bit back a sharp retort. She refused to give him the satisfaction of knowing he'd upset her. Somehow she managed to control her irritation through Ben's appointment, but it continued to gnaw at her the rest of the day. Every time her thoughts turned to the detective, anger knotted her stomach.

She was still fuming the next afternoon in the reception area of Westing Electronics. Seated on a sleek leather couch, she thumbed through a trade magazine and waited for Connor to appear.

He hadn't played fair.

Grudgingly she admitted she'd been far too complacent. Instead of taking action, she'd counted on Ben's turning him down flat. She hadn't been prepared. But that didn't change the fact that Connor had taken advantage of an inexperienced boy, manipulating Ben for his own ends. How had Connor known just the right things to say? It still galled her to remember how quickly he'd breached the boy's defenses.

Well, he wouldn't catch her flat-footed today.

She slapped the magazine down on the glass table and assessed her surroundings. Chrome and glass and black leather. Stark white walls, relieved only by prints of what she supposed to be electronic equipment. She felt chilled in spite of her warm clothing. If the sterile environment was any reflection of the owner of the company, it was no wonder Ben was so starved for approval.

The street door swung open, and Connor sauntered in. His scuffed tennis shoes squeaked across the imitation marble floor to the receptionist's desk. Laura drew small satisfaction that the Gorgon seated there seemed unimpressed by his lopsided smile and polite inquiry. Stiff faced, the woman acknowledged his presence and motioned him to the waiting area.

Laura watched him cross the lobby toward her. Today, in deference to the crisp bite of autumn in the air, he wore a dark green sweatshirt and denim jacket. Not quite the attire one chose to meet the president of a small company, she thought, but then, he didn't seem to need fashionable clothing to be impressive. The man himself was compelling enough.

His piercing blue eyes met hers. With a start, she realized she was staring. Self-consciously, she smoothed her gray wool skirt over her knees and pasted an aloof expression on her face.

Obviously undeterred, Connor relaxed into the chair across from her and smiled a greeting. "Glad you could make it."

Glad? She doubted it. Not trusting herself to respond in a pleasant manner, Laura nodded and reached for the same magazine she'd discarded moments before. It was no more interesting than the first time she'd looked at it, but it gave her something to do. Let him think her rude; it was better than giving him the advantage of seeing the effect he had on her.

The pages rustled loudly in the silence. Peeking over the magazine, Laura caught Connor studying her, an indecipherable expression on his face. His gaze made her uneasy. She quickly lowered her lashes and shifted against the slippery leather. What was it about this man that made her lose all poise?

"Laura."

His voice made her name a soft caress. Shivering, she looked up.

"We don't need to be adversaries."

She stared at him blankly.

"We're on the same side."

Same side? Ben's face rose in her mind. She shook her head.

"Yes," he insisted. "We're both trying to build a better society. We just approach problems from different angles."

His words had a certain logic, but his motives were suspect. He wanted Ben and had already proved he'd use any means available to get him. Laura wouldn't allow herself to be taken in.

"The angles are what bother me, Detective McCormack."

"You can go in now."

The receptionist's announcement floated across the room, postponing further discussion, but a last glance at Connor's hooded eyes informed Laura that he was not through arguing his case. Bracing for battle, she preceded him into Tom Westing's office.

Ben's father was an imposing figure in dressed-for-success dark suit and tie. An older, harder version of his son, he had Ben's platinum hair and hazel eyes. Pressed to pick a word to describe him, Laura would have chosen "controlled." It was her first impression at their one previous meeting, and nothing today altered her opinion. He was the kind of man she'd dealt with daily in her former job: businesslike, predictable—familiar.

Rounding the massive desk, he apologized for the delay. "I had a long-distance call that couldn't wait."

Automatically, Laura shook his proffered hand, aware of his swift inspection. He made no overt sign of approval, but interest flickered in his cool eyes. Controlled. Familiar.

"Miss Douglass, good to see you again." He turned to Connor. "And you must be Detective McCormack."

Laura compared the two men as they shook hands. Westing topped Connor by a good four inches, but Connor had the advantage in breadth. Strangely, when she observed the two together, Tom Westing's polish seemed superficial in the face of Connor's casual assurance.

The businessman showed them to a low couch in a corner of the spacious room. Though Laura would have preferred to distance herself from Connor, Westing staked claim to the only available chair. Resigned to sharing the couch, she perched as close to one end as possible.

"I must admit, Detective McCormack, your call yesterday alarmed me." Westing settled more comfortably against the padded leather, one sharp-creased pant leg crossed over the other. His appearance was anything but worried. "You were so cryptic, I assumed Ben was in some new kind of trouble."

"Nothing like that," the detective assured him, angling his solid frame into the cushions.

Laura shifted uncomfortably as Connor draped an arm across the top of the couch. His hand rested inches from the nape of her neck.

"I know," said Westing. "I spoke with him last night. I gather you want him to keep an eye on my nephew."

Connor nodded.

"Why?" With an index finger, Ben's father rubbed at an invisible smudge on the wooden arm of his chair.

Casual as the question seemed, Laura sensed a certain tension behind the word.

"Todd Billings is involved in drugs."

Westing appeared unsurprised by Connor's statement. "I figured as much."

"You never observed anything?"

"No."

The answer was quick. Too quick, thought Laura. Connor's next statement confirmed that he thought so, too.

"But you suspected."

"Yes," Westing admitted.

Connor's thumb brushed absently back and forth across the corduroy nap at Laura's shoulder. The rhythmic rasp, so close to her ear, was oddly distracting. She tried to block it out by concentrating on the detective's line of questioning.

"Why didn't you notify the police of your suspicions?"

"About what? Vague feelings? Unfounded guesses? There was no proof." His expression bland, Westing returned Connor's stare. "Besides, he's my sister's son."

"What about your own son?"

For the first time, Westing looked uncomfortable. His gaze shifted from Connor to Laura, then back. A defensive note crept into his voice. "I did what I could. I kicked Todd out and forbade Ben to see him."

"And you think that solves the problem?"

The question was gently spoken, but Laura sensed the sneer beneath. Evidently Westing did, too. His lips thinned, but he didn't rise to the bait.

"Ben is not a defiant boy. Impulsive, stubborn at times, but definitely not defiant."

The detective's thumb stilled, and though the persistent movement had made Laura edgy, its cessation was unnerving. Even before Connor spoke, she knew Westing's declaration had given him the opening he sought.

"Mr. Westing, Ben is still seeing Todd."

Westing gazed out the window for several moments, digesting the information.

"Do you realize that Todd is probably the person responsible for Ben's involvement in the burglary?"

Meeting Connor's eyes, Westing nodded curtly. No further elaboration was necessary. They both knew what the detective was getting at.

"So my son's to be a snitch." The words were devoid of emotion, spoken in the same way one might say that it looked like rain or the carpet needed shampooing.

Ben's father was not putting up the fight Laura expected. Alarmed, she spoke. "That's not been settled yet, Mr. Westing. You can still veto the idea."

Raising an eyebrow, Westing looked at her in surprise. "Why would I want to do that, Miss Douglass?"

Was the man dense? "Because it's dangerous! Because Ben could get hurt!"

"*Life* is dangerous," Westing said calmly.

The platitude stirred Laura's ire. "Don't be ridiculous," she snapped. "You don't shove a child into a deadly situation for a learning experience."

"The risks are minimal," Connor interjected. Laura glared at him, but he calmly continued. "Ben's only contact will be his cousin. And we'll keep a close watch on him if he goes anywhere with Todd."

"You can't allow this," Laura pleaded with the father. "Ben's doing so well. This could jeopardize all the progress he's made."

Westing was conciliatory. "I understand your concern, Miss Douglass, but Ben is not a child anymore. I can no longer protect him from things. Some lessons he has to learn on his own."

Astonishment battled with anger. The man didn't care. He was willing to let his only son get mixed up with drug dealers, and for what? A growth experience?

Turning his attention back to Connor, Westing agreed to sign a consent form. "Tell me," he asked in conversational tones, his pen gliding across the paper, "just how did you manage to convince Ben to do this? I can't see him betraying Todd willingly. He thinks his cousin is perfect."

"He's proving it," replied Connor.

Westing looked thoughtful. "Yes, that would work." He returned the signed form and stood, signaling an end to the appointment. "You'll keep me apprised of things?"

"Of course." Connor pocketed the paper.

Numbly, Laura rose from the couch. *How could they converse like two business associates who'd closed a deal when they'd just sealed Ben's fate?* Making one last attempt, she met Tom Westing's eyes. "You can still change your mind. Think of Ben."

"I am."

Nothing she could say was going to alter his decision. She regarded him with pity. "Maybe so, but what if you're wrong?"

He didn't answer.

Defeated, Laura stalked from the office.

Anger carried her through the front door and onto the sidewalk; despair halted her there. Hands knotted into fists, she stared across the parking lot. Open fields, dotted with trees, separated this industrial area from town. Her gaze skimmed the treetops to the foothills where the sun had already set. In the gathering dusk, the landscape looked bleak and lifeless. Leached of color, it matched her mood. Hopeless.

What was she going to do? If his father didn't care, how could she save Ben alone?

As if in response to her dark thoughts, a dry wind sprang to life. It swirled around her, tugging at her skirt and whipping strands of hair across her face. Chilled, she clutched the lapels of her jacket together and, head bent, scurried toward her car.

"Laura! Wait."

Fumbling to fit the car key into the lock, she pretended not to hear the call. Connor was the last person she wanted to talk to right now. Behind her she heard the slap of shoes against asphalt as he sprinted across the parking lot, and her fingers grew clumsy with haste. The lock finally turned, and she yanked up on the handle.

Too late.

He reached past her and caught the opening door, preventing her from slipping inside. "Laura—"

"I have to get home." Stubbornly she refused to turn, unwilling to meet the gloating look she knew she'd find on his face. He'd won. Did he have to rub it in?

"We need to talk."

"Forget it, Detective."

"No."

Irritated by his insistence, she pivoted, prepared to give him a piece of her mind, and collided with his chest. A hasty step backward brought her against the car door, but not before her senses registered his solid strength. Awareness pulsed through her, startling in its intensity. Confused, she drew a shaky breath. "Look, you got what you wanted. Now, please—leave me alone."

Connor sighed, his expression troubled. Tentatively he touched her shoulder in a gesture of comfort. "Laura, I'm sorry."

The gentle tone, the pressure of his fingers, worked a powerful magic. For a fraction of a moment she believed him. "Sorry enough to—" She halted when he dropped his hand and shook his head.

"I can't."

"You won't even reconsider?"

Connor hesitated, troubled by the expectant look in her eyes. Somehow he knew what it cost her to plead with him. All she asked was that he think things over. He considered agreeing just to erase the look of vulnerability from her face. But it would have been a hollow promise that would raise false hopes. In the long run, it would only have hurt her more.

Again he shook his head, attempting to soften his refusal with explanation. "Try to understand, Laura. I've lived with this case for months, tried everything I know of to get close to the center of things. Nothing's worked. If I pass up this opportunity..."

It was no use. He could see she wasn't listening to him. He wanted to grab her, shake some sense into her head, but instead he kept his arms rigidly at his sides. "Can't you see this is bigger than any one person?"

"All I see is a man so hell-bent on having his way that he won't even consider other possibilities."

The unfairness of her accusation stung him to anger despite his good intentions. He took a step toward her, one part of his mind relishing the way she shrank beneath his glare. From between clenched teeth he spat out words intended to hurt. "It must be wonderful to always be right—sort of like being God. Tell me, do you ever get lonely up there, so high above the rest of us ordinary mortals?"

No sooner had he spoken than he regretted the impulse.

Her head lifted defiantly, but he was close enough to register the slight quiver of her chin and the glint of tears in her liquid eyes. Pressing her lips together, she turned her back and slid into the car. Connor remained frozen to the spot as she started the engine and drove away without a backward glance.

Damn it to hell. Long strides carried him back across the nearly empty lot. Without thought he belted himself in his seat and turned on the ignition. The car leaped forward and swerved onto the street.

What was wrong with him? He never lost his temper. Not anymore. There was something about Laura Douglass that brought out the worst in him, even when he wanted to do the right thing. He wasn't the kind of man to browbeat a woman—he didn't have to. But there he'd stood, making her cringe, while cruel, vindictive words spewed from his mouth. What had become of his celebrated charm, his easygoing way with women? Blown away. All because of a mouthy, stubborn female.

It seemed he'd forgotten the lesson Meg had taught so well. There was no such thing as a defenseless woman. The more vulnerable they seemed, the more they worked you over. He refused to get caught in that trap again, especially when he was on a case. There'd be no more Sams in his life.

A glittering line of taillights warned him the traffic light ahead was turning red. He stomped on the brake, his hands tightening on the steering wheel. Maybe he couldn't avoid Laura, but he sure as hell could ignore her. From now on, she'd get polite civility from him, careful courtesy. Nothing more.

Chapter 4

Weekends were the worst.

Especially weekends when family duty called.

It wasn't that she didn't love her parents, Laura thought as she ran the vacuum across the living room carpet. But with Jared gone, all their attention and their hopes were focused on her.

It wasn't right. It wasn't fair. But it was fact.

Laura unplugged the vacuum and attacked the furniture with a dust rag.

During the week, her father was immersed in his law practice, and Mom kept busy with bridge clubs and volunteer hospital work. Weekends they set aside for Laura.

She had tried to tell herself they were just concerned parents, but it wasn't normal and she knew it. They should have been living their own lives, not hers. Once they'd been involved in a whirl of social and civic activities. Now they sat at home and tried not to notice that the antique grandfather clock in the living room ticked off the minutes of their lives.

Marking time.

What were they waiting for?

In a gesture that had long ago become habit, Laura lifted the silver-framed photograph of her brother from the bookshelf to slip it out of sight. Exactly as she did every time Mom and Dad came over. But this time something made her hesitate before hiding it away.

It was Jared's high school graduation picture. Laura studied his face, searching for a hint of discontent, a clue to inner turmoil. But there was nothing to foreshadow the tragedy that would occur less than a year later. He appeared relaxed and carefree.

Suddenly she was tired of the lie, tired of playing the game. She slammed the cabinet door shut and replaced the photo on the shelf. The small act of defiance made her feel better than she had in days. Maybe her parents could pretend they'd never had a son, but *she* couldn't forget him so easily.

The doorbell rang half an hour later while Laura was running a brush through her damp hair. Hastily she wriggled into clean jeans, pulled an ivory-tinted sweater over her head and padded down the hall as the bell sounded a second time.

She struggled to hook the silver links of a belt together with one hand and open the door with the other. "You're early."

"Not really."

Nonplussed, Laura looked up into the ultramarine eyes that had haunted her troubled dreams.

Connor surveyed her with cool interest, his gaze lingering on her bare feet before it returned to her face. "Aren't you going to invite me in?"

You must feel like God... Laura felt her face flush. "No. What are you doing here?"

"I figured you'd have cooled down by now. We still need to talk, remember?"

"Call me at work on Monday." She started to close the door, her words intended as a dismissal, but Connor stepped forward and inserted his sneaker between the moving door and the jamb.

"This won't take long."

Short of crushing his foot, a feat she wasn't sure was possible with a wooden door, it seemed she had no choice but to listen. Besides, he was just ornery enough to stand there until her parents showed up. Against her better judgment, she swung the door open. "It better not. I'm expecting company." Scowling, she followed him into the living room, where he took up residence on her couch.

His gaze swept the room, taking in the bright prints and neatly lined bookshelves. "Nice."

Laura was not in the mood for small talk. "How did you get my address?" she demanded.

"I'm a detective. I looked it up in the phone book."

He spoke with such solemnity that it was difficult not to laugh. Laura's irritation dissolved as her sense of humor reasserted itself. She fought to keep her expression stern, but a twitch at one corner of her mouth betrayed her.

"Okay, stupid question." Tucking one foot beneath her, she sank into the chair across from him. "Go ahead, Detective. Talk."

Suspicion flickered in his eyes.

Evidently he hadn't expected much cooperation. The thought of what her sudden reversal in attitude must have been doing to his mental balance caused her spirits to rise. It pleased her to think of his getting a taste of his own medicine.

"I'm sorry to bother you on Sunday, but I figured it'd be easier to talk now than to try to catch each other during the week."

Laura shrugged and wondered how much his polite manner cost him in light of the accusations she'd hurled the night before. He didn't appear to be under much strain. In fact, he looked rested and at ease, as though he'd had a better night's sleep than she'd had.

Her gaze wandered over his face, noting the lines etched between his brows and the imprint of laughter that framed his mouth like parentheses. This man, from all indications, smiled as frequently as he frowned. As he continued to speak, she watched his mouth curve and shift around the words he formed. His lips were full and mobile and mocked the hardness of his other features. In contrast to his wary, cynical eyes, his lips were full and sensual. She wondered what they would feel like—

In the same instant Laura became aware of two things: the timer on the stove was buzzing and she hadn't heard a thing Connor was saying.

She sprang to her feet. The hasty movement halted the flow of his words, and a startled expression flashed across his features.

"My pie," she mumbled and headed for the kitchen. Connor followed.

Armed with a pot holder, Laura opened the oven door to pull out the bubbling dessert. She welcomed the blast of hot air that greeted her, hoping it would be an adequate explanation for the color that suffused her face. How could she have let her mind wander that way? And in that direction?

She deposited the pie on a wire rack to cool.

"Apple?"

Nodding, Laura ignored the covetous note in his voice. She would not sacrifice her pie, no matter how pitiful he sounded.

"Lucky company."

Laura lifted the lid off a large pot on the oven's lower rack as Connor moved closer. Within touching distance. The oven's heat spread through her, and she wished the kitchen had a window she could open.

"Stew?"

"*Boeuf en daube,*" she corrected, motioning toward the open cookbook.

Connor leaned one hip against the adjacent counter and studied the ingredients. "Stew," he declared, a mischievous glint in his eyes.

She shot him a look of exasperation. The exotic-sounding French dish had taken hours to prepare, but he was right. It *was* a glorified stew.

Grabbing a wooden spoon from a drawer, she proceeded to stir vigorously. Too vigorously.

"Ouch!" Laura yelped, jerking back as hot gravy splashed across her hand. The spoon clattered to the floor.

"Watch out!" Connor caught Laura around the waist and pulled her out of range of airborne drops of gravy.

His hands cupped familiarly around her rib cage, nudging the undersides of her breasts, and her bottom rested intimately against his pelvis. All thought fled Laura's startled mind as her body molded itself to his. Then the pressure of his arms relaxed, and he set her carefully on her feet.

"Better get something cold on that hand."

While Connor searched in the freezer, Laura ran tap water, wincing when the cool liquid flowed over tender flesh.

"This should help." Grasping her wrist, he applied a cube of ice to the reddening area.

Laura gasped at the flash of pain that shot up her arm, but Connor held her firmly.

"Give it a chance to work. In a few seconds it'll feel better."

"Well, it can't feel much worse," she retorted, but she gritted her teeth and hung on.

When she no longer tried to pull away, he loosened his hold until her hand lay cradled within his. Laura concentrated on the strange sensations. As the back of her hand grew numb, the nerve endings on the other side seemed to become ultrasensitive. Warmth radiated from his fingers and palmed upward into hers. She felt soothed and comforted, the way she had as a child when her father took her hand to cross the street.

"There. That should do it." Connor removed the ice and studied the skin. "How does it feel?"

The burning had receded, leaving only a small ache of discomfort. Amazed, she raised her eyes and met his gaze. "Fine."

When he withdrew his hand to drop the melted ice cube into the sink, Laura suffered a pang of loss. The emotion confused her. Troubled, she turned to close the oven door, then rinsed out a sponge. Scrubbing at the congealed gravy on the floor, she voiced the first thing that came to mind. "Where did you learn that trick?"

"Grandma."

She glanced at him. "The one who knew the way to a woman's heart?"

For an instant, his expression softened. Then, as though embarrassed by her scrutiny, he grinned. "One and the same."

Before she could comment, the doorbell rang. Her heart sank. This was all she needed—Mom and Dad and Connor McCormack. She knew exactly what her parents would think and could only hope they didn't make it obvious to the detective.

"My mother and father," she told him, tossing the sponge into the sink.

Henry Douglass was leaning on the buzzer for the third time as Laura opened the door. Patience was *not* one of his strong points.

"I thought you might have forgotten we were coming," he explained, unfolding his lanky frame to plant a kiss on his daughter's forehead.

"Why would she have forgotten, dear? We talked just last night." Rose Douglass, fulfilling her customary role of peacemaker, favored her daughter with a smile that asked her to excuse her father.

Depositing an imitation fur jacket—Rose was vehemently opposed to killing animals for their skins—on the back of the couch, she shivered dramatically. The gesture was a little overdone, considering that she wore a layered wool outfit beneath. "The weather's turning. I wouldn't be surprised if it snowed tonight."

"Snow? Nonsense," contradicted her husband. "It never snows before Halloween."

"Dear, you're forgetting that ice storm a year ago Labor Day and the Columbus Day blizzard the year before that."

"Anomalies," declared Henry.

Laura sighed. The weather was one of her parents' favorite topics of disagreement. They continued to bicker as they trailed behind her, but the sight of a strange man in her kitchen brought the argument to an abrupt halt.

"Hello." Rose's tone was bright with interest.

"Dad, Mom, this is Connor McCormack. Detective McCormack, my mother and father."

"You didn't tell us you'd invited a friend, dear." Rose bestowed her best "pink-lady" smile on Connor, the same one she employed while working as a hospital volunteer.

Henry, who had caught the title, peered at him with suspicion.

Anxious to correct her mother's misconception, Laura blurted out, "No, Mom. We're not friends, just business acquaintances."

Connor's raised eyebrow reminded her of the good deed he'd just performed, and she guiltily amended her original statement. "That is—we're friendly business acquaintances. Sort of."

Her father rescued her from what threatened to be a bad case of foot-in-mouth disease. "You some kind of private investigator?"

Connor shook his head. "No, I'm with the Boulder Police Department."

"Humph."

The single sound spoke eloquently of Henry's feelings about policemen. As a criminal lawyer, he harbored a wariness of law enforcement officers that Laura never quite understood. The way she saw it, without the police, Dad wouldn't have had a job.

"How wonderful!" Rose exclaimed. Then, as the implications dawned, her expression grew troubled. "Are you here on a case?"

Quickly, Laura began to speak. "Detective McCormack—"

"Just passing on information," Connor supplied before she could finish. His gaze flicked toward her, daring her to dispute his explanation. "And in spite of your daughter's kind invitation..."

Laura blinked at the flash of deviltry on his face.

"I can't stay for dinner."

"Are you certain? We'd love to have you," Rose said.

The feeble attempt at matchmaking forced Laura to interrupt. "Detective McCormack has a previous engagement, Mom."

"Oh." Rose's disappointment was evident. "Well, perhaps another time."

"Perhaps," promised Connor vaguely, then he addressed Laura. "About that meeting next week . . . ?"

Meeting? Laura stared at him for an instant before she realized what he was talking about. "Oh, yes. I'll be there." She directed her parents to help themselves to coffee while she showed Detective McCormack out.

"Thanks for stopping by to remind me," Laura told Connor in a voice she knew carried easily into the kitchen. Opening the door, she leaned toward him and whispered, "When and where am I supposed to meet you?"

His initial look of puzzlement faded as he discerned her strategy and whispered back, "Eben Fine Park. Tuesday during your lunch hour. Ben needs to join us, too. Can you manage?"

Laura nodded.

Rose's voice called from the kitchen. "Dear, I'm taking the stew out for you. It seems to be scorching."

"Stew," he whispered.

In response to the twinkle of amusement in his eyes, Laura succumbed to a mischievous impulse. She raised her voice once more. "Give Myrna and the kids my love, Detective."

Grinning with smug satisfaction at his startled expression, she swung the door shut and returned to the kitchen to get dinner on the table.

Rose's curiosity resurfaced during dessert. As she poured everyone a second cup of coffee, she reintroduced the subject that had evidently been uppermost in her mind. "He was a nice man."

Laura looked up in surprise. Henry had just finished a story about his latest client, a man dubbed the Greedy Gourmet by the press for his penchant for stealing cookbooks along with jewels and silverware. For a moment Laura thought Rose was commenting on the accused burglar. It was several seconds before she realized her mother was making one of her odd conversational leaps.

Carefully stirring cream into her cup, Laura responded in what she hoped was a casual voice. "The Greedy Gourmet?"

"Don't be obtuse, dear. I'm referring to the young man we met earlier."

"Detective McCormack."

"Yes." Rose tilted her china cup toward her lips. "It's too bad he's married."

With her fork, Laura pushed an apple slice across her plate. "Actually, he's not."

"Oh? I thought I heard you mention a wife and children."

Although her sense of honesty prevented her from an outright lie, Laura was not above shading the truth in self-defense. "That was his sister we were talking about."

"Oh . . . so you've met the family?"

Now she was in for it. To Rose's thinking, introductions to one's family were tantamount to a declaration of intent. "Not exactly." Laura groped for a reply that would allay her mother's suspicions. "He mentioned them once."

"Then you've been seeing him for a while." Rose mulled over this bit of information as she sipped her coffee, her expression thoughtful. "Why haven't you told us about him?"

Hopelessly floundering in her deception, Laura resorted to the tactic of denial, something she'd practiced as a teen. "For crying out loud, Mom! I'm *not* dating Connor McCormack. I don't even like the man. If it weren't for one of my clients, I wouldn't have anything to do with him."

"Really, dear, you don't have to shout. I was only curious."

Henry, who'd been listening in silence to the exchange, chose that moment to enter the conversation. "Of course Laura wouldn't be interested in the man. After all, he's *only* a policeman."

Laura fought to control a surge of irritation. "What's wrong with being a policeman?"

A look of surprise crossed his face at his daughter's question. "Nothing on the surface, Laura. Most law-enforcement officers I know are solid, upstanding citizens. But it's apparent that your mother regards Detective McCormack as possible husband material."

"Don't be absurd, Henry!" Rose said indignantly. "I thought no such thing."

Laura's father ignored the interruption and continued as though making a summation to a jury. "The drawbacks inherent in such a liaison should be obvious. Police work is dangerous and stressful and not at all lucrative. All of which have a negative effect on a marriage." He paused with practiced habit and addressed his final remarks to his wife. "Laura is much too sensible to even consider such a man."

"Too sensible." Laura bristled. Though more subtle in his approach, Henry was just as guilty as Rose of trying to run her life. Maybe more so. At least Mom only aspired to marry her off to some poor slob. Dad, on the other hand, was still trying to stuff her into the neat little pattern he'd laid out years before. In spite of everything, he still viewed her changed lifestyle as a bit of delayed adolescent—regret-

table but understandable in light of the traumas they'd all endured.

Lips clamped tight, Laura rose to clear the table. She knew from past experience it was useless to try to best her father in a battle of words. Words were his specialty, and she would only end up frustrated. She shook her head at her mother's offer of help. "You two relax in the living room. This won't take a minute."

The sounds of the evening news drifted into the kitchen as Laura rinsed dishes under a running stream of hot water. *Sensible!* Was it sensible to grow warm at the memory of indigo eyes? Was it sensible to contemplate what would have happened if she'd twisted in Connor's arms as he caught her? Laura popped the last plate into the dishwasher and flipped the door closed.

Sensible, indeed!

The car rolled to a stop against the cement curbing, and Laura leaned forward to peer through the windshield. "I don't think he's here yet," she said, scanning the handful of people that dotted the long, narrow park. Actually, the survey was unnecessary. Her steady pulse was all she needed to assure herself he hadn't arrived.

Ben shrugged indifference, a gesture entirely at odds with his stiff, tense body, and opened the passenger door. "Let's go ahead and eat."

Dried leaves crackled beneath their feet as they walked across the grass toward a giant maple. Rose's dire predictions had proved groundless. Not only was there no snow, but the gentle blend of gold and brown, accented with an occasional splash of burnt sienna, announced that Indian Summer was in full swing. Colorado's autumn seemed subdued in comparison to the riot of colors Laura remembered from her time in New York State, but for some reason, she preferred the mellower effect.

Settling her back against the maple's trunk, Laura closed her eyes and turned her face to the sunlight that filtered through the branches. Surrounding trees muffled the sound of passing traffic, while Boulder Creek, which formed the northern border of the park, provided a faint musical background, punctuated by children's voices raised in play. Nearby, the rustle of waxed paper told her Ben was already unwrapping a hamburger.

The moment would have been idyllic, if only they'd really been here just for a picnic. She was not looking forward to this meeting. More than Ben's capitulation or his father's consent, today would mark the true beginning of an alliance with Connor McCormack. When lunch ended, there would be no turning back. Because she worried about Ben, she could not allow events to unfold without her, and that meant continuing to see Connor and contending with her own erratic emotions.

Sighing, she opened her eyes. "Ben, you don't have to go through with this."

Ben swallowed the mouthful of food he was chewing. "I have to."

"No, you don't. We'll just say you changed your mind."

"You don't understand," he mumbled.

"Yes, I do," she insisted. "You think you're protecting Todd."

He shook his head. "Todd needs me." His gaze dropped to the sandwich in his hands as he searched for the right words. "Nobody else cares about him. His dad left when he was little, and his mom threw him out. Even Dad just let him come as a favor to my aunt—he doesn't even like him. I'm the only one."

An echo of Todd's self-pity was evident in Ben's account, but Laura could think of no way to expose it without upsetting the delicate balance of her relationship with him. Overcome by a sense of helplessness, she studied Ben's bent head. He wouldn't believe her if she tried. Todd had found just the right means to ensure his cousin's loyalty. For now, all she could do was go along with the stupid plan and be there to make sure Ben wasn't harmed.

Looking up, she saw Connor approaching along the creek path at a steady run. The sight should have raised her anxiety level. Indeed, it would have if she'd not been mesmerized by the fluid motion of his body, apparent even beneath his gray sweats. While she watched, he raised a hand in greeting and broke stride.

Laura tore her gaze away and took a sip of cola to calm her skittering pulse.

Still panting, Connor lowered himself to the ground and reached for the drink Ben shoved in his direction. "Thanks." He raised the cup to his mouth, draining half its contents before speaking.

"How're you doing?" he asked Ben.

"Okay."

His breathing returned to normal, Connor indicated one of the still-wrapped burgers. "Mine?" At Laura's affirmative nod, he unwrapped it and took a bite, chewing with relish.

"When do you have to be back?"

Ben glanced at his watch, then at Laura. "Half an hour, I guess. I've got algebra."

It was bad enough, Laura decided, to feel as though her every nerve ending was being stroked by his presence, without the added agony of waiting to hear what plans he had for Ben. When Connor's last French fry disappeared, she dropped all pretense of eating. "Can we get down to business? I don't want Ben to be late for class."

"Sure." Catching the boy's eye, Connor quietly asked, "You still with me?"

"Yeah." Ben's voice was confident.

"Fine." Connor lay back, crossing his arms behind his head. "First, we need to stay in touch. But I don't think it's a good idea to take up your weekly time with your P.O., and I don't want people wondering why you're suddenly meeting a strange man all the time."

"Couldn't I just call you if I have any information?"

The hopeful note in Ben's voice clued Laura in. Left to himself, the teen wouldn't learn anything and, therefore, would never call. She waited for Connor's response. Would he fall for it?

"Good idea. I'll give you my number," said Connor, "but we need something else, something regular."

Damn. She should have known he would see through Ben's strategy. Glumly, she listened to them discuss possibilities.

"What about weekends? You busy?"

"Just with Eco-Cycle on Saturday mornings."

"Okay. What if you and Laura and I started doing some things together on Sundays, like taking hikes or going to movies?"

"It's all right with me."

Connor looked at Laura. "What about you?"

While she resented the assumption that she would participate in the plan, Laura knew Connor had hit on the perfect solution. She frequently joined her kids, singly or in groups, for various activities during her off-hours. No one would think anything of it if she spent Sundays with Ben. But Connor?

"How do we explain you," she asked.

"A friend."

A friend? Not by a long shot, but she supposed she could always pretend. The opportunity to keep an eye on Ben was hard to resist. And, she realized, the outings would give Connor a chance to see the teenager as a person instead of merely a means to an end. "It'll work," she agreed. "And you two can get better acquainted while we're at it."

"Great." Connor sat up, a smile lifting the corners of his mouth. "So where are we going?"

Chapter 5

Connor stepped on the brakes as the procession of vehicles ground to yet another halt. Wedged between a Cadillac and a station wagon loaded with kids, his car inched its way toward what had once been called the "richest square mile on Earth."

When Laura had suggested a ride through the mountains to view the aspens, he'd thought a visit to Central City would be just the thing to top off the afternoon. Now he wasn't so sure. Everyone in the state seemed to be up here today, and driving bumper to bumper wasn't exactly his idea of a good time.

Apparently it wasn't Ben's idea of a good time, either, Connor thought as he glanced at the boy in the rearview mirror. He looked bored. Connor couldn't blame him. How many green slopes slashed by spills of golden aspen could you look at before your senses grew numb? Well, they were almost to their destination. Maybe the historic gold-mining town would revive Ben's spirits.

In contrast to the two males, Laura seemed relaxed and content. She leaned forward to adjust the volume on the tape deck and Connor sniffed. A light lemony scent drifted to his nose. Her scent. He stared ahead but it did no good. He still itched to feel the weight of her hair glide across the back of his hand, to trace the shell of her ear with one finger. When she tilted her head to the side window, exposing the elegant line of her neck, he imagined his lips brushing lightly along the velvety skin. Would it feel as soft as it looked?

He tightened his grip on the steering wheel and wished he hadn't been so complacent when Laura had turned his plan for brief Sunday meetings into full-fledged outings so he and Ben could get to know each other. At the time he'd gone along with the idea to gain her cooperation with Ben. Now he wondered where his common sense had been. He should have known what proximity would do to his libido.

Damn it. He didn't need these feelings. Not now. He needed to concentrate on Ben—develop rapport, as they used to say in psych class. Today his job was to win Ben's trust.

And it wouldn't hurt, Connor reminded himself, if he also managed to catch a glimpse of Todd Billings's contact—a man who'd been seen with him up here on two previous Sundays. Sure, it was a long shot, but that's what this business was all about—following up on long shots. Central City might be a little out of the way for a drug buy, but it was safer than Boulder where Todd was known. Who'd think twice about two men among hundreds of tourists? Only his partner, Joe, who'd first spotted Todd and his contact two weekends ago while visiting the tourist attraction. It was pure luck that Joe had returned there the following weekend and had spotted Todd again with the same man.

Luck? No, Connor preferred to think of it as Fate. Luck came and went, but Fate was inevitable.

A little off-key, Laura hummed along with the music playing on the tape deck. A shiver of déjà vu rippled down his back. Meg used to hum, too, when she worked on a piece of jewelry—the same tune over and over. The repetition seemed to focus her energy on the task at hand.

Connor silently cursed and rubbed the muscles of his thigh in an effort to alleviate an ache of tension. Meg was intruding on his thoughts far too often of late. And he knew why.

Because no matter how hard he struggled to ignore it, something about Laura drew him, just as he'd been drawn to Meg all those years ago. Witty, beautiful Meg. The woman he'd planned to marry when he was young and foolish enough to still believe in things like love and forever. Well, she'd cured him of his illusions and left behind memories as a warning, a safeguard against temptation.

He cut a glance at Laura. No doubt about it, she was a distraction. One he couldn't afford. It had been stupid to include her. Her presence might make Ben more relaxed, but Connor felt darned uncomfortable.

They crept through Blackhawk, then rounded a bend in the road. Central City spread before them, clinging to the precipitous slopes of Gregory Gulch. On the outskirts of town, Connor swung the car into an open space and shut off the motor. "We're here," he announced unnecessarily. "Everybody out."

"This it?" Ben asked, a sneer in his tone.

Laura snapped a picture of one of the gingerbread houses that lined the street. "Yep. This is it."

"The main street's only three or four blocks ahead," Connor assured the teen as they made their way along the narrow, uneven sidewalk.

Ben merely grunted.

Even this late in the season, the downtown was crowded with casino enthusiasts and tourists who drifted in and out of specialty shops. With habitual caution, Connor scanned the street, automatically checking for anything out of the ordinary. The air was redolent with the aroma of draft beer and frying hamburger intermingled with the scents of cinnamon and nutmeg. Caught in the procession of people, the three strolled along, examining the storefronts until Ben spied a display of geodes. Spurred by the look of interest that lit the teen's face, Connor suggested they go inside.

Connor's glance swept the shop as they entered. The interior was a hodgepodge of rocks, minerals and antique mining equipment, scattered with no discernible order. Ben moved from one pile to another, pausing to examine an occasional specimen with rapt interest. For the first time, Connor glimpsed an ordinary boy beneath his protective armor.

"You collect rocks?"

"I used to," Ben responded, polishing a piece of amber on his sleeve, "but I don't know much about them. When I was a kid, I picked up rocks that looked interesting. Kept cardboard boxes of them under my bed until Mrs. White went into a cleaning frenzy."

"Jared always said rocks were magic." Laura turned toward the grimy front windows, holding a rock in her uplifted hand. Its hollowed interior was encrusted with crystals, and sparks of amethyst light flashed when she turned it.

Telling himself it was only casual interest, Connor asked, "Jared?"

"My brother."

His tension eased. "Younger, right?"

Laura looked at him in surprise. "How—"

"The picture in your office."

"The blond kid?" Ben edged closer to touch the crystal facets of Laura's specimen. "Does he collect rocks?"

If he hadn't been used to reading people, Connor never would have noticed the expression of pain that flickered across Laura's face. As it was, it passed so quickly that he almost thought he'd imagined it.

"No," Laura replied in a low voice.

"How come? Did you have a fussy housekeeper, too?"

It was a natural enough response, spoken in jest, but something in Laura's tense stance made Connor wish the boy had not asked.

Laura shook her head, her mouth tightening, and looked down at the rock she held, but not before Connor caught a shimmer of tears. Carefully, as though it were a fragile egg, she replaced the geode in its box, then took a deep breath and met Ben's stare. "My brother died four years ago of a drug overdose."

Ben's smile froze, turning his face into a grotesque caricature of mirth. He swallowed convulsively, and his gaze flickered from Laura to Connor and back.

Connor felt a pang of pity for the boy as he fumbled for words. For most teenagers, dying was something that happened to old people—grandparents or elderly neighbors— not to someone their own age. The idea of one of their own facing the awful specter of death struck at the very core of their strength—their sense of invincibility.

He could understand Ben's loss of speech; Connor himself could think of nothing adequate to say. He finally settled for a simple "I'm sorry."

The phrase sounded trite and hollow to his ears, but Laura nodded and managed a tremulous smile. Moving back along the aisle, she picked up the piece of amber Ben had examined earlier.

"Do you like it?" she asked him.

"Sure," Ben replied. His animated tone was a measure of the relief he felt at the change of subject. "But I think I'll buy the geode and start a new collection. It'll drive Mrs. White up the wall." He beat a hasty retreat down the aisle.

Connor scooped the golden stone from Laura's hand. "Looks like a great worry stone." At her quizzical expression, he explained. "Some people carry worry beads that they run through their fingers. It's supposed to relieve tension. I've found that a stone works just as well." Reaching into his pocket, he pulled out a small dark stone.

Laura smoothed the talisman between thumb and fingers, a smile on her lips. "Magic," she said as she gave it back to him.

He grinned at her whimsy and closed his fingers around the stone. Warmed by her touch, it pressed reassuringly into his palm. His glance traced the curve of her mouth, then lifted to her eyes.

Dark eyes.

Hypnotic eyes.

Ben returned with his package.

With a start, Connor broke eye contact and released the breath he'd been unaware of holding. He opened his fingers.

Nothing strange or supernatural. Just a piece of rock, polished by frequent touch. He slipped it into his pocket, where it rested familiarly against his thigh. Thoughtfully, he weighed the rejected piece of amber in his hand. Magic lay in the mind, not the rock, but maybe everyone needed a little fantasy now and then.

A few minutes later he emerged from the store to find Laura and Ben bickering like a pair of kids. Laura wanted to take a tour of the Opera House or visit the museum in the old high school, while Ben contended both would be boring.

Laura radiated indignation. "Boring! They're history."

"You said it. They're boring history."

Appointing himself arbitrator, Connor stepped into the fray. "*I* say we get something to eat."

Ben needed no convincing, but Laura only allowed herself to be persuaded after they agreed to let her take pictures in front of the Opera House.

"I have to have *something* to prove I was here," she insisted.

In front of the historic building, Laura issued orders like a drill sergeant. "Stand there. No, more to the left. Look interested."

Bossy, Connor thought in amusement. But he didn't mind. While she fiddled with the focus and adjusted the lens, he watched the way the late-afternoon breeze played with her hair and plastered her windbreaker to her softly curved breasts, and... A tightening in his groin warned him to turn his attention to more mundane things before he embarrassed himself.

Looking down the long block, he watched a small girl tug at her mother's hand and point to the corner toy store with a dripping ice cream cone. With a resigned slump to her shoulders, the woman let herself be dragged around two men and into the shop.

Two men.

All thoughts of Laura fled. Senses on alert, Connor used every break in the flow of humanity to study them. There was something familiar...

His patience was finally rewarded with another clear look when the younger man glanced across the street and nodded.

Todd Billings.

And he'd almost missed him, thanks to Laura.

"Okay," called Laura, lowering the camera. "I got it."

Connor turned his head, an idea percolating in his brain. Hell, why not? It was worth a try.

He crossed with quick strides to where she stood. "How about one with you and Ben now?"

"Great. Have you used one of these before?" At his nod of assurance, she passed the camera to him, pausing to point out the shutter release. "Actually, everything's set already. You just have to push the button."

While she hurried to Ben's side, Connor flipped the focus to distance. A swift glance toward the corner informed him the angle was acceptable. Not great, but it would do. Now, if Todd would just move back a little...

He snapped a fuzzy picture of Laura and Ben while his attention remained riveted on the two men at the edge of his vision. Waving his companions to remain where they were, he again raised the camera.

Come on, he silently urged Todd. *Step aside.*

As if on command, Todd moved and pointed down the street. The other man followed the direction of his hand, turning his back on Connor.

Son of a—

Click. Another blurred snapshot. At this rate, Laura would get nothing but out-of-focus memories.

With a raised finger he signaled "One more," noting Laura's grim expression. Fortunately, she didn't argue. Playing for time, Connor fiddled with the light setting while Todd's friend pulled a cigarette from his jacket. Backing into the breeze to light it, he finally presented Connor with a front view, just as more tourists erupted from the adjacent store. Connor gauged their speed. He took one more picture in Laura and Ben's general direction before the procession came between the lens and the Opera House, then swung to his left.

Click. Click. Click. Three shots in rapid succession before he lowered the camera and recrossed the street.

Laura snatched her camera from him. "I thought you said you knew how to use this!"

"Sorry," Connor said with an apologetic grin. "Put a camera in my hands, and I go crazy."

"Crazy is right," she muttered, checking the frame counter. "You took half a dozen pictures of us."

Unperturbed, Connor hooked his thumbs in the front beltloops of his jeans. "The scenery was irresistible."

Laura flashed him a look, heavy with suspicion, but was prevented from further comment by Ben.

"*Now* can we eat?"

"Sure thing," Connor replied easily, knowing their route would take them in front of Todd and his companion. Connor maneuvered himself between Laura and Ben and slipped an arm around Laura's shoulders. When she started to protest, he pulled her snug against his side and lowered his head within inches of her ear.

"Play along," he whispered.

Her muscles tensed, and he knew she was about to search the street. "Just two lovers on a Sunday outing," he warned, sliding his hand from her shoulder to her jeans-clad hip. Looking up, he saw a stunned expression cross Ben's face at the intimacy.

If the moment had been less dangerous, Connor would have laughed. Instead, he raised a quizzical eyebrow. "You want to eat? Let's go."

Laura marched with rigid precision at his side, her head bobbing next to his shoulder.

"Relax," Connor hissed. "Put your arm around my waist. Lovers, remember?"

She did as commanded and even managed to smile up at him.

"Much better," he murmured, conscious of the sway of her rounded bottom beneath his hand.

It was hard to say who was more startled by their meeting—Ben or Todd. A few yards apart, Ben recognized his cousin and faltered midstride. "Todd. What—"

Todd jerked as though stung. Taking in Ben's companions, he nodded curtly, then turned away.

And Connor kept walking, propelling Laura along with him. He wasn't worried about Todd. It was the other man—the same man whose gaze now bored into Connor's back—who concerned him. How good a look had he gotten? Connor had been careful to angle his face toward Laura at the moment the man looked his way, but he had no way of telling if he'd been recognized. It was one of the hazards of the job; you never knew when some two-bit hood would ID you and blow your cover.

A quick look over his shoulder informed him Ben was behind him, walking with his head bent. Connor stopped to allow the boy to catch up.

Todd and friend had disappeared.

"Don't say anything."

"But what if Todd asks?"

"Then you just say Laura's your probation officer and I'm her boyfriend."

Laura sat in the darkened interior of the car and waited while Ben considered Connor's advice. The heater blew warm air across her legs, its hum weaving around the sound of the purring engine. Minutes before, they'd pulled up in front of Ben's house, but he seemed reluctant to go inside. Laura couldn't blame him. Except for the porch light, the house sat dark and quiet. Where was everyone?

"Is your father home?" Laura asked.

"He left on a business trip this afternoon," Ben replied.

"You're alone?"

"Nah. Mrs. White stays over when he's gone." Resentment filled his voice. "Fat lot of good *she* does."

"Maybe your father doesn't want you to get lonely."

"Are you kidding? He just doesn't trust me."

Why should he? Laura resisted the urge to speak the words aloud. For a while this afternoon, Ben had been a normal teenage boy, joking and clowning in a way she remembered Jared had done. But after the encounter with Todd, he'd withdrawn. While Laura and Connor chatted through dinner, Ben sullenly shoveled food into his mouth. And since he'd responded to direct questions with monosyllables, they eventually quit trying to include him in the conversation. On the ride home, he slept—or pretended to. It was only as they entered town that he pulled himself out of his dark mood to quiz Connor.

"He'll ask, you know. He'll want to know what you do."

Connor's tone was reassuring. "Tell him I'm a psychologist."

Laura couldn't help herself. She laughed. The image of Connor McCormack taking notes next to a leather couch was ludicrous.

"What's so funny?" Connor asked.

"You. Practicing psychology."

"I happen to have a master's degree in the field."

Surprise cut off her humor. "You do?"

He nodded. "It comes in handy in police work." Turning to the back seat, he continued, "Don't worry, Ben. Todd's not going to be suspicious unless you act like you're hiding something. Just act natural."

Ben scooted across the seat. "Thanks for dinner," he mumbled in Laura's direction and climbed from the car.

One hand on the door, he hesitated, then poked his head back inside. "The other guy..."

Connor waited.

"He was probably a friend. See, Todd's funny sometimes when he's with friends. He doesn't always want me tagging along."

"Sure."

"I don't want you getting the wrong idea."

"I didn't."

"Okay." Ben pulled his head out and straightened. "See ya."

With an efficiency of motion, Connor pulled away from the curb. Laura studied his profile as they sped down quiet residential streets. Hard and unyielding, his face was that of a man schooled in self-discipline, a man who'd let nothing stand in the way of what he wanted. What would it be like...?

As if conscious of her stare, he glanced sideways. His eyes pierced the darkness and caught her midthought. Then, just as quickly, he looked away, a slight smile curving his mouth.

Dangerous.

Her heart thudded. Tension curled in her stomach, a warm ache that left her breathless. What was wrong with her?

"Laura's too sensible..."

Dragging her gaze away, she spoke to break the spell she'd woven for herself. "Do you think they're just friends?"

"No."

Connor's hand released the steering wheel and moved to his thigh. Fascinated, Laura watched him massage the muscle through the denim of his jeans. As he replaced his hand on the wheel, a mental image formed of the same hand sliding up the length of her leg.

"Too sensible..."

She ran the tip of her tongue over her dry lips. "That's the first time I've seen Todd. He didn't look like I expected."

"Oh?" They rolled to a standstill at a stoplight, and Connor turned his head. "What did you expect?"

Her stomach flipped.

I expect . . .

I want . . .

Laura stared at the stoplight, willing it to turn green so he'd quit looking at her with those damned eyes. He was turning her into a basket case. She took a calming breath.

"*Sensible.*"

"Oh, someone sort of sinister and—"

"Menacing?"

The light changed. He stepped on the gas.

Relief turned her limp. "Yes. He seemed a lot younger and more benign than I'd pictured."

"You'll find, Laura, that the bad guys come in all sizes and shapes. The friendliest-looking kid you'd ever want to meet tried to blow my head off with a .357 Magnum."

Startled, she asked, "What did you do?"

"I ducked."

The comical picture he painted restored Laura's equilibrium. The pressure in her chest eased; her lungs resumed their normal activity. She grinned. "Faster than a speeding bullet, huh?"

Connor shrugged. "Luckily, his aim wasn't too good."

"You're being modest."

"No one's ever accused me of *that* before."

A moment later, Connor pulled up in front of Laura's apartment building and turned off the engine. "I'll walk you up." Before she could protest, he nabbed her camera off the back seat and followed her across the grass.

A single low-watt bulb burned in the second-floor hallway and the worn dark carpeting swallowed the sound of their footsteps. During the day, sunlight poured in through high south-facing windows, but most nights, Laura found herself glancing nervously into the shadows as she made her way to her apartment.

"Poor lighting," Connor said. His eyes swept the corridor as he leaned one shoulder against the wall and waited for her to find her key.

How reassuring, she thought, digging in her purse. *Even the police don't think it's safe.* She unlocked the door. Pushing it ajar, she turned to him. "Can I have my camera?"

He hesitated an instant, then passed it to her.

"I'll show you the pictures after I take the last—" She glanced down to check how many frames were left. A red *S* showed in the tiny window.

Perplexed, she looked up. "I'm positive I had several more—"

Connor's eyelids dropped.

Confusion solidified into suspicion. She fumbled with the film release knob, knowing before she opened the back what she would find.

Nothing.

"Where's my film?"

Sliding one hand into the pocket of his windbreaker, Connor tried for a nonchalant attitude. Laura wasn't fooled. She remembered his offer to bring the car and save them the long walk back after supper. She'd thought him considerate when he took their packages.

And her camera.

Her eyes narrowed. "I think you'd better come inside."

A kid caught hiding his broccoli couldn't have looked guiltier. Without a word, Connor followed her into the apartment.

"Well?"

"Have you got a beer?"

"Never drink the stuff," she said through gritted teeth.

"Coffee?" He smiled engagingly. "I'm really thirsty."

Stalking to the cupboard, she grabbed the can and slammed it down on the counter. Dishes rattled on their shelves.

"Talk!"

Connor pressed the button on the stove hood, and the light flared. "Would you believe I wanted to get it developed to surprise you?"

Laura crossed her arms over her chest. This was worse than getting a confession from a three-year-old.

"No? I didn't think you would." He poured water into the coffeemaker, then measured coffee in. Flipping the switch to On, he turned and studied her face.

"Okay." He pulled the film canister from his pocket and set it on the counter. "I took it."

Laura resisted the urge to snatch it up. "Why?"

"I need the shots I took."

The events of the afternoon flashed through her mind. Connor offering to take a picture. Connor fiddling endlessly with her camera settings. Six used frames.

He'd taken pictures of Todd and his friend.

"Why didn't you ask?"

"Habit." He shrugged. "The less you knew, the better."

The memory of him whispering "Play along" sliced through her mind, and with it, the throat-clutching terror that had gripped her. Even after they'd rounded the corner and he'd explained about Todd and his friend, her legs had shaken for what seemed like hours.

"Sort of what I don't know can't hurt me." Sarcasm laced her words.

He'd asked for her help with Ben, then set her up. He'd used her for his own ends. But he didn't trust her enough to tell her the truth. He was a manipulator, just like her father.

Raking his fingers through his hair, Connor sighed. He shook his head. "I wanted to protect you."

Water bubbled noisily in the coffee maker, the only sound in the silent kitchen. She stared into his eyes, wishing she could believe him but knowing he lied. He hadn't worried about her. He'd only thought about his damned drug case.

Betrayal twisted in her stomach.

At least her father tried to manipulate because he wanted what he thought was best for her. Connor used her because it was expedient. She meant nothing to him. How could she have been foolish enough to think otherwise, even for a single, breathless moment when their eyes had met in the car?

Laura drew a deep breath, ignoring the hollow feeling that had taken up residence in her chest. With a slight movement of her head, she indicated the film on the counter. "I'd like the rest of the pictures when you've finished with the film."

He nodded, but instead of the self-satisfaction she expected, his eyes reflected regret. "Laura—"

Her mouth tightened. Lifting her chin, she willed her face to convey nothing but polite disinterest. "Yes?"

For the space of a heartbeat, as he narrowed the gap between them, her resolve wavered. She tried to focus on what he was saying but was only conscious of a desire to sway closer.

He pressed something into her hand and closed her fingers around it. His warm breath tickled at her ear as he whispered, "For you."

The front door closed. Behind her, the coffeemaker ceased to burble.

Slowly she lifted her hand and unclenched her fingers.

In her palm lay a piece of amber.

Chapter 6

Joe pulled the print from the developer bath and examined it in the light of the desk lamp. He nodded. "Same guy."

"Can you enlarge it?" Connor asked.

"No problem."

"Make me two—no, three—copies. We'll fax one out to other police departments in the state while we wait for CBI to run a check. I'll go back up to Central City and ask around. He may be a local."

"Better let me do that," Joe said. "You don't know how good a look this guy got. No sense in him starting to wonder about you."

A knock sounded at the door, and Brenda's muffled voice asked, "You men about finished? I've got hot coffee ready."

"We'll be right up, honey," Joe called.

They listened to Brenda's footsteps shuffle back up the basement steps.

Joe set the finished pictures to dry, then held up the rest of the negatives. "What do you want done with these?"

Connor stared at them glumly, disturbed by the memory of Laura's anger. Why did she have to take it so personally? He was only doing his job. "How about double prints of each? Cut out our shots, though. She doesn't need those around."

"Sure thing." He tossed the negatives into a plastic bin and opened the door to the darkroom. "I'll have them ready in the morning. You want them delivered?"

"No. I'll take them over."

"She got to you, huh?" A glance at Connor's impassive face made Joe grin as he started up the stairs. "You can't say I didn't warn you."

Brenda looked up from a crossword puzzle. "Warn him about what?" She laid down her pencil and rose to pour two cups of coffee.

Just because she'd grown up next door to Connor, Brenda seemed to think she had the right to pry into his private affairs. And unfortunately, Joe did little to discourage her. As a matter of fact, he seemed to find his wife's nosiness amusing.

Joe chuckled. "Connor's having himself a little female trouble."

"Female trouble?" She set a plate of cookies in the middle of the table and stood, one hand resting lightly on her husband's shoulder.

"Remember the probation officer I was telling you about?"

"The one who was giving him a hard time about her client?" At Joe's nod she shot a look of concern at Connor. "I thought you'd worked that out."

"I did," he replied, flashing his partner a warning glance.

Ignoring him, Joe continued. "Well, it seems that she caught him stealing film from her camera."

"I didn't steal it—I borrowed it. It had shots I took of a suspect."

"Did you explain?" Brenda asked.

"I tried, but..."

"But," said Joe, pulling his wife into his lap and patting her protruding belly, "Unlike some women, she wasn't very understanding."

"Leave Napoleon alone," she warned. "This is the first time he's been quiet all day."

Connor seized the diversion in the hope of heading off her curiosity. "Napoleon?"

Smiling smugly at Joe's obvious discomfort, Brenda explained, "Yes, we figured if he inherited his father's height and machismo, we'd have a mini-dictator on our hands."

"Seems appropriate," Connor replied, straight-faced. He helped himself to a cookie, brushing aside a twinge of envy at their affectionate interplay. Times like this made him question his solitary existence.

For some unknown reason, Laura's face flickered across his mind.

He snuffed it out. No, he'd made his decision years ago when Meg left, and his life was better for its lack of strings. No one made impossible demands on his time. No one played head games with him. And no one interfered with his job.

"I think you should apologize."

Connor suppressed a groan. When Brenda got an idea in her head, she was worse than his mother.

"I was doing my job," he reminded her.

Brenda slid off Joe's lap and faced Connor, head cocked, hands on hips—a miniature red-haired Buddha. "Maybe,

but that doesn't matter. If you want her to listen, you've got
to apologize. She'll like you better for it."

"I don't really care." That was a lie, but he'd be damned
if he'd admit it. Joe was getting a big enough laugh over his
discomfort without giving him more ammunition.

"But you *do* want her to cooperate, don't you?" Evidently taking his silence for acquiescence, she repeated her
earlier command. "Then apologize."

"Darn it, Brenda!"

Joe chortled. "Take my advice, Mac. You might as well
give up. She won't quit till you do."

What the hell. It was what he planned to do, anyway. To
keep Laura from causing problems with Ben, he assured
himself. "Okay, okay, I'll apologize. As soon as Joe devel-
ops the pictures."

Brenda smiled sweetly.

Women!

Laura fingered the piece of amber in her hand and tried
to concentrate as her last client of the day explained why she
hadn't been home for two nights. The problem was,
thoughts of Connor kept intruding, just as they had every
waking hour since Sunday.

"And then my step-dad starts yelling how I never help
around the house. Never help? I do everything—clean my
room, cook dinner, do the dishes. What am I, a maid or
something? Why doesn't he get off his fat—"

"All right, Joyce," Laura interrupted. "I get the picture. But when we left you at home, you agreed to try to get
along with your stepdad."

"He doesn't try to get along with me—always griping and
complaining. He's never satisfied."

Satisfied? Laura didn't feel the least bit satisfied at discovering Connor's true character. Not when other memories of him haunted her.

Stop it! She mentally gave herself a shake and tried to focus on Joyce's problems.

"What about your mother?"

Lank hair flapped around the girl's face as she vigorously shook her head. "She doesn't do anything. She's on his side."

"It sounds like an impasse."

"Thing's'd be fine if *he* wasn't there. Can't you make him move out?"

Move him out? How did you move someone out of your dreams, erase the heat of his hand on your hip?

Willing herself to concentrate, Laura shook her head. "You know I can't do that, but I'll try to think of something. In the meantime, try to get along with them. And no more disappearing, understand?"

After making a note to check out family counseling, Laura dismissed her remaining paperwork. It could wait. On the way out, she stopped at the front desk for her messages. There was another one from Connor McCormack, the third this week. Guilt nudged her, but she dropped the slip into her mailbox with the others. Tomorrow.

You can't procrastinate any longer, she told herself as she tossed chopped onions into a frying pan an hour later. *You're supposed to be working with him.*

Her anger had cooled the first night, replaced by embarrassment. Embarrassment for the way she'd let her mind build fantasies, for the way she'd embellished his every look into something more than it was. Embarrassment that despite her best efforts, she couldn't banish him from her mind. What had gotten into her? It wasn't like her to let her imagination run wild.

Hamburger hissed as it joined the onion and garlic in the pan.

So he didn't trust her. What did she expect? She'd done nothing but throw obstacles into his path since their first meeting. Just because she was now cooperating for Ben's sake didn't erase that fact.

The doorbell rang as Laura set a pan of water to boil. Frowning, she went to answer it.

"You really should find out who's at the door before you open it."

Laura couldn't decide if it was Connor's presence or the note of concern in his voice that made her pulse race. Whatever the cause, the affect was unwelcome, considering the time it had taken her to regain her senses after last Sunday. Irritation made her flippant. "Hello to you, too."

Connor acknowledged his blunder with a grimace as he came inside. "Sorry. It's the cop in me."

The cop in him didn't bother her nearly as much as the man. She stepped back, hoping distance would calm her rattled nerves. Instead, she felt stalked as he moved closer.

"I tried to reach you at work, but you must have been busy."

Unable to think of a plausible excuse, she bluntly agreed. "Yes."

"I brought your pictures." The manila envelope he handed her was devoid of markings. As if sensing her curiosity, he added, "A friend developed them in his darkroom."

Wishing for something—anything—to alleviate the tension in the room, Laura pulled out the snapshots and rifled through them. "He did a good job," she commented before coming to several hazy pictures that looked as if someone had tried and succeeded in catching an apparition on film. Puzzled, she fanned the six photos and studied them while Connor peered over her shoulder.

"Um, those are the ones I took of you and Ben."

His tone was so sheepish that it brought a smile to her lips. By fixing her gaze on the ghostlike figures, she managed to keep from laughing aloud. "I hope your shots of Todd and his friend turned out better than these."

"A bit."

"Only a bit?" Eyes widened in mock horror, Laura tilted her head. Her smile froze as she became conscious of how close he stood. Close enough for her to see the thick lashes framing his blue eyes. Close enough to wonder what the dark stubble along his jaw would feel like if she raised a hand.

"I thought you said you knew how to operate a camera." In spite of her jumbled thoughts, her voice sounded amazingly normal.

"I do, but I'd already set the focus for the corner, waiting for a clear shot. I intended to take at least one good one of you and Ben, but you got tired of waiting."

"If I remember correctly, you seemed to take forever." She slid the photos back into the envelope and laid it on the end table. "Well, thank you for getting these developed."

Connor nodded and pulled a box of film from his jacket pocket. He placed it atop the envelope. "To make up for the shots I wasted."

"That's not necessary." She tried to return the film, but he shook his head.

"No. It's little enough for the trouble I caused you." He paused and cleared his throat. "Besides, I owe you an apology."

Apology? Connor? It was the last thing she'd have expected. He was a man who did what he had to, without excuse or defense. As for saying he was sorry... Would wonders never cease.

"Look," he said, the words falling awkwardly from his lips, "I appreciate what you did Sunday. I was asking a lot and you... well, you have a right to be mad. I should have told you about the pictures."

"It wasn't your taking the pictures. I know you were doing your job. I even understand why you wouldn't want Ben to realize what you were doing. It just hit me wrong that you were hiding the whole thing from *me.*"

When he opened his mouth to speak, she raised a hand. "No. Let me finish." She drew a breath and rushed on. "I know I haven't given you any reason to trust me—I was against the whole plan from the start. But Ben's agreed to do this—and as long as he's cooperating, I will, too. Just don't lump me in with the opposition. I need to know what's happening."

Brows knit, Connor stared past her shoulder while he rubbed the back of his neck. "I hear what you're saying, but in this job, the more people who know what's going down, the more chance to mess up." Abruptly, his eyes shifted to meet hers. "I'll tell you what I can, but I can't make promises. You'll have to trust me."

Trust him? Trust wasn't a one-way street, not in her book. It was something you gave and received in return.

But what choice did she have? If she refused, she'd remain on the fringe of events, watching from the sidelines instead of joining the action. What good would she be to Ben then?

The thought of the boy stamped out her remaining hesitancy. Squaring her shoulders, she nodded. "All right."

Connor visibly relaxed, a hint of approval evident in his gaze. He made her feel she'd passed a secret test, though for the life of her she couldn't figure out what it might have been. She'd only agreed to trust his judgment, nothing else.

A memory nudged her—the sensation of his hand curving over her moving hip as they passed Todd in Central City. A breathless shiver, almost of anticipation, chased along her spine, followed by the distinct impression that she'd promised more than she intended. Alarmed at the direction of her thoughts, she glanced away. Only then did her mind register a rhythmic rattle of metal, like distant cymbals.

"My water's boiling."

Seizing the diversion, she escaped to the kitchen, away from her confusing thoughts. The band of tension around her chest loosened as she removed the lid from the pot of steaming water and set it on the counter. She opened the cupboard next to the stove and stretched toward the top shelf.

"Here, let me."

Connor's hand grazed her shoulder, sending a shock like electricity through her. Startled, she stepped back and watched him snag the spaghetti package, then present it to her with a flourish. Her fingers closed automatically around the plastic as her gaze riveted on his slanted lips. "Thank you," she mumbled, turning to hide the flush rising in her cheeks.

Beside her, Connor bent over the simmering spaghetti sauce and sniffed. "Smells good. A special recipe?"

"No, just ordinary sauce."

"It can't be as ordinary as what I make. Mine comes from a jar."

Was that a hint of longing she heard? While she fumbled to open one end of the package, she peeked sideways at him.

He was staring wistfully at her sauce.

"I guess I'd better get home."

About to dump a handful of noodles into the boiling water, Laura hesitated. It *was* after six. "Why don't you stay for dinner?" she heard herself ask.

"Do you have enough?"

He had to be kidding. Since she always doubled the recipe to save cooking later in the week, there was enough for an army. Hiding a smile, she assured him, "I can stretch it with bread and salad."

"Well, if you're sure . . ." he began, then grinned, giving up all pretense of reluctance. "Okay, but only if you let me make the salad."

Shrugging out of his parka, he looked around for a place to hang it.

"Just throw it on the chair."

Laura swung open the refrigerator door and grabbed a loaf of French bread. From the corner of her eye, she saw Connor hesitate, then reach behind his back to slip something from his waistband. Metal glinted in his palm as he transferred the object to his coat pocket.

A chill chased down her spine.

She told herself she was being ridiculous. Cops carried guns. Why should it matter that his was concealed? She shook off her unease and closed the refrigerator.

Connor anywhere was difficult to ignore, but in close quarters Laura found it impossible. The sheer breadth of his shoulders made her small kitchen seem to shrink around her. She slid the French bread from its wrapper and picked up a knife as he pushed up his sweatshirt sleeves to wash at the sink. Her gaze was drawn to the dusting of dark hair along his forearms where muscles played beneath the skin as he lathered and rinsed. When he reached for a towel, she looked up to find him studying her. His mouth tilted at one corner.

"Is that for me?"

Following the direction of his gaze, she realized she still gripped the knife in one tense hand. Feeling like an idiot, she shook her head and pulled a second knife from a drawer. "Here's yours."

The kitchen had not been designed for two people, Laura decided. While she tried unsuccessfully to concentrate on cutting neat diagonal slashes across the top of the bread, Connor attacked lettuce and tomatoes with the vigor of a karate instructor. In a matter of minutes, he was done. He swept the vegetables off the cutting board into a wooden bowl with the blade of his knife, then looked at her expectantly.

"Mind if I add some more stuff?"

"Help yourself."

By the time she popped foil-wrapped bread into the oven, Connor had assembled a variety of items. Not only had he raided the refrigerator, but the cupboards, as well. A can of mandarin oranges, and a jar of salted peanuts sat next to some leftovers—lunch meat, green beans and cooked noodles.

"Are you saving any of these?"

Laura regarded the odd assortment with trepidation. "No, but you're not planning on using all that, are you?"

"Sure. Salads are a great way to use leftovers." He began to toss things into the bowl. "Fewer dishes to clean up, too."

Thirty minutes later, Laura had to agree his logic was brilliant. "We could have eliminated the rest of the meal entirely."

"No way," declared Connor as he worked his way through his second helping of spaghetti. "This is great. It doesn't taste like ordinary spaghetti."

"Well," she confessed, "a friend showed me how to make it. He learned how from his grandmother."

"Friend?"

"A lawyer I knew in New York—Rob Mazetti. We did accounting work for his firm. He had this huge Italian family that got together Sundays out on Long Island— brothers, sisters, aunts, uncles. Grandma and the daughters always prepared a gigantic meal."

"Sunday dinner, huh?" Connor swirled strands of spaghetti around his fork. "You must have been pretty close."

"We were." Laura paused, thinking about the plans she and Rob had made together. A feeling of melancholy settled on her shoulders. It all seemed so long ago, like something that had happened to another person in another lifetime. Abruptly, she shook off her pensive mood. "We still exchange Christmas cards."

"Humph." Seeming satisfied with her answer he reached for the basket of bread. "So you were an accountant in New York. That's a far cry from Boulder."

"I suppose so." Laura cut spaghetti into bite-size pieces with the side of her fork. "But at the time it seemed the thing to do. Everyone hoped to go with one of the big firms, so when I got an offer, I jumped at the chance."

"Did you like it? New York, I mean."

"It was different. Some things I really enjoyed—the theaters, the night life. And there's a quality to the city that's hard to explain—an energy and drive. Everything moves at such a fast pace. I really got caught up in that."

"But..." Connor prompted.

"But nothing. The job was interesting, and the money was good. I had a nice apartment, lots of friends."

Connor paused in the process of breaking off a piece of bread. "Then why did you leave?"

She shrugged, wishing the topic hadn't come up. It was a natural enough question—why she'd left a comfortable position with a major firm in an exciting city to work in a field where the monetary rewards were secondary. People always asked. But she didn't think Connor would be satisfied with her standard reply, that she'd missed Colorado. Cops were used to ferreting out information, and he would read as much into her omissions as what she actually said. And, for some reason, she felt compelled to tell him the truth. He deserved to know the whole story. Then he might understand the reason Ben was so important to her, why she worried about him.

"Jared."

The name hung like a storm cloud in the air between them.

Connor leaned forward and rested his chin on his folded hands, his expression encouraging. "What happened?"

"I'm not sure. I only have bits and pieces, information I've patched together. Mom and Dad won't talk about it." Years of practice had taught her control, and she managed to sound casual in spite of the ache in her throat. "Sometimes it's almost as though they never had a son."

"A defense mechanism. People think if they pretend something bad didn't happen, then it won't hurt so much. Only instead of going away, it just festers."

"The psychologist talking?"

Connor shook his head. "The man. We all suffer the problem. It's hard to acknowledge pain, and we're afraid we'll scare people off." He drew invisible designs on the place mat with the handle of his spoon. "So tell me. I don't scare easy."

"Well . . ." She stared across the room, focused on the past. "Jared was always the rebellious one. Me, I just went along with whatever Dad suggested." She gave him a rueful smile, knowing she sounded like a Goody Two-Shoes. "That's not to say I never did anything wrong. There were lots of times I got mad at the restrictions and expectations.

It's just that, for me, it was easier to not fight things too much. Most of the time, what he said made sense—get good grades to get into business school, go with a Top 10 firm, make lots of money, marry the right kind of man. It all seemed so logical at the time."

Sadness washed over her as she remembered how her brother, in direct contrast, had run headlong into every obstacle in his path. "Jared was different. From the time he was little he did things his own way. If someone said tree climbing was dangerous for a five-year-old, Jared would be halfway up the biggest one in the neighborhood in a flash. When he was four, Dad told him he was too little for a two-wheeler, so he took mine—I was ten—and secretly practiced for days, then rode it down the driveway as Dad pulled up after work." A pensive smile tugged at her lips. Jared had always refused to listen to his older, more experienced sister, even when his actions were sure to result in punishment.

"The older he got, the more defiant he became. Dad valued education, so Jared did as little work in school as possible. The teachers were always saying it was a waste of a good mind. 'If he'd only apply himself . . .' they'd say."

Connor grimaced. "I know the lines. I heard them often enough."

The tone, more than what he said, told her he wasn't just mouthing empty phrases, and for an instant, Laura pictured him rebelling against the established order of things. Somehow, it helped her go on. "Finally, when Jared was a sophomore in high school, Dad decided it was time to take matters in hand. He enrolled Jared in a private school in Colorado Springs. After that, Jared seemed to settle down— at least there were no more bad reports."

She took a steadying drink of water, then placed the glass on the table before smiling apologetically at Connor. "I told you once it was a long, boring story."

He touched her wrist in a gesture of reassurance. "And I told *you* that nothing about you could be boring."

Laura's pulse quickened, throbbing so strongly beneath his fingers that she knew Connor could feel it, too.

The moment spun out like silken thread as he caught her gaze. The thread stretched taut and a near-tangible current of understanding flowed between them. In a single, fragile moment, something new and tentative took root, something that might flourish and grow if carefully nurtured.

Tracing a feather-light path across the back of her hand, he opened his mouth to say more, then apparently thought better of it. Instead he settled into his chair. "Go on."

Although she regretted his withdrawal, the lingering comfort of his touch reassured her. And she needed reassurance. Up to this point, all the memories she shared had been bittersweet, but now began the part that she always shied away from, even in her own reminiscing.

"By then, when Jared was in high school, my parents had moved to Denver. I was going to Colorado University and living in Boulder, so Jared and I only saw each other during vacations. He seemed quieter, more self-contained. I guess I should have wondered at the change, but you know how college kids are—I was all wrapped up in my own life." Self-reproach twisted in her stomach. If only she'd been more aware, more receptive.

"You were only a kid yourself."

"Yeah, I suppose you're right."

She wasn't convinced. Pulling the amber stone from her pocket, she rubbed its cool surface in an attempt to calm her nerves. "Anyway, I think it was during high school that he started using drugs, although we didn't realize it at the time.

He did talk to me once about smoking marijuana—said everyone did it. Unfortunately, all I said was *I* didn't, so he shut up." A sharp, bitter bark of laughter escaped from her throat.

"What did he die of?" Connor asked suddenly.

For four years she'd lived with the hurt, kept her lips sealed, like a wild animal protecting itself. It hadn't helped; the wound was as raw as if it had just been inflicted. "Coke overdose."

"Then he was experimenting with more than marijuana."

"I know—now."

"How did it happen?"

Laura took a shuddering breath, determined to hang on to her composure. As though aware how difficult it was for her to speak, Connor fixed his attention on his water glass, tracing a line down the film of moisture on the outside, and waited.

"Well, I'd been in New York for three years, and Jared was in his freshman year at Berkeley." She looked up. "Did I tell you how smart he was? His grades weren't the best, but he blew the top off the SATs, and with some pull from friends of Dad's, he got accepted. Dad really didn't want Jared going so far away—I guess he still wanted to keep an eye on him—but Jared insisted and Dad finally gave in. It *is* a pretty prestigious school."

Connor nodded.

"The first semester he ended up on academic probation. Dad had a fit. Said he wouldn't keep putting out that kind of money if Jared didn't shape up. Jared just said college was a real adjustment for everyone and promised to buckle down second semester.

"Mom and Dad got a call from the university in March, just before spring break. All they said was Mom and Dad had better come because Jared was extremely ill, so they flew out.''

The tightness in her throat now extended into her chest, pushing against her lungs until she couldn't draw a breath. Bile nudged upward from deep in her stomach, and she clamped her teeth tight against it. Faster and faster she turned the stone in her hand, seeking strength to speak. She raised her head to look at Connor through a haze of tears.

''That's all they said—extremely ill. He was dead!''

Chapter 7

Her anguish tore at Connor's heart. He covered her hand with his. "They have to say that, Laura. You can't break news like that over the phone."

"Oh, I know." She rubbed at her eyes with the back of her free hand. "It just seemed so callous."

Silent, he clasped her hand, giving her time to finish. After a few moments, she started speaking again.

"It was a heart attack. Isn't that funny? Nineteen, and he had a heart attack." She tried to smile, but her face couldn't quite manage the movement. Suddenly, she wrenched away and sprang from the chair. "Coffee. I bet you'd like some coffee."

Connor stood. "Laura."

She halted, her face averted.

He pulled her into his arms, turning her to his chest, holding her rigid body. For an instant, he thought she'd maintain her control, but then her shoulders began to shake.

She lifted her arms and clung to him as strangled sobs tore from her throat.

His palm slid in repetitive motion over her back while soothing, unintelligible sounds came from his mouth. Anger churned in his gut. Not at her, but at the scum who dealt in death and destruction. God, he hated them!

People like Laura were one of the reasons he worked in Special Enforcement. Victims of drug abusers—the parents, husbands, wives, the sisters and brothers left behind.

"That's it," he murmured as her tremors vibrated through his body. "Let it all out." Hell, it'd been four years, but to her it was yesterday. Only someone who'd bottled grief inside broke down like this. Who did she think she was— Superwoman?

Gradually her harsh sobs tapered off, replaced by quiet tears that signaled the storm's end. His arm tightened around her, as she slumped against him, her muscles limp with fatigue. Patiently he waited, massaging her neck and shoulders until she drew a deep breath and released it in a long, shuddering sigh.

Gentling his hand, he stroked lightly down the length of her curved back, the way he would a small, frightened animal. "Better?"

Her head bobbed against his chest.

He smoothed back her hair, thinking how vulnerable she was and how well she hid it from the rest of the world. Never again could he look at her without glimpsing the hurt she covered with a sensible exterior, without remembering the helpless woman he'd held in his arms. She moved beneath his hand and he deepened the caress, massaging her scalp and letting her soft hair slide through his fingers. It was as silken as he'd imagined.

Like the whisper of night wind, a sigh fanned from her lips and she shifted slightly, relaxing against him. His body stirred in automatic response to her soft curves; his thumb traced the slope of her neck, from earlobe to the hidden hollow of her throat.

An alarm sounded in his brain, jerking him sharply back to reality. What was he doing? She'd come to him for solace, not seduction.

Knowing he should let her go, he found himself unable to take the step that would separate them. Her arms held him with sweet insistence, and beneath his thumb, he felt the flutter of her pulse. Helpless, he breathed in the fresh scent of her hair.

He was no saint. She sought comfort, and what better way to provide it than with his hands and lips and . . .

The ache in his groin intensified.

Before he could change his mind, he gripped her upper arms and forced her back a step. His nerves protested vigorously, then accepted the inevitable as she released her hold.

Avoiding his eyes, she pulled a tissue from her pocket and made a production of blowing her nose. "Your sweatshirt's soaked," she mumbled, risking a glance just above his belt buckle.

"No problem. It'll dry."

His response drew a self-conscious smile from her. "I don't know what happened. I've never broken down like that before."

Her swollen eyelids and blotchy face made her look like a heartbroken ten-year-old. It was all he could do to keep from sweeping her back into his embrace. He shoved his hands into his pockets. "Everyone needs to grieve."

"I have grieved—inside."

"Maybe that's the problem." In spite of his reluctance to pry, he found himself unable to resist questioning her further. "Tell me, didn't you ever cry with your parents?"

She shook her head swiftly. "They were trying so hard to be strong, I couldn't do less." She stared across the living room.

When she didn't continue, Connor followed her gaze to the bookcase on the far wall. He walked over and picked up a silver-framed photograph he'd barely noticed during his earlier visit. "Jared?"

"Yes." She moved to join him. "Do you understand why it's so important that I help Ben?"

Though the youth bore little similarity to the boy he'd seen in the photo in her office, he seemed familiar. Like a blow to the solar plexus, it hit him. Startled, he glanced at Laura, then back at the picture. Did she see it, too? The shape of the face and the coloring were different but the hooded eyes and the twist of the mouth—they were Ben's.

"You aren't to blame for what happened to your brother, Laura." He returned the photo to the shelf.

"I should have been there for him."

Connor ran his knuckles over her cheek and captured her chin, tilting her face up. The tears were gone, but a residue of sadness haunted the deep brown eyes. Slowly, emphasizing each word, he repeated, "It's not your fault."

For several moments, she remained silent, studying him, her head tilted to one side. Though she gave no indication she believed him, her eyes darkened. Unexpectedly, she lifted a hand to caress his jaw.

Connor froze.

"Detective McCormack?" Her voice was no more than a whisper. "Do you know what a good person you are?"

He'd been called a lot of things—hard, cynical, even stubborn—but good? Never. He opened his mouth to set her straight, but she laid a finger across his lips.

"Shh."

While her eyes held him captive, her hands stole around his neck, urging him closer. He yielded to their insistent pressure and slowly lowered his head, giving her the chance to change her mind.

She didn't.

Her mouth was softer than he'd dreamed, plush velvet beneath his, tasting faintly of tears. He thought to exchange no more than a gentle kiss of friendship, but his good intentions were washed away with her sigh when their lips met.

The kiss deepened as his fingers tangled in her hair and he slanted his mouth hungrily over hers, demanding a response. A flame flickered. She opened her mouth, granting him access to the sweet recesses.

He took it.

His hands sought the contours of her back and moved lower to cup her bottom. She strained against him.

The fire leaped.

A heart hammered against his ribs. His or hers? He couldn't tell. All he knew was fierce desire that threatened to drown out the voice of caution inside his head.

Remember. Remember. Remember. In faint tempo the words battled his growing need. A vision of Meg, her face wet with tears, and the memory of Sam, forced him to lift his head and drag his hands up to rest on the curve of Laura's hips. His breathing came in ragged bursts.

Damn, he didn't know how much more of this he could take. He wanted her. Here. Now. In spite of the case. In spite of Ben.

"Connor." Her words, soft with entreaty, were muffled against his chest. "I need you."

He tensed, hearing the pain in her voice, knowing her need to blot out memories. How could he refuse to give her the comfort she begged for?

As though aware of his ambivalence, she worked her hands beneath the ribbing of his sweatshirt. The touch of her fingers on his skin, soft and teasing, proved his undoing. With a growl of capitulation, he reclaimed her lips, giving himself up to the taste, the smell, the feel of her. Her mouth, her body, her rising passion sent a clear message—she wanted him as much as he wanted her.

Laura was the one to pull back the second time, but only long enough to lace her fingers through his and silently urge him toward the bedroom. At the side of her bed she swung back into his arms and raised on her toes, begging for more.

Connor obliged. Cupping her face in his palms and running his tongue lightly over her eager lips, he paused to murmur, "Are you sure?"

In a heart-stopping motion, she twisted out of his grasp and took a single step back. Connor's chest constricted as their gazes locked. The taut lines of her body, the quick rise and fall of her breasts and the solemn look on her face made him painfully aware of the silence surrounding them. His stomach knotted as he prepared for the words he dreaded. In his mind he heard her admit it was all a mistake, tell him he'd better leave. Though, in his present condition, he didn't know how the hell he'd do it.

"I'm sure."

A shy smile touched her face. With deliberate slowness she began to unbutton her blouse. Connor hardened in anticipation as the gap widened, revealing a tantalizing glimpse of pale skin, the swell of her breasts. Air caught in his lungs as she shrugged free of the garment and arched to reach the back of her bra.

Only then did his muscles break free of paralysis. Breathing with shallow, controlled care, he reached out and brushed her velvety skin with his fingertips, impatiently pushing at the lacy fabric that clung to the slope of her bosom. It fell away and he watched her nipples pebble beneath his gaze. His body ached to pull her into his arms, but he let his hand drop to his side, knowing there was more to come.

Unfastening the button of her skirt, Laura hesitated, searching his face. Apparently reassured by what she saw, she slid down the zipper and released the skirt from her grasp. It rustled to the floor and she stepped free. Perching on the edge of the bed, she peeled off shoes and hose, then stood, clad only in the briefest scrap of panty.

Connor felt as though someone had grabbed him around the throat and squeezed.

She was gorgeous.

Hungrily, his gaze skimmed her while he battled an impulse to take her without preliminaries. His jaw ached with the effort. How was it possible to become so aroused without even touching her?

Uncertainty flickered across her face and he realized she'd mistaken what had to be superhuman control for rejection. Her arms curved over her breasts in an age-old feminine response of shame as her lashes brushed her reddened cheeks.

"Don't!"

Her eyes flew open.

Striving to temper the harshness of his tone, he managed to speak with only a gravelly rasp in his voice. "I want to look at you." Then, following her lead, he pulled his sweatshirt over his head and undid the buttons on his jeans.

Comprehension replaced her wariness as he stripped off his clothes with far more haste than she had. Watching him, her lips curled in a secret smile. "Beautiful."

It was Connor's turn to feel self-conscious. He'd never thought much about his looks. Indeed, if asked, he'd have counted himself fairly average-looking. Beautiful? Men weren't supposed to be beautiful.

To cover his embarrassment, he laughed. "You're crazy, lady. And—" he caught her, pulling her with him to the bed "—I think you stole my line."

She didn't seem inclined to argue, especially when he silenced any possible retort with his mouth. Soft against hard, she sprawled across his chest in feminine abandon, the sweetness of her breath mingling with his as their tongues met in an intricate dance of seduction.

Warmth radiated into his pores, obliterating any remaining doubts from Connor's mind. Right or wrong, whatever her motives, he was beyond caring. At this moment, he'd grant her anything.

A purr vibrated in her throat as he stroked her body, learning the shape and feel of her—the sweep of her spine, the hollow at its base, and the rise of her buttocks. Like grass bending beneath the wind's gentle touch, her skin quivered in the wake of his hand, and he thrilled to the sensation.

Rolling her to her back, he trailed moist kisses along the side of her throat while his hand cupped the fullness of one breast. With the pad of his thumb, he gently flicked the nipple, felt it harden and peak and finally took it into his mouth.

She arched beneath him, nails digging into his shoulders. "Connor!"

He relaxed the pressure of his lips, letting her nipple slide free, and raised on one elbow to gaze innocently into her flushed face. "You don't like it?"

"I don't..." The words caught in her throat as he tongued her other breast. "I don't..."

"Don't what?"

Catching her lower lip between her teeth, she met his teasing glance. The look she gave him was so intense that he forgot to breathe. His hand stilled.

And then she touched his cheek, her expression rife with longing. "Don't want you . . . to stop."

Pent-up air burst from his lungs in a ragged laugh. "Stop? I don't think I could, even if I wanted to."

And the truth was, he didn't want to. Didn't want to stop. Didn't want to let her go. Didn't care that his control was strained to the breaking point. Her hands, her voice, the intoxicating scent of her arousal, chased all rational thought from his brain.

It was years since his first sexual encounter, an eternity of partners whose faces blurred in his mind. But Laura made him feel like a teenager again. Every nerve in his body prickled with the need to be closer, to bury himself within her. It wasn't sane, it wasn't logical. It just *was*.

Entering Laura was like coming home.

Warm, welcoming.

Her face mirrored pleasure as he thrust inside, then wonder, as the rhythm built, and finally, ecstasy, as they rode the crest of their passion to mutual fulfillment.

Limbs entangled, they clung together, neither willing to hasten the moment of separation. His chest still heaving, Connor listened to Laura's ragged breath. Gradually it slowed, ending on a sigh that echoed his own contentment. Tenderly, he kissed the moist skin of her shoulder.

She shivered.

"Cold?"

She shook her head, but he didn't believe her. Reaching over the side of the bed, he caught the edge of the comforter and rolled, drawing it with them. Laura curled into his embrace, her head tucked beneath his chin, one arm flung across him. Then, as he languidly massaged her back, she drifted asleep. Her muted breath softly stirred the hair on his chest.

Their bodies meshed like the pieces of one of those friendship medallions kids wore, he thought. Two different halves, melded into a smooth-edged whole. He stirred restlessly at the memory of just how well they fit together. Renewed desire stirred within him. In spite of the fatigue that claimed his every muscle. In spite of a voice that cautioned restraint. In spite of his better judgement.

Damn. He was already addicted to her.

Dismay washed over him. He'd let emotion overrule common sense once before and look what had happened—an old man with a penchant for booze, who'd never harmed anyone but himself, had died. Well, it wouldn't happen again.

Connor eased from the covers, hoping distance would strengthen his resolve. Laura murmured an incoherent protest, then quieted at the touch of his hand. From beside the bed, he studied her shadowed form, strangely reluctant to leave. Instinct told him Laura was different, that she wasn't manipulative like Meg, that she cared about others. But he couldn't take the chance of getting involved with her. He'd slipped tonight.

Slipped, he reminded himself, not fallen.

And one slip need not prove fatal.

Releasing his pent-up breath, he left the room.

Laura tugged the comforter higher and inhaled the musky odor that clung to the fabric. A feeling of well-being enveloped her. She reached out drowsily, seeking the warmth of another body. She grasped empty air. Startled, she peered through the dark for the luminous numbers on the clock radio. Nearly eight. And she was alone.

She burrowed deeper to ward off the chill creeping through her veins, but it was no use. He was gone.

Memories of his mouth, his hands, his hard, masculine body lingered in her mind. Moments before, the thoughts had warmed her as she slept; now they pricked her conscience, filling her with doubts. What had she expected? She'd used him to forget her pain. Even sensing his reluctance, she'd thrown herself at him, turning his male instincts to her own ends. The caresses, the whispered words, meant little in the heat of passion. Their coupling had been nothing more than a physical act. Hadn't it?

A muffled sound, out of place in her empty apartment, intruded on her thoughts. Laura rolled over to search for its source, her gaze leaping to the half-opened door. Light spilled across the floor from the living room beyond. The noise came again—a faint rush of water and the clatter of dishes. Hope caught in her throat as she identified the sound. Her heart's rhythm accelerated.

He was still there.

She threw off the covers and hastily pulled on a sweatshirt and pants. Combing her hair with her fingers, she padded from the bedroom, the carpet absorbing her footsteps.

Barefoot, dressed only in low-slung jeans, Connor worked at the kitchen sink, his back turned. More exuberant than efficient, he scrubbed at a pan, splashing soapy water on the countertops. Laura stopped. Mornings after—or nights after, she corrected—were not her forte.

Some sixth sense must have alerted him to her presence because he abruptly swung around. His features relaxed when he caught sight of her in the doorway.

"You're awake."

Her breath stuck in her throat at the sight of his bare chest. She remembered the play of muscles beneath her fingers, the feel of the crisp hair that trailed down...

Guiltily, she tore her gaze from the unbuttoned waistband and nodded.

"I made coffee."

Thankful to have something ordinary to occupy her mind, she poured a mug while he finished rinsing the pan and placed it in the drainer.

"You didn't have to do the dishes. I usually leave them till morning."

"I couldn't sleep." He dried his hands on a towel and studied her with watchful, unsmiling eyes.

What was he thinking? Did he regret what had happened the way she did?

She curled both hands around the mug and looked away, trying to tell herself it didn't matter, as a lump formed in her chest.

Connor reached for the coffeepot and poured a mug for himself. His voice, beside her, was subdued. "Laura, we have to talk."

She led the way to the living room, feeling like a patient about to be told she had three months to live. After a moment's hesitation, Connor settled at the opposite end of the couch from her, creating an illusion of distance that made her spirits sink even lower.

A sudden anger rose in her, irritation at her juvenile reactions. Here she sat, like nothing more than some pathetic schoolgirl, waiting to be dumped by a boy she had a crush on. Her teeth clenched. She'd gone into this with open eyes, and by God, she was going to start acting like a grown woman instead of a lovesick teenager.

"Okay. Talk."

He took a swallow from his mug, then set it on the coffee table and leaned back against the cushions, eyes closed. He blew air from his lungs in a heavy sigh. "Look, Laura, I don't know how to say this."

"I'm a big girl. How about starting at the beginning and going until you reach the end."

He tilted his head sideways to meet her gaze. Laura's face remained impassive, but she had the feeling he knew exactly what she was thinking.

"Yeah. I guess I owe you that." Rubbing his whisker-shadowed jaw, he stared into the distance. "Eleven years ago, I joined the police force . . ."

Laura choked on a spurt of hysterical laughter. "That wasn't exactly what I had in mind when I suggested you start at the beginning."

"I know." A half smile formed on his lips, and he took her hand. "But it's where I need to start."

She waited silently.

"I joined the police force eleven years ago," he repeated, stroking the back of her hand, "and I've worked undercover for eight of those years."

A shiver raced along her arm at the light touch of his fingers. She tried to ignore it and concentrate on his words.

"Eight years." He turned her palm up and ran the pad of his thumb over the life line. "I'm good at what I do, but it's not easy. When you're working a case, you have to live, eat and breathe it. Nothing can interfere. Because the stakes aren't just lost money or damaged property—they're people's lives."

"Sounds pretty tough," she said, intent on the tickling sensation his touch evoked. "Do all undercover cops feel the same way?"

"I don't know, but it's the way *I* have to do things. Years ago, I set up some rules for myself—rules that help me survive."

A premonition inched its way along Laura's spine. This was going to be something she wouldn't like, something she didn't want to hear. She slid her hand free of his, clasped her mug tightly in front of her and stared into its murky depths.

"Rule number one—keep your own counsel. Rule two—don't get emotionally involved. Three—expect the unexpected."

He paused and Laura felt his gaze on her. She took a sip of coffee, then placed the mug on the table next to his.

"Laura . . ." Low but insistent, his tone compelled her to raise her eyes. "Tonight, with you, I broke all three rules."

With a shake of her head, she denied his words.

"I suppose, technically, I didn't break number one, but I as much as agreed to. Don't worry," he hastened to add when she started to speak. "I won't go back on my word. I'll let you know what's going on. But rules two and three—" Resting his elbows on his knees, he leaned forward and inspected his laced fingers for several seconds. "It's not your fault. I take full blame for what happened tonight. I took advantage of your emotional state." A rueful smile touched his lips and he cut her a glance over his shoulder. "But you are definitely a distraction, lady."

Laura didn't know if she was more stunned by his accepting responsibility for their lovemaking or at being labeled a distraction. The former denied her any will; the latter made her sound trivial. Indignant, she drew herself up, eyes snapping.

"Rest assured, Detective McCormack, I have no intention of taking your mind off your work. You and your damned rules are safe."

"You don't get it, do you?" Irony edged his harsh laugh. "You don't have to do anything. You just have to *be* there."

With a twist of his body, he braced his palms against the couch on either side of her, his face inches from hers. Frozen, unable to protest, Laura stared into his flinty blue eyes.

There was nothing gentle in the mouth that met hers, only barely leashed power that caused her pulse to thunder in her ear. For an instant, shock held her immobile. Then, with a small moan, she wrapped her arms around his neck and returned his kiss with a ferocity that matched his own. Her breasts flattened against the firm wall of his chest, and she felt the blatant rise of his sex press hard against her stomach.

Muttering a curse, he wrenched free and flung himself to the far end of the couch, his breathing ragged.

Laura rubbed her arms, wishing the ache could mask the throbbing in her pelvis. She could no longer delude herself. It wasn't grief over Jared that was responsible for her throwing herself at Connor. It was desire, pure and simple.

"You still think there's no problem?"

The bitterness in his voice fed her guilt, making her response sharp. "I can control myself if you can."

"Hell, lady, control's my middle name. If it weren't, we'd be rolling on the floor naked."

Laura felt her face flame. No one had ever talked to her that way before, not even Rob—and she'd planned to *marry* him. Not for the first time, she realized how dangerous this man was. Not because she feared he'd harm her, but because of the emotions he kindled in her.

And, she suddenly remembered as reason reasserted itself, he had the authority to exclude her from keeping an eye on Ben. Her heart clenched. As much as she wanted to respond caustically to Connor's statement, she didn't dare. Somehow, she had to assure him that they could work together without passion interfering.

It took only a moment for Laura to seize on a convincing argument, an argument that Connor himself had provided. Her emotional state.

"All right, things got out of hand earlier tonight," she admitted, "but I really don't make a habit of throwing myself at everyone who offers sympathy. Let's chalk it up to stress—or temporary insanity—and forget it. I promise it won't happen again."

Connor stared at her for long seconds before releasing a harsh puff of air. "Okay. We agree we made a mistake. But there's more involved here than a simple case of misdirected hormones. There's Ben."

Laura stiffened. "This has nothing to do with Ben."

"No, it has to do with you."

The sharpness of his reply made her jump, and Connor modulated his tone. "Look, Laura. I said I'd take care of Ben, and I will. But things can happen. And if they do, I can't afford to worry about you, too."

"You don't have to. I won't get in the way."

"Right. Because you're not going to be there."

"Wrong." No one, not even Connor, had the right to dictate to her. As long as she broke no laws and no one was hurt, she was free to do what she felt best. Icy determination fueled her courage. "Without me, you lose Ben. I guarantee it."

Connor's eyes narrowed.

Laura raised her chin, waiting for him to concede defeat.

And when he did, she wondered why victory left such a sour taste in her mouth.

Chapter 8

Seated in his parents' living room two weeks later, surrounded by hordes of relatives, Connor faced the fact he'd been a fool. Control was one thing; torture was another. Only a masochist could have endured what he had without complaint.

The first weekend after their night together, he and Laura had taken Ben bowling—an ordinary enough proposition. Or so he'd believed when he suggested it. Who'd have thought it would be erotic to watch a woman bowl? Well, not any woman, he admitted. Laura. The way her snug jeans stretched across her rounded bottom when she bent to release the ball, the excited look on her face after picking up a split... Was it any wonder he'd ended up with the lowest score of the three?

And last Sunday had been nothing sort of a disaster, at least as far as his libido was concerned. They'd spent the afternoon at her apartment, playing Scrabble and Pictionary and eating gooey slices of pepperoni pizza. He hadn't considered ahead of time the memories that might be stirred by the familiar surroundings—the glimpse of her floral bedspread through the half-open bedroom door, the pillow-strewn couch where he'd been tempted to abandon his damned rules a second time.

Pure hell.

Connor glanced at the mob that had descended for Big Mac's birthday and cursed himself for deciding to bring Ben and Laura here for the afternoon. It had seemed such a good idea when Mom had called to remind him of the party, the perfect solution to his dilemma. Among all his relatives, he'd reasoned, he wouldn't have time to dwell on Laura's tempting curves, her provocative smile.

Wrong again. For all the good distance did, she might have been sprawled naked across his lap.

He glumly stared at the television, only half listening to the men around him. Normally, he liked nothing better than watching a good football game. Today...

Laura, he noticed, had been cornered near the dining room table by Aunt Harriet and his sister Kelly, both of whom would know even her shoe size by the time the afternoon was over. Briefly he considered rescuing her, but thought better of it. He hadn't brought a woman home with him in twelve years, not since his abortive effort to introduce Meg to the family, and nothing was guaranteed to raise speculation more than an attempt to head off his inquisitive relatives.

Shifting his attention back to the screen, Connor tried to work up some enthusiasm for the game. Was it his imagination, or were the Broncos supremely uninspired this afternoon?

The sound of Laura's laughter, light and teasing, echoed over the din of voices.

His neck muscles tensed. He took a long pull from the beer he was nursing and slouched lower in the armchair. Hell, if this case didn't end soon, he'd be ready for a straitjacket.

"Case not going well?" Big Mac hunkered beside his chair.

"About the same."

"Well, hang in there. You'll get 'em." He patted his son on the shoulder and lumbered off toward the kitchen.

Connor watched him go. Except for the white hair and slower pace, his father didn't seem much different from when Connor was a boy, growing up in Denver. Retired after thirty years on the police force, Big Mac carried himself with an air of quiet authority. A man of few words, he still managed to let his kids know he was there for them. The fact that he'd made a point of saying anything to Connor indicated he sensed his son's black mood.

Standing in the kitchen doorway, Laura tried to keep her mind on the conversation around her. It wasn't easy with all her senses focused on the man in the living room. The same man who, after introducing her to a bewildering assortment of relatives, abandoned her for a football game. Not that she expected him to stay glued to her side. That would have been a little too close for comfort. But it wouldn't have killed him to act a bit... friendlier. After all, she and Ben were here at *his* invitation.

"Don't you agree, Laura?"

For a moment, Laura stared blankly at the two women in front of her. She had no idea what she'd just been asked. "I'm sorry. I'm afraid my mind was wandering. What did you say?"

Aunt Harriet and Kelly exchanged knowing looks.

"It's all right, dear," Aunt Harriet assured Laura with a pat on the arm. "We understand. I felt the same way when

my George took me to meet his family for the first time.
Families can be a little overwhelming."

They'd obviously put their own interpretation on Laura's
presence. It made her uncomfortable, as though she were
here under false pretenses, especially since sisters Erin and
Lee had already informed her that Connor *never* brought his
girlfriends to these gatherings. But Laura saw no way of
clearing up the misconception without going into a lot of
awkward explanations.

"Have you considered that you might be speaking of
yourself?" Connor's mother, on her way to the kitchen with
a stack of dirty plates, gave her sister an exasperated look.
"Why don't you leave the poor girl alone?"

Indignation lit Harriet's wrinkled face. "Sharon Noreen!
I'm only trying to make her feel at home."

"Is that what you call it? Humph." She turned to Laura.
"Come with me, dear. I could use some help in the
kitchen." With a baleful look at the other two women, she
marched through the doorway, Laura close on her heels.

Sharon McCormack scraped remnants of food from the
plates and plunged them into a pan of soapy water. When
Laura picked up a dish towel, she shook her head. "No, no,
dear. I merely thought you could use some rescuing."

"I'd like to help, Mrs. McCormack."

"If you really want to, go ahead. And the name's Sharon.
Mrs. McCormack always reminds me of my mother-in-law,
God rest her soul."

Sharon attacked the dirty dishes, keeping up a running
stream of chatter. "I've never known anyone as nosy as that
sister of mine. She can't stand not knowing everything that's
going on, whether it's her business or not. But don't you
mind her. She has a good heart."

Laura picked up a plate from the drainer and smiled. "I
could tell that."

"And that daughter of mine! I think she spent too much time around Harriet when she was growing up. She certainly doesn't take after me. 'Live and let live' is *my* motto."

"I think your family's very interesting."

"But a little overwhelming, to borrow a phrase."

"A little," Laura admitted.

"You don't come from a large family, do you?"

"No."

"I didn't think so." Sharon turned on the faucet and began to rinse off soapy plates. "You can always tell the ones from small families—they're quiet. In a large family, if you're quiet, you get lost." Her hands paused beneath the stream of water as a thought struck her. "It's kind of funny, though. Mine have all married quiet ones."

Laura met Sharon's assessing glance and smiled politely.

The older woman shook her head as though clearing her mind, then, with a short laugh, turned her attention back to rinsing. "Of course, it could be that none of their spouses can get a word in edgewise."

A distinct possibility. Laura had never known anyone who ran on the way Sharon did, not even her own mother. But it was kind of nice—made you feel . . . welcome.

Returning to the soapy dishpan, Sharon changed the subject with a swiftness that caught Laura unaware. "Connor said he met you at work. Are you a policewoman?"

Laura shook her head.

"Oh, good. I don't know if I could handle another one. Not that cops aren't wonderful people, but I do think variety's the spice of life."

"How many law officers are there in your family?" Laura asked curiously.

"Let's see. Big Mac and his brothers—of course, they're all retired now, but I still count them. My son Jimmy—he lives in Dallas—and my niece Catherine, who's with the

Denver force, and Connor, of course. That's six. Now who am I forgetting? Oh yes, Harriet's grandson Kevin's at the academy. Seven. Seven cops."

"My God. It's like your own private police force."

"Precisely. And let me tell you a secret." A twinkle sparkled in her eyes as she lowered her voice. "It's also what's kept me on the straight and narrow all these years."

Only after their laughter finally faded, did Sharon return to her earlier line of questioning. "So what *do* you do for a living, Laura Douglass?"

"I'm a probation officer."

"Ah. That explains Ben." A note of pride crept into her tone. "Connor always was the one to care about kids." She rinsed and stacked the last plate in the drainer. "There. That's enough for now. Leave the rest to air dry and go find my son."

Laura's smile was strained as she left the kitchen. It was apparent that Sharon was blind to her children's faults. The idea that Connor might be using Ben had never entered her mind. Well, Laura wouldn't be the one to disillusion her. After all, the woman *was* Connor's mother.

Feeling guilty at having left Ben to fend for himself for so long, she made her way to the low-beamed basement.

She needn't have worried. Ben was crouched over an ancient pool table at one end of the room, getting instructions on play from a petite blonde who hovered at his side. As Laura watched from the foot of the stairs, Ben aimed his cue and missed the shot.

"Tough luck, man," sympathized a scrawny boy, who then dropped the next two balls into corner pockets.

Ben tried again after listening intently to suggestions from the girl. This time he managed to sink one ball before giving up his turn. A sheepish grin lit his face when the girl applauded his effort.

"You've got a good teacher, Ben."

Laura jerked her head around to see Connor on the steps, directly behind her. The teenagers greeted him with an enthusiasm that told her he was well liked.

"Wanna play, Uncle Connor? We're starting a new game?"

He shook his head. "You kids go ahead. I'll watch."

"Ben's never played before. You should give him some pointers."

"He's doing fine, Ally. I saw that last shot."

A flicker of surprise crossed Ben's face at the words of approval. Laura could almost see his shoulders straighten with confidence when he turned back to the pool table. Did Connor realize what he'd done? Maybe so. And maybe Sharon McCormack hadn't been so far off base when she said that Connor cared. The thought made her feel closer to him, as though they shared a common goal.

Connor leaned against the wall beside her, hands shoved deep in the pockets of his jeans. At Laura's prodding, he identified some of the dozen or so kids in the room, linking names to others she'd heard upstairs.

"And that's Ally, Lee's oldest," he said, inclining his head toward the blonde who was helping Ben. "She's Big Mac's prize pupil."

Laura watched as Ally chalked the end of her stick with a flip of the wrist. Bending low over the table, she sent the cue ball spinning across the felt. The racked balls broke with a satisfying crack, scattering around the table. Stepping back, she let Ben take a shot.

"Rather young."

"She's fourteen. Big Mac teaches the game to all the grandkids as soon as their heads clear the table."

An army of lilliputian pool players marched through Laura's imagination. She smiled. "Well, I suppose it keeps them out of mischief."

"And off the streets."

Connor's breath puffed against Laura's ear, light and distracting. Crossing her arms over her chest, she tried to ignore her jumpy pulses. She shot a swift glance sideways to discover his attention wasn't on the game. Her tongue flicked out to lick her lower lip, and his eyes followed the movement, then rose to meet hers.

The din of voices receded, stranding them in a pocket of private awareness, a place where they communicated without sound.

I've missed you.

You've been avoiding me.

Because when you're near, I want to touch you.

Go ahead. Touching can't hurt.

But when I touch, I want more.

Is that so wrong?

Even before he turned away, Laura read the answer in his eyes. For him, the act would be a betrayal of principles, principles that shaped the very fabric of his life. The strength they gave him was part of what first attracted her to him, and she couldn't ask him to give them up.

But what was wrong with bending them a little?

"Cake time," called a voice from above.

The announcement started a stampede for the stairs. Stepping quickly out of the way, Laura bumped against Connor. Automatically, he grasped her shoulders in a steadying movement. Only when the last kid had rushed past did his hands reluctantly release their hold. It might have been wishful thinking, but Laura thought she felt the brush of his fingers against the nape of her neck as she started to climb the stairs. Afraid she might be wrong, she didn't look back.

Everyone crowded into the dining room to sing "Happy Birthday" while two of Connor's sisters carried in the cake, ablaze with sixty-eight candles. Connor's father, looking appropriately self-conscious, took a deep breath and blew. The candles flickered and went out to a roar of cheers.

"What did you wish for?" asked one of the littlest girls.

"If I tell, the wish won't come true," Big Mac told her solemnly, but a mischievous grin lit his face as his glance slid from his youngest son to the woman at his side.

Laura reddened. Was the whole family crazy? All she'd done was come to a birthday party and they all jumped to conclusions.

The front door opened and a bearded man stuck his head in. From behind him peeked a tiny red-haired figure in a long coat and mittens. "Are we too late?"

Connor crossed the room to meet them, giving the rotund woman a hug. "Nope. You timed it exactly right as usual. We're just having cake."

The redhead returned his hug and planted a kiss on his cheek. A *warm* kiss, Laura decided, as she eyed the woman suspiciously.

"Joe, Brenda." Connor's father hurried over to help the woman off with her coat. "I thought you weren't going to make it."

"We wouldn't miss your birthday for anything," Brenda responded with a bright smile. "The McCormack cops would probably arrest us if we did."

Big Mac put his arm around her and drew her into the living room, providing Laura with her first clear view of the woman. Brenda wasn't plump; she was pregnant—very pregnant.

The noise level rose as people greeted the newly arrived pair. From remarks made, it was obvious they were old friends. A gaggle of chattering women quickly surrounded Brenda, asking how she was doing and comparing notes on pregnancies.

Connor, Laura noted, was still in the hall with Joe. Heads bent, they appeared to be engaged in earnest conversation. Connor said something and Joe nodded, scanning the room. His gaze lingered for a second on Ben, whose back was to him, and then moved on to seek out Laura.

Not sure why his look made her uneasy, Laura pretended to be engrossed in the cake she'd just been handed. When she peeked a moment later, the two men were making their way toward her.

Up close, there was nothing about Joe to warrant her earlier attack of apprehension. He acknowledged Connor's introductions with a warm smile that completely transformed his plain features. "So you're the lady who's keeping Mac on his toes. Brenda's been dying to meet you."

"Blabbermouth." Brenda slipped her arms around Joe's waist and grinned at Laura. "You'd think a cop would know when to keep his mouth shut."

"After you get to know them better," Connor said, "you'll learn who's the real blabbermouth in their family."

Brenda shot him a look of exasperation. "Remarks like that are what made me decide *not* to marry you."

Joe and Connor exchanged raised eyebrows over the top of Brenda's head.

It was easy to see that the three were good friends, although Laura couldn't understand how Brenda could joke about a broken engagement.

As if sensing her confusion, Brenda explained. "Connor and I grew up next door to each other. Our dads were partners on the force—sort of like Connor and Joe, except they worked homicide. I spent as much time over here as I did in my own house. Connor even baby-sat me on occasion. You wouldn't believe how sweet he was back *then*."

"If I'd known how you were going to turn out, I would have been nastier," Connor said.

Brenda ignored the gibe. "And he promised to marry me."

"I did no such thing."

"You did, too! I remember it as though it were yesterday. I was six and I asked you to marry me. You said you weren't going to marry anyone, but if you ever changed your mind, I'd be your first choice."

"Sounds like a real declaration of love," Joe said. "Think it'd hold up in court?"

"I doubt it," Connor replied. "I was underage. Not more than sixteen. Anyway, she's already married to you, so I couldn't have her if I wanted her—which I don't."

He glowered at Brenda, but Laura saw affection in his glance. There was an easy camaraderie among the trio that bespoke years of shared experiences. It was the same bond she sensed among everyone in this house—a guarantee that in spite of any differences, in the end they liked and supported one another.

"She'd drive me nuts in two weeks," Connor muttered under his breath.

Joe smiled down at his wife. "Didn't take her nearly that long with me. I was a goner the first time we met."

Brenda gave him a hug. "You and Connor go and find something to drink and let me get acquainted with Laura."

Looking as though he weren't certain that was such a good idea, Connor followed Joe to the kitchen. As soon as they were out of earshot, Brenda edged closer to Laura.

"Did he apologize?"

"Apologize?" Laura looked at her in confusion.

Brenda's eyes darted around the room and she lowered her voice like some modern-day Mata Hari. "For stealing your film."

"Oh." The discovery that Connor had told Brenda about the film was disconcerting. "Yes, he did."

"Good. I told him he should, if he wanted your help."

A chill spread through Laura's body at the implication of Brenda's words. Connor had only apologized because he wanted Laura's help. To keep her cooperation.

And if the apology was a fake, how much else was, too? How could she trust anything he said or did? A sick feeling settled in her stomach as doubts crowded her mind, taking root like bind weed, wrapping tenacious tentacles around each memory Laura had stored away. The amber worry stone, the sympathy, the kindness to Ben. The loving.

All lies.

Laura glanced around the crowded living room. What would these people say if she told them Connor was a liar? Would their faces reflect shock, disappointment? Or would they stare at her with disbelieving, pitying eyes. A liar? Our Connor? Never.

But Laura knew otherwise. And she knew why. Like her father, Connor was cursed with the need to control. Though he used different tactics, his motive was the same—to manipulate people and events so that things turned out the way he thought they should.

"Laura? Is something wrong?"

Laura managed a weak smile. "Nothing. I guess I just need to sit down." She sank into the nearest vacant chair, discovering that her legs did, indeed, feel wobbly. Suddenly, she wanted nothing more than to go home, to escape the cloying, friendly atmosphere of the house.

Concerned, Brenda hovered over her. "Is it that time of the month?" she whispered. "I know I always get woozy then. Or at least I did before this." She pointed to her protruding stomach.

In spite of herself, Laura had to chuckle at the other woman's bluntness. "No, Brenda, it's not 'that time of the month.'"

"Then it's something I said." Lines of worry furrowed between her brows. "Joe's always saying my mouth gets me into more trouble than a herd of elephants."

Before Laura could puzzle through the fractured analogy, Brenda shrewdly guessed the source of the trouble. "It's what I said about Connor apologizing, isn't it?"

Laura's swift denial didn't convince her. "He would have done it without me. I could see he felt bad. I just gave him the push he needed. I guess it's a male trait—they don't like to admit they make mistakes. And since Meg . . ."

The reference to a woman piqued Laura's curiosity. "Meg?"

Brenda pressed her lips together, for once reticent to divulge all she knew. "All I can say is Connor has more cause than most to be cautious of women."

Whatever the mysterious Meg had done, Laura decided, gave Connor no excuse to manipulate others. She tried to summon up righteous indignation, but all she felt was numbing gloom and a sense of foreboding.

On the drive back to Boulder, Laura discerned a new ease between Ben and Connor, as though something in their relationship had shifted during the course of the day. She should have been glad for Ben's sake—he needed a friend, someone who could wean him from his dependence on Todd—but mistrust of Connor's motives made her wary.

As though prompted by her thoughts, Connor casually questioned Ben about Todd's activities that week. He seemed unperturbed when Ben responded with only mundane goings-on, and shifted the conversation around to a discussion of pool strategy.

Pool reminded her of the basement and the moment of recognition that had passed between her and Connor. Was she being foolish to think he felt the same hunger, the same regret as she did? She sighed, not realizing the sound was audible until Connor glanced her way.

"I take that to mean you're not in favor of an afternoon of pool next Sunday."

"I don't play," Laura admitted.

"I could give you lessons."

Laura envisioned herself bent over a pool table, braced within the curve of Connor's body. The thrill that chased along her backbone warned her how dangerous that suggestion was. "I don't think so, but you and Ben go ahead if you want."

"No, we'll think of something else."

Leaning her head back against the seat, Laura closed her eyes. These Sunday outings were proving to be more wearing than she'd anticipated. Ben wasn't the problem; he embraced every plan with the eagerness of a neglected puppy. It was a joy to see him slowly losing his hostile attitude, to watch the mask of indifference slip more and more often from his face.

No, the real problem was Connor. Or if she were being truthful, herself. For in spite of her suspicion that he was only using them, she couldn't help being drawn to him, lured by fleeting glimpses of a side he kept hidden from the world. The man who stroked her hair and kissed away her tears. The man who took a moment to give a word of praise to a praise-starved boy. The man who told a six-year-old he'd marry her.

"Skiing!"

Laura's eyes popped open. A shower of snowflakes reflected in the headlights of the car, the obvious cue for Connor's train of thought. The curtain grew visibly heavier with each passing moment although there wasn't much accumulation on the road. Connor dimmed the lights to low beam to lessen the hypnotic effect of the falling flakes.

"What do you think? The reports from ski areas are good. There's been plenty of snow already in the high country."

"Great idea," Ben said. "I haven't been on the slopes since last spring."

"Well," Connor said, "I was kind of thinking along the lines of cross-country skiing. There are some good trails above Eldora, and I know of a place where we can stop for a meal if you want—a small cabin."

"Sounds fine to me," Ben said. "What about you, Laura?"

"Sure." Laura hadn't been skiing in years, not since leaving Colorado for New York City, and these past two years she'd been so busy with her job that she hadn't taken the time. Besides, the cost of lift tickets had gone up so drastically that she had trouble justifying the money when there were so many other, less expensive sports. Cross-country skiing, she'd heard, was a more economical route to go. "But what about equipment?"

"We can rent stuff in town," Ben said. "I've done it before."

"It's settled, then," said Connor. "We'll head out around seven next Sunday. I'll take care of lunch."

Chapter 9

It'd been a hell of a week, Connor thought as he drove across town Sunday morning. Nothing exceptional. A drug raid that netted weapons and a few grams of coke, surveillance of a suspected dope house frequented by college kids and endless hours of inventorying confiscated money. Another ordinary week in the glamorous life of a narc.

Nothing unusual. Except for the feeling of restlessness that came over him whenever Laura slipped into his thoughts. Which happened constantly.

With one exception, he'd never allowed anything to interfere with his job. Mind over matter. But Laura was fast becoming an obsession. For the first time since Meg, he considered breaking his rules. Maybe all he needed to regain perspective was to let things take their course. Then he might be able to focus on his work. Right, sneered a more rational segment of his mind. And while you're at it, you might as well shove Ben down a mine shaft!

The shiver that ran down his back had nothing to do with outside temperature.

In front of Laura's apartment, Connor turned off the engine and checked his watch: 7:00 a.m. Hunching his shoulders against the sudden bite of chill wind, he tromped toward the building. Week-old snow crunched beneath his boots.

The sight of Laura's cheerful face did strange things to his insides. He wanted to sweep her into his arms, sample the taste of her delicious mouth, explore the curves...

"Come in. I'll be ready in a minute."

His gut twisted as rumpled sheets and her naked body floated through his mind, but he managed a smile. "Take your time."

While she slipped into a multicolored parka and pulled a knit cap over her ponytailed hair, he forced himself to think of harsh wind and cold snow.

It helped.

A little.

"I've got a thermos of coffee and doughnuts and fruit for the ride up," she said, when he offered to take her backpack.

Connor hefted it appraisingly as they walked downstairs and out of the building. "What else? This must weigh ten pounds."

"Oh, some candy bars and juice, granola and another thermos with cocoa—in case we need a snack—a pair of binoculars and my camera."

He looked at her with exaggerated disbelief. "You're taking all that?"

"Hey, this is nothing. You're looking at a veteran backpacker. When Dad and Jared and I went camping, I used to carry a forty-pound pack and bedroll."

"Poor thing," Connor sympathized, unlocking the passenger door of his car for her. "McCormacks camp the easy way—pop-up tent trailer, gas grill—all the amenities of home. It was the only way we could get Mom to agree to go."

"*My* mother didn't—go, that is. She said if God had meant her to cook over an open fire, she'd have been born in the Stone Age."

Chuckling at the image of Laura's well-groomed mother crouched in a dark cave, Connor shifted the car into low gear and headed toward Ben's.

The streets were nearly deserted beneath a lowering, dismal sky. A lighter gray in the east attested to the fact that the sun had risen, but its rays were unable to break through the heavy layers of clouds. Except for a few brave souls like themselves, the city slept peacefully behind drawn curtains.

Connor rapped at the Westings' front door and rocked on the balls of his feet, studying the single set of boot prints that marred the snow-dusted brick terrace. His gaze followed the fresh tracks to where they disappeared around the corner of the house. He raised his hand to knock again, but before knuckles met wood, the door inched open.

"I can't go," Ben said hoarsely. "I don't feel good."

A shadow wavered behind him in the dim hallway. Connor felt the hairs on his neck prickle as he realized it wasn't Ben's. Mrs. White, the housekeeper? No, the shadow belonged to someone who preferred to remain anonymous.

Connor kept his tone sympathetic, while his mind raced over the possibilities. "You should have called."

"It just hit a couple of minutes ago."

"We could wait for a while, see if you feel better."

Ben's eyes flickered away from Connor's gaze. "Naw. It's probably the flu."

Or nerves, Connor silently amended. "A lot of that going around. Laura'll be disappointed, though."

"Yeah?" Ben glanced toward the car. "Well, you guys can still go."

Connor looked down, unsurprised to note that Ben wore tennis shoes, not boots. "Don't know if she'll want to without you."

"Hey, man. You don't need me."

Ben's words were edged with impatience, and something else that Connor couldn't quite put his finger on—tension, maybe. It didn't take an expert to sense something wrong. The signs were too obvious. Ben wasn't sick; he just wanted them out of there. "Okay. I'll try to convince her. Take care of yourself."

The door whispered shut.

Connor stared at the carved surface. Ben's nervousness might have any number of explanations—a girl, or just rebellion at spending the day with two adults. But Connor doubted it. Instinct told him Todd was inside the house.

His gut knotted. He tried to convince himself the pain had nothing to do with worry for Ben. The kid was all right. Just rapidly approaching a moment of truth. Soon he'd have to choose between what was right and his cousin. Much as Connor would like to give Ben a shove in the right direction, he couldn't. Not without tipping off Todd. He couldn't even wait around to make sure Ben was all right, though a voice in his head kept insisting he ignore his training and do exactly that.

He looked back at the car. Laura's promise to stay out of the way wouldn't be worth a damn if she thought Ben was about to get into trouble, and her meddling might blow the whole thing. Somehow Connor had to keep her away without raising her suspicions. And since he didn't dare leave the kid entirely to his own devices, he also had to arrange for surveillance. Frowning, Connor retraced his steps down the walk.

"He's sick," he announced as he climbed into the car.

Concern creased Laura's brow. "Maybe we should keep him company. His father doesn't get in till tonight."

"The housekeeper's there most of the time," Connor pointed out, alarm stabbing at the knot in his stomach.

One hand on the door latch, Laura hesitated. "It's not the same as having friends."

Inwardly cursing her mothering instincts, he turned the key in the ignition. "When was the last time you wanted friends around when you were puking?"

"Well . . ."

While she wavered, he drove home his argument. "Besides, he'll just sleep, and I can't think of anything more boring than watching a teenager sleep."

Although clearly not convinced, she settled back as he pulled away from the curb. "I suppose I can call later and see how he's doing."

Connor groaned silently. Having grown up surrounded by females, he knew that it would take very little to send Laura scurrying back to the Westings', and the last thing he needed at this point was her well-intentioned interference.

"Let's get your equipment over to the rental store. Since it's so early, maybe we can talk them into refunding your money."

The speedometer inched upward, keeping pace with his growing fears for Ben, but it wasn't until he took a corner on two wheels that Laura complained.

"Do you have to drive so fast? I don't think a few minutes will make that much difference."

Given the circumstances, Connor heartily disagreed, but he obliged by easing up on the gas pedal a little. Too little, he could tell by her compressed lips and dashboard-clutching fingers, but thankfully she kept any further complaints to herself.

He sped down Arapahoe and pulled into the ski rental parking lot, braking into an empty space at the side of the building. "Can you get your things inside? I've gotta make a phone call."

Without further explanation, he sprinted to the glass-enclosed booth. His fingers thrummed impatiently on the side of the box while the phone rang.

Joe finally answered on the third ring.

"Get up. I need a favor."

"It's seven-thirty, you sleazeball."

"If I'd wanted the time, I'd have called 'Time and Temperature.' Now listen, then get your butt in gear." Quickly, Connor sketched the morning's events and related his suspicions. "There was someone else in the house, someone he didn't want me to see, and my money says that someone was Todd Billings."

"What're they gonna do on a Sunday morning—rob a church?" Joe chortled at his own humor.

"I don't know, but I can't stick around to find out. Todd's seen me once. How'd it look if he spotted Laura's boyfriend the psychologist snooping around?"

"Like you were trying to drum up business?"

Connor swore.

"Okay, okay. Where do I reach you when I'm done?"

"You don't. I'll be in Central City trying to ID the guy I saw with Todd."

"It's a waste of time. I've tried twice."

"I know. But I have to keep Laura away from Ben, and it's the best I can come up with on such short notice. I'll check in when I get back."

"Oh, great." Sarcasm dripped from Joe's voice. "You hit the casinos and I freeze my tail off."

"I owe you one, buddy."

"You bet you do. You owe Brenda, too." With that, he hung up.

Empty-handed, Laura rounded the corner just as Connor stepped from the booth.

"They give you any trouble?"

She shook her head, her gaze darting from Connor to the phone. He could almost see the wheels grinding in her mind.

"I left the burner on under the coffeepot. My neighbor's got a key." He could tell she didn't buy the explanation, but except for a sidelong glance, she let the matter drop.

"It's probably just as well we aren't going," Laura said as they climbed into the car. "I've got a stack of reports to do and a week's worth of laundry." Sighing, she leaned against the headrest and closed her eyes. "But right now, a nap sounds wonderful."

It sounded wonderful to him, too. Especially if he were curled against her, touching her velvety skin, stroking... Quickly, he blocked the evocative scene from his mind. Being around her without Ben's inhibiting presence was going to be rough. Connor cleared his throat. "I need to drive up to Central City."

When he failed to turn on the engine, Laura opened her eyes and looked at him questioningly.

"Since we're already out, I thought you might like to go along." Fool, he thought. You sound like a bumbling teenager asking for a date.

Laura shook her head. "No thanks. I want to be around if Ben needs me."

So do I, he wanted to snap, but he managed to keep the frustration from his voice. "Ben'll be fine, and you can call when we get back. Besides, I owe you for canceling our plans."

"You didn't cancel. Ben did."

Great! Now she had to be logical. "Whatever. You're still missing an outing. The least we can do is salvage lunch." Laura followed his gaze to the bulging pack in the back seat. "I'd hate to see it go to waste."

Unexpectedly, Laura's lips quivered. If he didn't know better, he'd guess she was trying to keep from laughing. Suddenly, he remembered wolfing down her spaghetti and realized how ludicrous his last statement sounded.

"I certainly wouldn't want that to happen," she replied solemnly.

Connor grinned. "Okay, ridiculous, I know. But I *do* have to see if anyone up there can identify the guy in the pictures—the one with Todd. And, with two of us asking..."

"We'd finish in half the time."

He nodded, aware that she found the idea of helping appealing.

Finally she agreed. "But you have to promise I'll be back at a decent hour. I've got a lot to do."

Connor smiled, feeling the fire in his gut ease a fraction. As he dropped the transmission into reverse, he wondered if an ulcer was the price he'd pay for doing his job despite his feelings for Ben.

"Any luck?"

"Nothing."

The clamor of slot machines in a nonstop feeding frenzy spilled from the Red Dog Saloon and Gambling Hall behind them. Laura raised her voice a little to be heard over the din. "What now?"

"Now, we call it a day."

"Thank God." She wiggled her toes inside her tennis shoes, trying to relieve the ache produced by three hours of pavement pounding. Three *unsatisfactory* hours, she thought.

Taking different sides of each block, she and Connor had systematically covered Central City, showing the snapshots of Todd and his companion in every shop, restaurant and casino. For nothing. If this was a sample of Connor's job, he could keep it. All she wanted was a bathtub full of hot soapy water. "So, what are we waiting for? Let's head home. We can eat in the car."

"I've got a better idea," he said as they started down the sidewalk.

Laura broke stride. She wasn't sure she wanted to hear another inspiration. Especially if it included more walking.

"What do you say we wait and eat at the cabin?"

Cabin? What cabin?

Correctly interpreting her puzzled expression, he added, "The cabin where the three of us were going to stop for lunch."

"I thought we had to ski to get there."

"It's accessible by road, too. At least when the weather's good, it is."

Lunch in a cozy mountain cabin. The appeal was undeniable. Laura could almost smell the scent of pine and hear the crackle of burning logs in the fireplace as she imagined the scene.

Just the two of them.

For a moment she hesitated, remembering the fire that had ignited the last time they'd been alone together. Hot kisses and lingering caresses—a memory made bittersweet by what had followed. It wouldn't happen again.

"And it's right on the way home."

Hunger and her aching feet won out. She sighed in resignation. "All right. Just give me a second to call Ben."

Connor looked as though he wanted to protest but apparently thought better of it. While she dialed, he leaned against the booth and waited with a stoic expression on his face.

"Mrs. White? It's Laura Douglass. I'm just calling to see how Ben's doing?"

The housekeeper assured her Ben was fine. She hadn't heard a peep from him all morning. In fact, she'd just peeked in, and he hadn't even stirred. "Burrowed in like a hibernating bear" was her description.

"What'd I tell you?" Connor said as they drove down the canyon. "He didn't need us hanging around when he'd only think we were there because we didn't trust him."

Laura agreed, amused by the relief Connor had tried to hide from her. He'd been just as concerned as she.

"Just a couple more miles," Connor announced when he pulled off the highway less than an hour later.

Laura's teeth jarred together as the car bounced over the corrugated surface of a dirt road. She craned her neck to study the sky through the close-set lodgepole pines. The sun had long since disappeared behind a lowering bank of dull gray clouds. As she watched, large fat flakes began to fall. They gathered, then slid in watery clumps down the glass, distorting the scene outside.

She shot Connor a sidelong glance. Why did men refuse to turn on the windshield wipers until it was nearly impossible to see? Almost as though their masculinity might be called into question if they gave in to the elements. Just when she decided to speak up, they rounded a curve and rolled to a stop. A small, log cabin crouched on the other side of a narrow clearing.

Stepping out of the car was like leaving a sauna for a plunge in an unheated pool. The cold air raised goose bumps across Laura's skin. She hunched her shoulders and brushed at the feather-light snowflakes that settled on her face.

The hard-packed dirt was slippery with pine needles and a light dusting of snow. Head down, Laura followed Connor across the clearing and bumped into him when he stopped to unlock the door.

"Careful." He wrapped an arm around her to prevent her from slipping again, then shouldered open the weathered door. Light from a window to one side of the single room cast a ghostly glow across the dark interior. While Laura waited in the doorway, he retrieved a kerosene lamp from the mantel and placed it on a small oak table. Striking a kitchen match, he lit the wick. The lamp flared to life, casting a circle of buttery gold.

"Okay, you can come in now."

Laura gave the door a shove, and it creaked shut behind her. She took a step forward, then stopped.

All alone in the middle of nowhere.

They'd already spent several hours cooped up in much closer quarters in the car, Laura realized. But for some strange reason, being in the cabin made her acutely conscious of their isolation. She told herself she was being ridiculous, but the feeling persisted.

Unaware of her hesitation, Connor crossed to the stone fireplace and soon had a fire started. Tendrils of warmth spread through the chilly room.

Seated on the raised hearth, he unlaced his boots. "Better get out of those wet shoes."

His practical suggestion cut through Laura's thoughts, and the room seemed to snap back into focus. Ordinary. Comfortable.

She removed her hat, then gulped as he peeled off both parka and sweater. The swell of muscles were clearly delineated beneath his black turtleneck. Heat that had nothing to do with the fire blazing in the grate surged through her.

Dragging her gaze away, she fumbled with her laces, kicked off her soggy tennis shoes, then silently handed him her coat. When he turned to drape their things over a chair, her attention was caught by the leather holster hanging from one shoulder.

Did he wear his gun everywhere?

Shaking off the tickle of unease, she knelt before the fire and listened to Connor move around the kitchen. Unable to identify the strange metallic clanking behind her, Laura glanced over her shoulder. Connor was testing an iron hand pump. Satisfied when water spurted into the sink, he removed dishes from a shelf above the wood-burning stove.

"Do you want to eat at the table, or picnic in front of the fire?"

At the mention of food, her stomach growled. "Let's picnic."

"Your wish is my command." With a grin, he spread a checkered cloth and deposited dishes atop it.

Following his lead, Laura sat cross-legged on the floor, curious to see what he had brought. Like a magician pulling rabbits from a hat, he emptied two thermoses, bottles of seltzer water and a variety of foil-wrapped packages from his backpack.

"And you grumbled about what *I* packed?" she couldn't help teasing.

"Absolute necessities," he insisted.

The packages turned out to hold individual-size Italian loaves, cheeses and wafer-thin slices of turkey, from which he assembled gigantic sandwiches. After handing her one, he poured vegetable soup from one of the thermoses.

A short time later, Laura leaned back on her elbows and stretched her legs toward the dying fire, too full to take another bite. Eyelids drooping, she watched the dancing fire-light and let her thoughts drift.

Although concern for Ben still nibbled at the edge of her mind, she wasn't really worried. Mrs. White seemed quite competent, and Laura's initial reservations had faded. The truth be told, she was glad she'd had the opportunity to see a new side of Connor—a mellower, more relaxed side. And she liked not needing to fill the silence with idle chatter.

Covertly, she studied his profile and wondered what their relationship would have been like without the continual sparring over Ben.

Sweet and sudden, memories of their lovemaking flooded through her—his hand brushing the side of her breast, his mouth, fierce with demand, and the fiery heat of possession...

Abruptly, she corralled her wandering thoughts. *Impossible*. They were too different. On opposite sides of the fence. Where she believed in giving kids a second chance, he, as a cop, was more interested in putting them away. How could she even think for a second that she and Connor would overcome the problems between them? Although, for a while today...

As though sensing her scrutiny, Connor turned. For a long moment, he gazed at her, and Laura imagined she saw desire flash in the dark depths of his eyes.

Her heart hammered wildly against her ribs as he slowly leaned toward her. His warm breath caressed her cheek and she closed her eyes, waiting for the touch of his lips. It came, so light and fleeting that it could have been the whisper of a night breeze.

Laura's eyes snapped open, but Connor had already stood and crossed to the kitchen without a word. Frustrated, she willed herself not to moan.

Behind her, the pump screeched as Connor filled a cast-iron pot with water. Laura drew air deep into her lungs and searched wildly for something to break the tension. "Do you know the owner?"

The squealing stopped, but there was no answer.

She peeked over her shoulder. Connor faced the window, one hand gripping the pump handle. Something in his stance sounded an alarm, and she rose to her knees. "Connor, what's wrong?"

The sound of her voice broke through his preoccupation. "What? Oh, nothing. Just checking outside. It's still snowing. But nothing to worry about." He lifted the heavy pot from the sink with two hands and carried it to the fireplace. "What were you saying?"

"I asked if you knew the owner of the cabin?"

He hung the pot on a metal rod bolted into the stone and swung it out over the fire. "Yes." Settling beside her, he stared at the flickering flames with a distracted air.

"Well, who is it? A friend?"

"What?" His eyes focused on her face, and he seemed to pull his thoughts from a long way off. "Who owns the cabin?"

Laura gave him an emphatic nod.

"I do."

"Why didn't you say so?"

"You didn't ask. What difference does it make?"

"None, I guess." She looked around at the stark, unadorned interior. It reminded her of a monk's cell, a place for atonement. "Have you had it long?"

"A few years. I come here when I want to get away."

Get away from whom? From what? He didn't elaborate, and she shied from asking, afraid to hear the answer. "How did you find it?"

Connor picked up a log from the hearth and poked at the half burned wood in the fireplace. Sparks scattered up the chimney.

"Summers, I used to come up to the area to fish. Then one day, when nothing was biting, I hiked upstream and found the cabin. It hadn't been lived in for years. I kind of liked the way it sat off all by itself, so I asked around down in Nederland. Learned it'd been built in the twenties by a recluse. Some say he was one of the convict laborers from the Colorado State Penitentiary who helped lay the road between Boulder and Nederland in 1915. Came back because he liked the area."

"And I suppose that appealed to the cop in you."

Amusement sparked in Connor's eyes. "You bet it did. Almost as much as the other story that circulated about him—that he was a prospector, still dreaming of making his fortune. Whoever he was, he didn't like people. Only went to town for supplies a couple of times a year. When he died in the sixties, the property passed to a distant relative in Denver, who used it for a fishing retreat when he was younger. He hadn't seen the place in ten years and was glad to sell it to me."

Abruptly, Connor checked his watch, then paced to the windows, gazing out into the gray world beyond. "I spent most of my free time up here that first summer, doing repairs, fixing up the place. Mom and Big Mac donated the furniture." He returned to the hearth to swing the pot of water away from the heat with a piece of kindling, which he then added to the dying fire.

Using a rag to carry the steaming pot to the sink, he poured part of the water into a dishpan and added some soap.

Laura stacked dirty dishes and carried them to the sink. "Why don't you let me clean up? Since you provided the meal and the picnic site..." Smiling, she echoed his frequently used cajolery and looked up. "It's the least I can—"

The smile faded from her face.

Disbelieving, she stared through the window. The snow swirled and leaped in an erratic dance outside. Icy pellets buffeted the glass. Squinting hard, she could make out the first line of trees beyond the cabin.

But past them, the world had disappeared.

Chapter 10

"**W**e're snowed in!"

Laura paced the floor, berating herself for giving in to his cajolery. "We should never have stopped for lunch. As soon as the snow started, we should have turned around."

"Laura, you heard the radio on our way down—light flurries. No one was expecting this."

"You should have known. You come up here all the time." She knew she was being illogical. Colorado was famous for its unpredictable weather, and Connor couldn't be expected to have more insight than experienced weathermen. But she hated feeling helpless. "Surely, if we drive carefully—"

"The road's impassable in weather like this. It's too risky. The snow should stop before morning. We'll try then."

"Morning!" Arms akimbo, she glared at him. "I have appointments in the morning."

Connor shrugged. "I guess they'll have to wait."

"Couldn't we call someone?"

He shook his head. "No phone. I come here to get away. Remember?"

"But surely you have some way to contact people in an emergency."

"If I'm going to stay, I bring a CB." His expression was apologetic. "But our original plans called for skiing in..." He didn't need to complete his explanation. They were stuck. But good.

"Look, Laura, we've got a roof over our heads, plenty of firewood, even a little food. Since there's nothing else we can do, we might as well make the best of things."

Her glance swung back to the frost-covered window, and she sighed. He was right; it would have been foolish to venture out in the storm. But admitting it made her feel impotent, frustrated. Staring at the floor, she allowed herself one last grumble. "What if it doesn't? We could be here for days."

Laughter rumbled in Connor's chest, and before she realized what he was about, he gripped her shoulders, pulling her toward him. "I promise it'll be over by morning. If it isn't, I'll fight my way to the highway and hijack the first snowplow that comes along. Okay?"

Trapped between his muscular thighs, Laura discovered it was impossible to remain irritated. Her objections and arguments were lost in an avalanche of sensations—his masculine scent, the vibration of his chest beneath her open palm as he spoke, the pressure of his callused fingers on her chin gently yet inexorably forcing her to look up.

"Okay?" he repeated, his amusement evident.

Lost in the depths of his navy eyes, Laura struggled to remember the question. She looked at his curved lips.

"All right," she replied, her voice oddly husky. "Whatever you say."

Drawing an unsteady breath, Connor wondered how long he could keep his feelings in check. And why was he even trying? She couldn't possibly wreak more havoc than she already had, invading his dreams and intruding on his waking thoughts. What could it hurt, just this once, to give in?

Drawn by the promise in her eyes, he sought the delicious, remembered taste of her mouth and found reality even better than memory. Her lips moved, soft and pliant, and parted to allow her tongue to dart in a teasing, tantalizing dance with his. She moved impatiently, her pelvis rubbing intimately against his swollen crotch, filling him with a heavy ache. Even through her bulky sweater, he felt her breasts strain and swell against his chest and imagined drawing the pebble hardness of her nipples into his mouth. He inhaled the enticing, feminine scent clinging to her skin...

In the fireplace, a log popped and splintered, shattering the intimacy of the moment. Brief as it was, the sound nudged at Connor, reminding him of his surroundings—the edge of the sink digging insistently into his backside, the draft from the window.

He tried to ignore the intrusion of common sense. Bare wood floor, lumpy couch—the place didn't matter. Hell, he was willing to take her standing up, against the kitchen counter. But reason, once granted a toehold, refused to be silenced.

He drew back and filled his lungs with air, struggling to dull the clamor of his protesting body. It was agony just being this close. Unable to resist one last touch, he ran the pad of his thumb lightly along her jaw and dropped a chaste kiss on her moist mouth.

"I say we take care of these dishes before the water gets cold."

As confusion flitted across Laura's face, he curbed the urge to gather her back into his embrace.

"The towels are in the bottom drawer."

Biting her lower lip, she retrieved a dish towel and moved stiffly to the sink.

In silence, they washed and dried the dishes.

Connor felt like a jerk. She'd taken his restraint for rejection, and there was no way to explain without making matters worse.

Later... he thought. Later, he'd build a roaring fire, dig out the blankets, lace the thermos of coffee with brandy from the cupboard...

Later, he'd make it up to her.

Laura placed the six of hearts on a black seven, then counted out three more cards. A red five. She studied the array of cards on the floor in front of her for a moment, then wiped a trickle of sweat from her forehead.

A fire blazed in the hearth, testimony to Connor's labors. Standing, Laura pulled her sweater over her head and tossed it on the couch.

Since they'd finished the dishes, Connor had occupied his time hauling in more firewood, dragging the couch closer to the fire and checking the food supply. Right now he was in the loft, searching for heaven knew what else.

Anything to avoid being near her.

When she'd offered to help, he'd handed her a deck of cards and told her to relax. How the heck was she supposed to relax with a tiger prowling overhead?

Frustrated, she wandered to the window. The wind had let up, but the snow still fell in fat fuzzy flakes that coated the trees with a layer of whipping cream. She scraped her fingernail across the frost on the inside of the glass, etching designs. A heart. An arrow.

Guiltily, she rubbed at the drawing with the heel of her hand, then wiped her hand on her jeans while she skimmed over the nearly empty shelves. Four cans of soup, a box of pancake mix, an unopened glass of jam, flour, sugar and a jar of instant coffee.

Her gaze returned to the pancake mix, then leaped to the stove. Did it work? She pried up one of the iron circles from the top and peered inside. This had to be where you built the fire.

Something thudded on the floor behind her, and she whirled in time to see several blankets drop to the cabin floor. Connor's legs appeared at the top of the ladder, and she watched him descend, pillows and sheets tucked under one arm.

"Our bed," he explained, piling blankets on the couch with the rest of his load. "It'll be warmer down here by the fire. There's no heat in the loft."

Our bed? Not if she had anything to say about it! Twice today she'd abandoned her reserve, only to be slapped in the face with his damned control. And now he wanted to sleep together? No way. She might be many things, but a masochist wasn't one of them. "I can sleep on the couch. It looks a little short for you."

Connor looked startled. Obviously, separate beds hadn't occurred to him. "Don't be ridiculous. Sharing body heat will help when the fire dies down."

"I'll take my chances."

"I can't let you. You could get hypothermia."

"Then we'll flip for it." Laura bent to pick up the cards strewn on the floor, hiding a smile of satisfaction.

Muttering something about stubborn females, Connor gave in. "Okay, but I'd rather leave the choice to a friendly game of poker."

"Never play."

"Gin rummy?"

Laura shook her head.

"War? Concentration?"

"Kids' games."

"Not the way I play them." His eyes glinted wickedly.

Unsettled by his swift change in mood, she refused to even ask the obvious question. "I know," she said suddenly. "Double Solitaire. You do have another deck somewhere, don't you?"

"In the kitchen drawer."

"Super. We'll play right after dinner."

A look of disbelief crossed Connor's face. "Dinner? We just ate a couple of hours ago."

"Three to be exact," Laura corrected, after checking her watch. "And by the time you get a fire going in the stove so I can make pancakes, it'll be after five. Dinnertime."

"Now just a minute." Connor's voice was firm. "There's no sense in making more of a mess than necessary. We'll just finish off the lunch things I brought."

"There's not enough left for two of us. Besides, what do you plan to do for breakfast?"

Connor glanced toward the shelves. "Heat a couple of cans of soup in the fireplace?" he suggested hopefully. "Like the pioneers."

"I doubt pioneers carried cans of soup on the trail. Too heavy. Nope, I think it's pancake and soup for dinner, left-over lunch meat and bread for breakfast."

"You don't know what you're letting yourself in for."

Laura blithely ignored his ominous tone. "It can't be any worse than cooking over a campstove."

It was.

In the first place, it was hot. Hot enough that the phrase "slaving over the kitchen stove" took on new meaning. And not just around the area where she was cooking. The whole stove glowed, lying in wait for an unsuspecting part of her body to come in contact with it—a fact she discovered when she accidentally leaned against the front. Luckily, she'd jumped back before the heat penetrated her jeans, or she'd have been sporting a nasty burn in a highly vulnerable spot.

In the second place, Connor was no help at all. After building the fire in the iron monstrosity, he declared his part of the job done, settled on his stomach in front of the fireplace and promptly fell asleep. At least she assumed he was asleep, in spite of the suspicious quiver of his shoulders whenever she muttered a curse.

By the time dinner was prepared, she was a sticky, irritable mess.

Balancing bowls of soup, she nudged Connor awake with an impatient toe. He grunted and rolled over, taking in her disheveled appearance. Wisely, he refrained from making a comment. But his eyebrow lifted when she deposited the plate of pancakes on the table.

"I couldn't regulate the heat," she explained defensively as he forked two scorched disks onto his plate.

"I'm sure they'll taste fine."

He slathered strawberry jam on the pancakes, then reached for his knife while Laura watched. Slicing off a bite, he stabbed it with his fork and popped it into his mouth. "Great," he pronounced, after swallowing the piece.

Laura managed to finish one chewy pancake before conceding defeat. Glumly, she stared at the pile left in the middle of the table.

"Don't feel bad. The squirrels will eat them."

Grateful for his attempt to make her feel better, she met his twinkling gaze.

"Or use them to play Frisbee."

For an instant, before her sense of humor intervened, she considered aiming a pancake at his head. But it would probably knock him out cold, and then what would she do? She picked up her empty plate and rose with a grin.

"You could always use them for target practice," she said, reaching to pat his holstered gun as she passed by.

His hand snaked out, clamping around her wrist in a viselike grip.

Raw shock obliterated her smile. Seconds before, he'd been relaxed, teasing. Now his face wore the cold mask of a stranger. As her brain registered pain, a whimper escaped from her throat, and the pressure on her wrist eased a fraction.

"Don't ever do that again."

His tone was harsh and menacing, unlike anything Laura had ever heard from him before. She shook her head, biting her lip to prevent tears from falling.

A jolt of horror crossed Connor's face. With a jerky motion, he let go, then released a ragged breath.

Laura carefully set her plate back on the table and cradled her throbbing wrist.

"Laura, I'm sorry. It was pure reflex."

When she didn't respond, he slid his fingers over hers, interrupting her massaging motion.

Their eyes met, and Laura felt the icy chill around her heart begin to melt at his visible remorse.

"I would never intentionally hurt you. Never."

She shivered as his lips grazed the tender skin of her wrist. "Forgive me?"

How could she do otherwise when he looked at her like that? "Yes."

"Thank you."

His gratitude surprised her so much that she didn't protest when he insisted on cleaning up alone. Dropping to the sofa, she folded her legs beneath her and stared into the fire. Her wrist still burned, though the physical ache was secondary to the pain she'd felt at seeing him change before her eyes. In that awful moment, when he turned on her, he'd become someone to fear, someone she'd have run from if she met him on a dark street. The image bothered her. During the weeks since they'd met, as she'd allowed herself to forget what he was trained to do, the cop had slipped from her mind, replaced by a man she liked and respected.

A man she could easily love.

The admission fell like a pebble in placid water, the ripples spreading in ever-growing circles of disturbance.

Was it true? Was she falling in love? Or had she merely been enchanted by a clever facade? Was the real Connor gentle or violent, compassionate or ruthless, tender or cruel? Or... all of the above?

Connor's approach, minutes later, only added to Laura's confusion. Walking on silent cat feet, he leaned over the back of the couch, catching her unaware.

"How about a nightcap?"

At her nod of assent, he circled the couch and presented her with a mug of coffee.

Alerted by his expectant air, Laura took a cautious swallow, then gasped. "What did you put in this?"

"A little whiskey."

"There's more whiskey than coffee," she accused. "Are you trying to get me drunk?"

He smiled innocently. "How else am I supposed to beat you at cards?"

Another swallow and Laura decided she liked the way the beverage settled with a warm glow in her stomach. "I suppose 'all's fair...'" Her voice trailed off as she finished the saying in her head.

"Exactly," Connor agreed in a husky voice, meeting her flustered gaze.

The glow in her stomach spread outward.

Connor drained his mug and set it on the mantel, then eased another log on the fire.

Laura frowned at the weapon in his holster. "Do you always wear a gun?"

Eyes wary, he confronted her. "Only when I'm dressed."

She was about to laugh, but something about his expression stopped her. He was serious.

"Why?"

"Because I never know who's at my back, who might be around the next corner."

"That's paranoid."

"No. That's reality."

Troubled by his dulled response, Laura watched him pick up a blanket, shake it out and let it drift to the floor. She moved to the end of the improvised bed he was building and bent to straighten the corners, searching for words that would erase the harsh grooves around his mouth.

"Connor—"

"What do you think my job is, Laura—helping little old ladies cross the street?"

His attempt at humor was overdone, and she sensed that her comment had unintentionally hit a raw nerve. Her conclusion was confirmed when he continued.

"Well, it's not. It's dirty and dangerous, and the rewards are few and far between. The bad guys laugh at you, and the decent people don't give a shit until their own homes and families are terrorized."

A second blanket was flung open like a challenge. Laura caught one edge and lowered it atop the first, wrestling with the resentment his words unleashed in her. The sneer he'd given to the word "decent" stung. She'd heard his attitude expressed more than once, but the thought that he lumped her in that category hurt. It was untrue and unfair. What made cops think they were the only ones who cared about crime? Wasn't she carrying on the same fight in a different way?

"So it's just you against the world."

"Damn right."

His antagonism crackled in the air. Laura bit back an angry retort, but her clenched jaw must have communicated her irritation, because Connor suddenly looked embarrassed.

"Hell, I've got a big mouth," he muttered as he crossed to the kitchen. Grabbing the bottle of whiskey, he returned to the fireplace and poured himself a generous portion.

Laura busied herself with spreading bedding on the floor and covertly watched him belt down the drink. Her heart sank when she saw him wipe his mouth with the back of a hand and pick up the bottle once more.

Abruptly, he raised his eyes and caught her worried look. He glanced from her to the bottle, hesitated, then replaced it on the mantel. Keeping his back turned, he braced his hands against the ledge, head bent.

The silence, punctuated by the intermittent crackle of fire, dragged out for several seconds while Laura sat back on her heels, her fingers rubbing uneasily over the nubby surface of a blanket. She'd never seen him this way before, so moody and withdrawn, as though he carried a weight that was too much to bear.

When he finally stirred, she held her breath, then watched in surprise as he took off the leather holster and gun and laid them on the mantel.

"There." He swung to face her. "Feel better now?"

"Immeasurably." She knew she was grinning like an idiot but couldn't help it. By removing the weapon, he was doing more than making allowances for what he saw as her squeamishness. The gesture told her he could change, *would* change—for her. His dark side was there, a part of who he was. She couldn't wish it away. But it didn't matter.

"Just keep in mind," he warned, kneeling in front of her, "that a gun is a cop's security blanket. Especially an undercover cop's. Without it, he feels naked. Soooo..."

He drew out the single syllable in time to the movement of his thumb tracing along her lower lip.

"...when I take it off..."

She shivered as his lips nibbled at her earlobe, then moved down the column of her neck.

"...you'll have to make extra certain..."

His fingers unbuttoned the front of her shirt and slipped inside to gently stroke.

"...I feel safe and protected."

Laura felt her breasts swell in his palms while beneath her hands, his biceps stretched and tensed. She wove urgent fingers in his thick hair as a tender, moist sensation blossomed at the juncture of her thighs, a heavy yearning that oozed like honey through every part of her.

Her breathing quickened as his tongue swept her aching nipples through the sheer lace of her bra, and when he unhooked the front clasp to suckle at her breast, she grew dizzy with longing. "How...how...?"

The question was no more than a puff of air, but he heard and raised passion-darkened eyes to hers. "Oh..."

Smiling at some inner secret, he unsnapped the fastening of her jeans and tugged down on the zipper. "I think you'll—" his hand slipped inside the elastic of her panties and brushed against her feminine mound, making her shudder with desire "—find a way."

Gasping, she arched against his palm as his fingers slid seductively inside her.

Her quivering thighs refused to support weight and she slumped against his chest, moaning in frustration when he withdrew his hand.

"Easy, easy," he whispered against her lips, then made it impossible by sweeping her mouth with his eager tongue.

His breath tasted of whiskey, but it was his tongue's teasing that made her giddy. Boldly, she ran a hand over the swell beneath his zipper, pleased when her movements made him groan.

"Now, who needs to take it easy?" she murmured with satisfaction, then gasped as he forced her jeans and panties to her knees and grasped her buttocks, pressing her against his arousal.

Her thighs and stomach tingled to the softly abrasive touch of stone-washed denim. But it wasn't enough. She needed to see him, touch him, breath in the warm, masculine scent of his skin or she'd shatter into a million pieces.

When she pushed insistently on his forearms, he reluctantly loosened his hold. With more haste than finesse, she shrugged out of shirt and bra, then sat on the blanket and swung her legs forward.

Connor stopped her as she grasped the wadded clothing to pull it off. "Let me." Encircling her legs with palms and fingers, he pushed her jeans and panties ahead of his hands, an inch at a time until they slid over her feet, together with her socks.

When he stood to strip off his turtleneck, she leaned back on her elbows to watch, her gaze skimming hungrily over the expanse of his chest. He balanced on first one foot then the other to peel off his socks, then reached for the waistband of his jeans.

"No. Let me."

Startled, he hesitated, but when she rose to her feet his hands dropped to his sides. She carefully worked each metal button from its hole and pushed the jeans over his hips, smiling when he impatiently kicked them free. His stomach muscles tightened at the touch of her fingers on the elastic of his shorts.

"Enough, Laura," he said through clenched teeth. "I'll take care of the rest, unless you want this to be over before it starts."

His body was beautiful, more beautiful than she remembered. For weeks, her mind had fed on memories—the play of hard muscles beneath her palms, the salty-sweet flavor of his skin, the scent of his masculine sweat. But now she needed more. She needed reality.

He stretched out his hand, guided her to the floor, firelight dancing in his eyes.

"We're not playing by the rules," she warned when he poised above her.

His gaze scorched her. "Rules be damned. We'll make our own."

She surged to meet him, wrapping around him, urging him deep within.

Later, she might regret. But for now, she surrendered to ecstasy.

Chapter 11

Sometime during the night the snow stopped.

Laura didn't care.

Through lowered lids she studied Connor's bare back as he poked at the glowing embers in the fireplace. Unable to resist temptation, she ran her palm down his spine, relishing the warm, smooth texture of his skin.

He shivered and turned, a half smile curving his lips. "Watch it, lady, or the fire will go out."

Propping herself on one elbow, she let the blanket slip to her waist and arched an eyebrow at him. "That tired?"

His gaze caressed her bared breasts, and Laura felt her nipples tighten.

"Hell, no, but you should be."

Laura yawned and stretched. "I *am* a little sleepy."

He caught her hands over her head and pinned her against the bedding. His mouth closed roughly over hers while he rubbed his chest against her breasts.

Desire raced like quicksilver through her veins. Feeling him harden against her stomach, she moaned and shifted restlessly under his weight.

"Oh, no you don't." He nipped her earlobe. "I have to bring in more firewood." With that he rolled away.

Laura drew the covers to her chin and watched him pull on his jeans, socks and boots. Her eyes widened when he bypassed jersey and sweater to slide directly into his parka. "Won't you get cold?"

"You'd better hope not," he replied. The door slammed behind him.

Laura squeezed her lids shut to block out the light from the kitchen window. It was morning already, and soon they'd have to start back. But she didn't want to think of that now. She didn't want to think at all. Feel. That's what she wanted to do. Feel Connor's mouth against her neck, feel his breath stirring her hair, feel his hands . . .

She wiggled onto her side and felt the blanket slide sensuously over her skin. Every nerve in her body was set to overload, so that the slightest touch made her delirious. That's what he'd done to her. Time after time, throughout the long night. Connor.

Just thinking about him . . .

Furtively, she touched a finger to the swollen spot between her legs. Her finger came away wet.

She was going to have a dreadful time when she got back to Boulder, if every time her thoughts strayed . . .

Discipline. That's all that was needed. She tried to clear her mind and think of mundane things—the state of the world, her job.

Her job.

Ben.

Oh, God. How could she do her best for Ben if she couldn't put her feelings for Connor out of her mind?

The door banged open, letting in a blast of cold air. Laura kept her eyes tightly closed, but it didn't do any good. She could still hear him moving around the room, dropping a load of wood on the hearth, adding a log to the fire.

The couch squeaked when he sat down. Thud. One boot hit the floor, and she held her breath until the second one followed. The rasp of a zipper told her he was taking off his coat; a rustling sound evoked an image of him removing his jeans. Then, silence.

Her heart pounded against her ribs, and she knew without looking that he was staring down at her. She feigned sleep.

A whisper of cool air touched her skin when he lifted the blanket to crawl in, spooning his body around hers. She jumped. His chest was like ice.

By sheer force of will, she lay quietly as his lips tickled the nape of her neck, but his hand, moving seductively over her breasts, wasn't so easy to ignore. And when his fingers glided down the curve of her belly to stroke across her hidden core, Laura knew her efforts were useless.

In a gesture of surrender, she rolled to her back.

"I wondered how long you'd pretend to sleep."

"Too long," she admitted, lacing her fingers together behind his neck.

With a gentle tug, she pulled his head down and brushed her lips across his, but when she sought to deepen the kiss, he pulled back and gazed into her eyes.

"I want to give you something."

"You've already given me everything."

"Shh," he whispered, covering her lips with one finger. "This is for the trip back..."

He trailed kisses along her neck, stopping to press his lips against the pulse in its hollow before moving down to her breasts.

"For tomorrow and the day after..."

His mouth swept down her rib cage, tasting and nibbling.

"...and the day after that."

Tension coiled in her stomach when his lips brushed lower still. He raised his head, his gaze dark and hypnotic.

"I want to see you burn, every time I look at you..."

His teeth grazed the soft inner flesh of her spread thighs and the coil tightened.

"...just the way you're doing now."

His tongue dipped.

Sensation ripped through her. She dug her nails into his shoulders, frantic with need. A scream tore from her throat. "Connor!"

Swiftly, he joined with her as her world exploded into a million shards of light.

"Connor?"

His name blew softly across his chest, piercing through his languor. Lazily, he stroked Laura's hair. "What?"

"Who's Meg?"

His hand froze, and Laura lifted her cheek, running her fingers through the flattened curls where she'd lain.

"Where did you hear that name?" he asked quietly, trying to still a flutter of apprehension.

"From Brenda. At Big Mac's party."

Silently he uttered a string of expletives. Someone should put a muzzle on that woman, and if it weren't for Joe, Connor would volunteer. Being an old friend didn't give her the right to meddle in his affairs.

"Who is she?" Laura persisted, resting her chin on his sternum and looking into his eyes.

"Part of the past, Laura."

"An important part?"

"Only as important as you make it."

His words came out flatter, colder than he'd intended. He could tell by the startled look on Laura's face, the way she glanced quickly away, that he'd hurt her. Why couldn't she leave well enough alone? He didn't want to think about Meg, relive the pain.

Intending to change the subject with a kiss, he slipped his arm around Laura's shoulder, but she shrugged him off with an apologetic smile.

"I need to visit the outhouse."

He sensed her excuse was a ploy to escape, but how could he argue? Silently, he watched her pull on her clothes, zip her parka to her chin and slip out the door.

It was an inauspicious ending to the weekend.

By the time Laura returned, Connor was dressed and had cleared away all evidence of their lovemaking. Her glance settled for a moment on the empty floor, but she said nothing, content, it appeared, to swallow a hasty breakfast and prepare to leave.

"I hope no one's worried," Laura said as she waited for him to lock up the cabin.

Connor dropped the cabin key into his pocket. "Who's to worry? You said you only had one appointment Monday morning, and we'll be in Boulder by ten."

"I just thought Ben might have tried to get in touch with me."

"Ben's fine," Connor said lightly, concealing his concern. Maybe Todd hadn't been at the house at all. But even if he had been, Connor trusted Joe to keep Ben out of trouble.

It took more than half an hour to negotiate the three miles back to the main highway. At times the car acted as though it had a mind of its own, straining to leave its designated route for the challenge of dodging pine trees. Twice, they had to haul out the bag Connor kept in the trunk for winter emergencies and spread sand under the tires. Each time they held their breath as the car scrabbled for traction, then regained the road.

"For a while, I thought you'd have to strap on your skis and make good on your promise to flag down a snowplow," Laura joked when they finally headed down the canyon.

Connor grinned. "Why do you think I worked so hard to get the car back on track?"

Low snow walls on either side of the highway attested to the passage of plows earlier in the morning, and the sun was already melting the last traces of precipitation from the asphalt surface. The trees flaunted mantles of white beneath a vivid blue sky. A perfect day, Connor decided. Or at least it would have been if it weren't for what awaited them.

Beside him, Laura sat lost in thought, and he wondered if she, too, hated the idea of returning to the real world. Things between them wouldn't be the same as before—last night had taken care of that—but he had to face facts. Neither of them would allow what had happened to interfere with responsibility, and the resulting conflict would strain their new relationship. Maybe beyond endurance.

He didn't want that. But how could she understand the forces that drove him, the memories that compelled him to put his job foremost in his life?

He had to tell her about Sam.

He couldn't.

His palms grew wet at the thought of breaking the years of silence. He'd never told the whole story to anyone, not even Joe. Never expressed the horror. Never voiced the guilt.

He couldn't do it. Not even if it meant losing her.

But it was the only way.

In the end, it boiled down to merely opening his mouth.

"Meg was the woman I lived with years ago, when I was in graduate school."

Laura fingered the mitten in her lap and stared out the front windshield.

"I thought I loved her."

Conscious of Laura's darted glance, he kept his attention on the road. If he stopped, he might never continue.

"I wanted to marry her, but Meg considered herself a free spirit. She said society's trappings were meaningless and that living together was commitment enough. I went along because I was afraid of losing her if I pressed too hard.

"I was going to get my doctorate and set up a counseling practice in Southern California because that's where Meg wanted to go. She made jewelry and felt the vibes were better there for what she called 'artistic types.'"

"Connor," Laura interrupted, "you don't have to tell me this."

His throat clenched at the sympathetic note in her voice, and he met her eyes for an instant. "Yes, I do."

She nodded and let him go on.

"She'd already alienated my family, although to be fair, I don't think she intended to. She just never considered other people's feelings when she spoke, and when I tried to suggest she be a little more diplomatic around my parents, she called them rigid and bourgeois. It was easier not to argue with her."

"I can't imagine *you* keeping quiet for anyone."

Connor laughed ironically. "I've learned."

The car emerged from the canyon and entered the city. Laura opened her mouth to protest when they sped by the Justice Center, but evidently thought better of it. "So... what happened?"

"She left me." His grip tightened on the steering wheel as he awaited the familiar surge of pain in his chest.

It didn't come.

Surprised, he smiled at Laura. "She ran off with a hippie she met in a coffee house. She was even thoughtful enough to leave me a note. Said it wouldn't work between us. I made her feel hemmed in, smothered. She wished me a good life."

"Did you look for her?"

"How could I, after that? When I came out of my depression, I decided I was a rotten judge of character and had no business becoming a psychologist, so I dropped out of grad school and joined the police force. Actually, I'd been toying with the idea for some time but had been afraid of Meg's reaction. She thought cops were sadistic pigs."

He swung the car into a space in front of Laura's apartment and shut off the engine, feeling suddenly drained.

"And you never saw her again?"

"Once." Apprehension dried his mouth and gave his voice a hard edge. "One night, after I'd been on the force a year, she called. She was back in town and had to see me. I had an urgent message on my answering machine I needed to follow up on, but she was insistent. She couldn't wait. I gave in."

Connor stared out the windshield, unwilling to watch Laura's sympathetic expression change to one of loathing, as it surely would when she heard the end of his story. Before he could chicken out, he rushed on. "I should have followed my instincts. She wanted money, not me, and when I got around to contacting the guy who'd called, he was dead."

Old Sam's grizzled face swam before his eyes. Not twisted by a wry grin, but frozen into a mask of horror, the way it had looked that day.

"Who was he?" Laura asked in a subdued voice.

"An old man. Sam. He used to come to me with information. Mostly worthless. But I'd stand him a couple of drinks and keep him company for a while." He paused, knowing his next words might drive the look of compassion from Laura's face. He steeled himself and continued. "Some kids messing around in the canyon discovered his body."

As vividly as if it were yesterday, he remembered standing on the hillside while they lifted Sam's body out of the abandoned mine shaft.

"The coroner said he'd died from a massive blow to the head, consistent with a fall, and his blood contained a high level of alcohol. Conclusion—death by misadventure. But I always wondered. And I never found out what he'd called about."

"You don't think . . ." Laura hesitated.

"I don't know. That's the problem. If I'd followed my instincts instead of my—"

Laura laid a hand on his forearm. "It's not your fault, Connor. You can't spend the rest of your life blaming yourself."

"But I do. Meg conned me into forgetting my instincts, but it was my own fault. I knew better."

"What happened to her?"

"Who knows. She disappeared again, this time for good—at least *I* haven't seen her since."

"Meg was stupid." Laura's eyes flared with anger, then softened as they met his. "But I'm glad she was or I wouldn't have found you. I've never even visited Southern California."

His heart swelled. He'd been right to tell her. Right to

trust in her understanding. "I'm glad, too," he whispered in the instant before their mouths joined in a lingering kiss.

"What do you mean, you don't know where they went?"

"Just what I said, Mac. I followed them to Todd's place and then they disappeared. Three hours later, some clown drops them back in front of the building." Joe shook his head regretfully. "I felt like an ass watching an empty apartment."

Uttering some choice expletives, Connor slammed his fist against the desk.

"Hey, chill out, man. What do you expect with a one-man surveillance team?"

"I expect... Oh, hell." Connor dragged his fingers through his hair. "I'm sorry, Joe. It's not you. I'm just tired."

"Didn't get much sleep, huh?"

Connor chose not to answer. He had enough trouble without being hassled about Laura. Besides, it was none of Joe's business.

"Think we can pull Ed and Mike off the Kelso thing?"

Joe shook his head. "We don't have enough to go on right now."

"How about you?"

"I'm okay. There's nothing that can't wait. I've tried to clear things for when Brenda has the baby."

Brenda wasn't due for another three weeks. That was plenty of time, because the way Connor's gut was twisting, something was going down soon. "Good. You keep an eye on Todd, and I'll work on Ben. Between the two of us, we'll manage." *We'd better,* he told himself. *Laura'll never forgive me if anything goes wrong.*

"As long as there aren't any back doors," Joe muttered morosely.

* * *

"You want to talk about it?"

"Talk about what?" Shoving a strand of hair behind one ear, Laura refocused her wandering attention on the telephone.

Her mother uttered a long-suffering sigh into her ear. "You just agreed that my chartreuse negligee would be ideal for the dinner with Judge Mason and his wife."

"You don't own a chartreuse negligee."

"Exactly. And you haven't heard a word I've said for the past five minutes."

"I'm sorry, Mom. It must be the weather. I can't seem to concentrate."

"Couldn't have something to do with a certain detective, could it?"

She felt heat rise in her cheeks and gave silent thanks that technology hadn't advanced far enough for video phones. "Now, when have I ever let a man interfere with my work?"

"Never. Maybe that's your problem. Maybe you need to cut loose once in a while, dear. It might help you put things in perspective."

"Advice to the lovelorn?"

"Okay, okay," Rose admonished. "I can take a hint. But if you ever *do* need advice..."

Biting back laughter, Laura said goodbye and stared at the pile of paperwork in front of her.

Mom was right; something *was* bothering Laura. But it wasn't Connor. In the week since they'd returned from his cabin, Connor had been...wonderful. Laura smiled. She'd never expected to sound like a giddy schoolgirl, but every time she thought about Connor, a feeling of warmth flooded through her.

No, Connor wasn't the problem. Ben was. Something about him was different, and the fact that she couldn't put her finger on it made her uneasy. At his appointment Friday, he seemed withdrawn, and then, on Sunday, he'd canceled again, even though she'd finally agreed to play pool.

She thumbed through her Rolodex until she located Tom Westing's business card. For several seconds, she stared at it, then punched the number in on her phone and asked to be put through.

"Miss Douglass. What can I do for you?"

Laura took a breath. "I just wanted to touch base with you about Ben."

"Is something wrong?"

"No," she assured him. Now that she had him on the phone, she wasn't sure how to begin. Tom Westing wasn't the kind of man to trust vague feelings and premonitions. Slipping her hand in her pocket, she touched the amber worry stone. "I just wondered how he's doing at home—keeping curfews, homework, things like that."

"Everything's fine. He's a little moody at times, but what sixteen-year-old isn't? Hormones, you know."

"I just got the impression Friday that he was still feeling under the weather after his bout of flu two Sundays ago."

"Flu?" Westing sounded puzzled. "Was that why he was home early? He told me the weather turned bad."

Her hand convulsed, and the edge of the worry stone dug into her palm. Why hadn't Ben told his father he'd stayed home sick? And why hadn't Mrs. White mentioned anything to Tom? Carefully, she let the amber slide until her fingers could rotate it. "The weather *was* pretty miserable. Did it delay your flight at all?"

"Only a little. I managed to get home by four. Ben had Mrs. White's roast reheated and dinner all ready to eat."

"Mrs. White wasn't there when you arrived?"

"No. Sundays, she leaves early to spend time with her son and daughter-in-law and her grandchildren."

Laura's throat went dry as she tried to make sense of what she'd learned. Ben had lied, both to his father and to Connor. He hadn't been sick. He'd made plans to leave the house after Mrs. White was gone.

Or before.

She strained to recall Mrs. White's exact words. Something about Ben burrowed beneath the covers like a hibernating bear.

What if he hadn't been there at all? Jared had once told Laura how he piled pillows under the covers when he wanted to sneak out. He'd laughed as he explained how simple it was to fool anyone checking on him. Was that what Ben had done? And if so, why?

A possible answer flashed across her mind—Todd.

"Strange, he didn't mention getting sick," Westing said.

"He probably didn't want to worry you. You know how sixteen-year-olds are."

Westing failed to catch the irony in her voice. "I do," he agreed with a short laugh. "Is there anything else you need?"

"No. Just please call me if you notice anything... out of the ordinary. Ben's a special boy, and I'm available to help if something's bothering him."

"Thank you, Miss Douglass. I know Ben appreciates all the time you spend with him. You're taking him out tonight again, am I right?" After Laura murmured an assent, he added, "You must be a real pool shark, playing two days in a row. You'll have to invite me along some time. I was a pretty good player in my day."

"How nice," Laura said faintly, pulling her hand from her pocket. "Well, I don't want to keep you any longer, but feel free to call anytime."

Glumly, she listened to the dial tone. She wasn't much of a detective. All she'd learned was that Ben had lied to his father about last Sunday and yesterday and that Mrs. White left early on Sundays. A few facts and a lot of supposition. She wondered if Connor would still say she worried too much.

"You worry too much," Connor told her later that night. He nuzzled her neck playfully, his fingers busy with the top button of her blouse.

"How can you say that?" she demanded. "Didn't you see how he acted tonight?"

"He's sixteen, Laura. He was afraid someone he knew would see him with two old folks." One finger slipped inside her blouse to tickle above her bra.

"He never acted that way before."

"We've never been out with him so close to home before."

"What difference does that make?"

"Stands to reason. He's more likely to run into friends around here."

Another button popped loose and Connor ran his tongue along the cleft of her breasts.

She shivered and drew the edges of her blouse together. "Connor, stop it. I'm trying to be serious."

"So am I." He caught the nape of her neck in his palm and slanted his mouth over hers.

Laura sighed when they finally drew apart, wanting the kiss to go on forever. But it couldn't. Her mind leaped back to Ben.

"You've got to help me work this out!"

"Okay, okay." Absently, he raked his fingers through his hair. "But you're making a mountain out of a molehill." Crossing his arms over his chest, he sank back into the couch cushions and watched her pace.

"Ben told his father he was with us the last two Sundays, and he never mentioned being sick. Don't you think that's odd?"

Connor shrugged noncommittally.

"He's being evasive. He said everything was fine at school, but I called the attendance office and he missed two days last week. His dad never mentioned that—probably doesn't even know." She halted in front of the bookshelf and ran her finger along the polished frame of Jared's picture. "I wonder what he's doing?"

A piece of lint on the shelf caught her eye, and she flicked it away. "You said you'd be keeping an eye on him. Do you know?"

Only the whir of the small enameled clock intruded on the silence. Laura pivoted.

A muscle ticked along Connor's jaw and his gaze shifted away.

Her stomach pitched. "You do know, don't you?"

He stood and crossed to the window. Drawing aside the curtain, he peered out into the dark.

"Not exactly."

"Connor, you promised you'd tell me."

He let the curtain fall back into place and turned, his face impassive. "No," he corrected, "I told you I'd tell you what I could."

A knot lodged in her chest at his cold response. She took a faltering step toward him. "You've got to call it off."

Shoving his hands deep in the pockets of his jeans, he hunched his shoulders. "I can't."

"Tell him you don't need him anymore. Tell him to stop."

"It won't work. Whatever he's doing, he's doing for Todd, not me. All I can do is wait and watch and hope he gets scared enough to ask for help."

Laura resumed pacing, her mind scrambling wildly for a solution. "I'll call his father. Better yet, you call. Tell him to keep Ben home."

"Laura, be sensible. What's Westing going to do, lock Ben in his room, hire a jailer?"

There was that damned word again—sensible. As if being sensible solved anything. Well, she wasn't sensible; she was scared.

"Laura." His tone was soothing, as if he were calming a skittish colt. "You have to trust me. I won't let anything happen to him."

She turned her back and stared at Jared's photo, holding back tears. Trust him? How could she, when he refused to do anything except wait?

His footsteps made no sound in the thick carpet, but she knew when he moved. Her muscles tensed as she felt his warm breath stir her hair.

"Laura, look at me."

With a strength born of desperation, she fought the seductive persuasion of his voice, sensing she'd be lost if she turned around. Because more than anything, she wanted to believe him, wanted to feel his arms wrap protectively around her, wanted to accept his assurances that Ben would be all right.

But words were easy.

"Laura."

She felt his fingers touch her shoulder in a brief caress, then drop away. Heard the whisper of Lycra as he pulled on his jacket. And listened to the echo of the closing door.

Chapter 12

"Are you sure you know how to play?" Ben eyed the box with skepticism.

Laura blew across the lid, raising a puff of dust, and closed the closet door. "Sure. My father taught me years ago." She didn't add that she'd been ten, and so disappointed at receiving a chess set for her birthday instead of the record album she'd wanted that she'd conveniently misplaced it after the first few lessons.

"I haven't played in a while," she admitted, dumping the carved wooden pieces onto the kitchen table, "but I'm sure it's like riding a bike—something you never forget."

"I guess so," Ben replied doubtfully. He arranged the men on the board while Laura filled glasses with ice and cola.

"How about some popcorn?"

"Sure."

The hamburgers, fries and milk shakes they'd just consumed at a nearby fast-food restaurant obviously hadn't dulled his appetite.

"I can't stay long," Ben reminded her as she tossed a package of popcorn into the microwave.

"No problem. A couple of games. Just enough to get me back in shape to beat Connor."

Her conscience pricked at invoking Connor's name. *He* wouldn't approve of her plan at all, but she refused to let Ben go down without a fight.

After Connor had left last night, she'd lain awake searching for ways to avert what she feared would be a disaster. Unable to sit and do nothing, she'd finally decided to catch Ben after school and take him to dinner. The chess idea was born when he made reference to school clubs.

"You first," she said, sliding in behind the row of black chess pieces.

Ben moved a pawn. Laura moved the corresponding man on her side. After mimicking his plays twice, she decided she'd better try something original. Hoping she remembered right, she moved her knight in an L and captured one of Ben's pawns. "One for my side," she announced gleefully.

Disgust marred the teen's classic features.

"How's your dad doing?"

"Fine." Ben studied the board.

"How about Todd?"

His gaze flickered up for a moment before he moved his bishop. "Okay. Why?"

"Oh, I just wondered." Laura kept her tone casual as she took his bishop with a pawn. "You seem distracted lately, and I thought there might be some problems between the two of you."

Ben shook back his hair, resentment flashing. "No. Everything's super. Now, can we just play?"

Laura smiled in resignation.

Nibbling at the popcorn, she contemplated Ben's bent head. When she'd suggested returning to her apartment, she'd forgotten chess was such a quiet game. How was she going to get Ben to open up if she had to keep her mouth closed? An eternity later, when he said, "Checkmate," she breathed a silent sigh of relief. Maybe now they could talk.

"I really gotta go. Homework." He shoved on his down jacket, poised for flight. "Thanks for dinner."

"Ben, wait." Laura laid a restraining hand on his arm. "Give me one minute."

Eyes wary, he hesitated, and Laura was encouraged that he didn't pull away.

"Are we friends?"

He nodded curtly.

"And friends are there for each other, right?"

"Hey, you need my help, just ask."

Laura ignored his attempt at flippancy. "I think you're the one who could use some help."

"Heck, no. I'm great." He accompanied his words with a stiff smile of bravado.

"If you say so. But if you need to talk, I'm always here. Okay?" When he didn't respond, she added, "I'm on *your* side."

He didn't move when she dropped her hand, but he took a breath as if to speak.

The phone rang. Laura ignored it.

His gaze jumped to the phone as it rang again. "Aren't you going to answer it?"

"Not if you want to say something."

"Nah." Pushing his hands deep into his coat pockets, he hunched his shoulders and inched toward the door. "See ya." He made his escape on the fourth ring.

Cursing the caller who'd rung at such an inopportune moment, Laura lifted the receiver. "Hello."

"I hope I didn't get you at a bad time, dear. You sound a little irritable."

"No, Mom. I'm just tired." Holding the phone against her ear with her shoulder, Laura cleared the glasses and bowl of popcorn from the table.

"Well, I can understand why. You're never home anymore. By the way, is your answering machine working properly? You haven't returned my calls."

Laura tried to blank out the thought of the half dozen or so messages she'd ignored in the past week. Did mothers go to a special school to learn how to install guilt in their children?

"I'm sorry—I've been busy."

"Too busy to call your own mother?"

"Mo-o-o-m!" She rolled her eyes heavenward and inhaled a calming lungful of air. "What are you calling about?"

"I merely wanted to chat." Rose sounded hurt. "It's been so long since we've seen you, I wondered what you'd been doing."

"Working."

"Weekends, too?"

Laura coiled the cord around one finger. "No. I went skiing, and I'm learning to play pool."

"Pool!" Rose's voice reflected horror. "I'm not sure that's quite the appropriate thing—"

"Mom, I'm twenty-nine years old. Don't you think it's time I made my own decisions about what I should or shouldn't do?"

The sudden silence on the other end of the line told her that she'd spoken more sharply than she'd intended. Maybe it was for the best. They had to face that fact she wasn't a child anymore. She only wished she'd been a little more diplomatic.

"Mother? Are you there?"

"Yes, dear." The words were subdued. "I was just thinking. For a moment you sounded..." She sighed, and Laura knew she was thinking about Jared. Then Rose seemed to collect herself. "You're absolutely right, Laura. You *should* be living your own life. I'd better go now."

"Bye, Mom."

"Laura... Call once in a while."

"I love you, too, Mom."

Laura stared at the phone. It was funny. For so many years she'd been afraid to speak up for herself, and when she'd finally done it, it hadn't been hard at all. Her mother hadn't screamed and fainted; she'd accepted. And still loved her.

She scooped a handful of chess pieces from the table and dropped them into their box, her thoughts returning to Ben. Everyone kept telling her it didn't pay to get emotionally involved, but how could she help it? Her clients weren't statistics—they were children. And Ben...something about him had drawn her from the moment she'd first seen him in court. It wasn't that he reminded her of Jared, though she had to admit there were striking resemblances; it was the need for approval that she sensed in him.

Tom Westing, if asked, would say he loved his son. But Westing was too wrapped up in his job to let a growing boy know he was more than an inconvenience, and Ben's mother had died when the boy was still a toddler. Laura tried hard not to lay blame. That wasn't her job. But she wondered how Ben would have been different if he'd had a father who spent less time running a company and more time showing he cared.

Ben was so afraid of not being loved that he'd latched on to the first person who showed him any attention. His loyalty to Todd wasn't so strange when you looked at it that way. She only prayed he'd see his cousin for what he was before it was too late.

And what of Connor?

She picked up the black king and rubbed a finger over its carved surface. She loved the way he made her feel and when they were apart, missed him with an intensity that tore at her heart. But that wasn't enough to build a relationship on. And how could she consider a future with a man whose ideals were more important than the people involved?

Slipping the king in with the other chess pieces, she returned the box to the closet.

"The doctor says the baby might be early." Joe's voice crackled over the portable radio.

"Figures," Connor shot back.

"How so?"

"No kid of Brenda's would dare drag its feet."

"Hey, that's my wife you're talking about."

"Case in point. How long did you say it took her to reel *you* in?"

Joe's chuckle echoed in the dark interior of the car.

Shoving his hands into his coat pockets, Connor slid lower in the seat. Damn, but it was cold. He considered pouring another cup of coffee, but he'd had too many already and his car wasn't equipped with a urinal.

Without turning his head, he checked the side and rear-view mirrors, then scanned the street. Nothing.

"Anything on your end?" he inquired softly into his transmitter.

From around the corner, a block and half away, Joe answered. "Just two cats circling each other. Wait. There's a

'78 Chevy turning onto the street. Looks like your boy's coming home.''

Connor picked up the night scope and focused it on the Westings' house. In an eerie wash of red light, Ben's car pulled into the driveway and the headlights blinked out. As Connor watched, Ben circled to the trunk to pull out a backpack. Swinging it to one shoulder, he made his way to the front door and inserted a key. A few minutes later, a light came on upstairs.

Placing the scope on the seat beside him, Connor settled back to wait. Within half an hour the upstairs light flicked off, followed by the rest of the lights an hour later.

''Looks like everyone's gone beddy-bye,'' he reported to Joe. ''We'll give it another hour, then call it a night.''

Memories of Laura teased him as the moon inched across the inky sky. The feather of dark lashes against flushed cheeks. The warm, fragrant scent of her skin. Chocolate eyes melting with desire.

He shifted uncomfortably against the vinyl seat and checked his watch. Eleven-thirty. Too late to drop by; she'd probably already gone to bed.

To bed. He imagined slipping naked beneath the covers to wrap himself around her sleeping form, and his mind filled with tantalizing, distracting images he had no business thinking of now.

''Damn.''

''Something happening?'' Joe asked.

''Nothing,'' Connor snapped. Nothing that a cold shower wouldn't take care of. Not that cold showers were remedy for much besides his physical reactions. They certainly didn't erase Laura from his thoughts.

Fighting his frustration, he uncapped his thermos and drained the last of the coffee. He never should have caved in at the cabin, never should have abandoned his principles, no matter how tempted he was. He'd been insane to think he could seal away the memories and go on as usual.

Hell, he couldn't even remain objective about Ben because of Laura. Her fears were a corrosive acid, eating away at his ability to remain neutral. Patience, which by now should have been second nature, was increasingly nerve-racking.

Why doesn't the kid phone?

Connor fished the river-washed stone from his pocket and let it dribble through his fingers. Till Ben decided to come to him, all Connor could do was watch . . .

. . . and wait.

The call came at ten o'clock the next morning.

"Mr. Westing? What can I do for you?" Laura asked.

"Ben asked me to call. You'd better come right away—to the house. And bring Detective McCormack with you."

Alarm quickened her pulse. "Is something wrong?"

"I'll explain when you get here."

Fingers fumbling in haste, Laura punched in the Special Enforcement number. Connor wasted no time with questions, simply agreed to meet her at Ben's in ten minutes. As she raced out of the probation department, she commanded the startled receptionist to cancel her appointments.

The cross-town traffic moved at an infuriatingly slow pace, punctuated by traffic lights that made Laura beat a nervous tattoo on the steering wheel every few blocks.

All Connor's talk of watching and waiting had failed. Ben was in serious trouble; nothing else could have produced the urgency she'd heard in Tom Westing's voice. And if anything happened to Ben because of Connor's refusal to act . . . Laura's mouth tightened. The car ahead signaled a turn and she whipped into the left lane, oblivious to the honking of the car she cut off.

Silently praying, Laura pulled to a screeching halt in front of the Westing house and climbed stiffly from her car. Relief washed over her when she spied Connor moving to intercept her. At least she didn't have to confront whatever waited inside alone.

"Do you know . . . ?"

He shook his head tersely, no hint of emotion marring his expressionless face.

Laura's heart sank as she fell in beside him.

Before they could knock, Ben's father opened the door and spoke in hushed tones. "He's in the living room."

"What happened?" Laura asked, modulating her voice in unconscious imitation.

"When I left this morning, he told me he was sick and couldn't go to school. Then at a quarter to ten, when I returned for some papers, I found him . . . Well, see for yourself." He urged them through an archway into the sunken living room.

Ben sat on the couch, his head in his hands. His crumpled backpack lay at his feet. In front of him, stacked high on the glass coffee table, was a small fortune in currency.

"He hasn't moved since I called you," his father whispered hoarsely.

Laura glanced quickly sideways, surprised to find lines of worry etched in his normally calm face.

"I didn't know what to do, so I just left him."

Connor crossed the velvet-napped carpet and touched Ben's shoulder.

"It wouldn't fit. I tried, but I couldn't make it fit."

Laura's heart wrenched at the plaintive sound of the boy's words.

Ben raised his head and stared at the mountain of money. "It won't fit," he repeated dully.

Tears welling in her eyes, she sat next to him and reached for his limp hand.

"We'll help," Connor said. When Ben didn't respond, Connor spoke more firmly. "Tell us what's wrong so we can help."

For several seconds, Ben was so quiet that Laura wondered if he'd even heard. She glanced up at Connor, but his gaze was fixed on the boy.

"Ben, tell us."

Laura felt a tremor race along Ben's arm at Connor's insistence. His shoulders shuddered as he drew in a lungful of air.

"He said I had to bring it in my backpack."

"Who said?" Connor's voice was calm and soothing. He sat down next to Ben as Tom Westing eased himself into an armchair. "Who, Ben?"

The teen's fingers tightened around Laura's, but after one darting glance his father, he looked at Connor. "Todd."

"Where are you supposed to take it?"

"To Todd's. I'm supposed to bring it to him."

"How did you get the money?"

The silent seconds strung together like beads of water on a spiderweb. Was Ben still intent on protecting his cousin?

"Todd's been giving it to me, a little at a time, to hide in my room. He said he was afraid of being robbed."

She released her pent-up breath in a whispered sigh, then stared in amazement at the pile of bills. There had to be several hundred thousand dollars. Where had it come from?

"Why does Todd need it today?"

Again, Ben hesitated, his face contorted by his inner struggle. Connor waited patiently, giving him the time he needed. Laura felt the boy's fingers flutter, then clutch hers for support.

"He's meeting someone."

"Who?"

"I don't know." Under Connor's compelling stare, Ben shifted uneasily. "I don't! I just know he's meeting someone at noon. I don't even know where."

"Ben," Laura interrupted, "what if someone had found out you had all this money?"

His hand dampened within her grasp, and he pulled it free to wipe on his jeans. Inhaling deeply, he looked at the floor.

"He gave me a gun."

Tom Westing's face blanched. "Son of a—"

Ben sent his father a pleading look. "I wouldn't have used it, Dad. I took out the bullets."

"You did the right thing, telling us," Laura said. "Now Connor can take the money—"

"I don't want the money."

Laura looked at him in surprise. "Of course you do. What else . . . ?"

A muscle ticked along Connor's jaw. His eyes were hard. "I want the men who'll be getting the money."

A trickle of fear shivered along the back of Laura's neck as she glimpsed the cold professional behind his familiar features. Reminding herself that he'd promised not to hurt her, she tried to keep her voice even. "Fine. Then follow Todd—"

"He won't go without the money."

Despair stabbed her. He claimed to care but refused to listen. He wanted her to trust him but couldn't meet her gaze.

"I'll take it." Ben's face wore a look of grim determination.

Laura fought to push back the panic twisting at her stomach. Her glance jerked from Connor to Tom as a silent message passed between them. Tom's gaze shifted to his son, and his eyes glinted for a moment as he noted Ben's raised chin. Then, with the slightest movement, he lowered his lids and nodded to Connor.

"Okay, let Ben deliver the money and come home." Not caring if they heard the frantic edge to her words, Laura plunged on. "You can put a bug or something in the backpack."

Connor refuted her logic. "Todd will check the bag to make sure all the money's there."

Ben nodded in agreement.

"I'm going to have to wire you," Connor continued, closely watching Ben's face. "I'll call Joe and have him bring over the equipment. Try to get Todd to tell you where he's going."

"He won't." Ben spoke with absolute certainty. "But he'll take me along if I ask."

Laura's heart lurched; her throat went dry with fear. Unable to speak, she shook her head from side to side, feeling like an invisible presence to which no one paid any attention.

His face devoid of emotion, Connor met the boy's steady gaze. "What made you change your mind?"

"I don't like drugs," Ben said bitterly. "And if I'm there, I can be sure Todd's safe."

How? Laura wanted to scream at him. *You can't protect Todd. You'll be lucky to take care of yourself.* But nothing came out.

Connor considered Ben's words carefully, then nodded and left to use the phone.

* * *

Joe was on his way.

In a matter of minutes, all the months of waiting and watching would end and the final phase of the operation would swing smoothly into motion. Connor hung up the receiver and leaned back against the counter, rubbing at his neck to relieve a knotted muscle, then helped himself to coffee from the machine on the counter, wincing when the hot brew ignited his stomach to fiery life.

Usually, at this stage in the game, he operated on high-octane adrenaline.

Not today.

Today, instead of exhilarated, he felt tired and edgy and tense. And, to be honest, scared.

Scared for Ben, who'd be right in the middle of the final act.

As though conjured up by Connor's thoughts, Ben entered the kitchen and filled a glass with water from the sink. "So, when does Joe get here?" he asked.

"Soon."

"The sooner the better."

Connor had thought nothing could make him feel worse, but Ben's efforts to act nonchalant tore at his insides. A month ago it wouldn't have mattered, but now, he knew Ben, cared about him. For an instant he considered calling off the whole operation, but doing so meant turning his back on his duty.

He couldn't do it.

He could only make damned sure nothing bad happened.

"Don't fool yourself. You're putting yourself in a dangerous situation. If Todd finds out you're working with us, he's not going to care how close you've been." Connor half hoped his words would frighten Ben into backing out, but Ben just waited for him to continue.

"Afraid?" Connor asked.

Ben hesitated, then nodded curtly. "But not enough to change my mind."

Connor sighed. "Okay, then let's get started." He set his empty mug on the counter. "Just keep in mind that you're more important to us than any drug bust and don't do anything foolish...."

Chapter 13

Laura watched numbly as Joe taped a body bug to the underside of Ben's arm and gave him instructions. Her body felt limp with fatigue, as though she'd run a marathon in the past hour.

She still couldn't believe this was happening. In spite of all of Connor's promises, Ben was being sent out alone into the heart of danger.

And for what?

She clenched her teeth against the bile that rose in her throat. No case was important enough to risk Ben's life.

Connor moved in front of Ben to get his attention. "Your wire's got a two-block range, so don't worry, and don't look for us or you'll make Todd suspicious."

He sounded like a football coach choreographing second-quarter plays. Laura listened with morbid fascination.

"When you get to the meeting, let Todd take the backpack." Connor paused, following Ben's gaze to the table where Tom Westing, with mathematical precision, counted and stacked bills before stuffing them into the bag.

"Say you're sick or something." Connor stepped into Ben's line of vision, giving him a stern look of warning. "Under no circumstances are you to leave the car. We'll be right behind you, and I don't want you in the way."

If there's any shooting, Laura finished for him. She stared at his implacable features, wondering where the gentle man she'd come to know had gone. This was the stranger she'd met at the cabin, the man who walked the fine edge of violence.

"I want you out of there before we move in, but that might not be possible. So no heroics. Stay with the car." His eyes narrowed. "I mean it, Ben."

Better yet, don't go. Laura stared at the lump of amber in her palm. Its surface looked the same as ever, but its power to comfort had fled. Magic, like love, couldn't survive without faith. Her hand convulsed around the stone as she struggled to beat back the shadows of doubt that threatened to smother her.

"All set." Joe stepped back and gave Ben a pat. "Sit down and relax for a bit."

Connor followed Ben to the couch and squatted, bringing his face level with Ben's. "Now, if you and Todd are still there when we round everyone up, we're going to have to take you both. If you play it cool, no one will guess who blew the whistle. Understand?" When Ben nodded, he patted him on the knee. "We'll release you after we get to the station and book everyone."

"What about afterward? Won't they put two and two together when Ben isn't charged, too?" Tom Westing leaned forward. Although at first glance he appeared as calm as ever, tension was evident in his rigidly held body.

"In cases like this," said Connor, rising, "someone Ben's age would be turned over to juvenile authorities and his identity protected. Don't worry—they won't think anything of it. They'll assume we've been watching Todd." Giving Ben a nod, Connor left to confer with Joe.

And what will Todd assume? The rounded edge of Laura's talisman dug into her hand. Her stomach constricted so painfully she wondered if she was getting an ulcer. She felt like the only sane person aboard a runaway train. While the rest of the passengers made plans for their arrival at the depot, only she was aware of disaster looming at the end of the line.

Afraid to look at Ben for fear she'd burst into tears, she followed Connor into the kitchen in time to hear Joe's rundown.

"CBI's positioning units north and south of town and on the turnpike, and Mike's got the Diagonal Highway. Ed and I'll cover west into the mountains."

Connor nodded grimly, ignoring Laura's presence. "I'm guessing they'll stay inside city limits. Plenty of places here to make the transfer."

"Too many, if you ask me, but I hope you're right. We'll have a hard time lying low and keeping in contact if they head out."

A whimper of distress escaped from Laura's throat.

Shifting uncomfortably, Joe glanced from her to Connor, then down at his watch. "I'd better get going. Ben's due at Todd's in thirty minutes. Good luck." He gave Laura a brief look of sympathy as he passed, then slipped out the back door.

Drawing a deep breath, Connor turned.

"Connor... Call it off." She hated the way her voice broke, hated the feeling of begging. But if it would keep Ben safe, she was willing to get down on her knees.

For just a moment, she thought she saw a flicker of response in Connor's eyes, a hint of compassion that he quickly concealed behind hooded lids.

"Surely, with all the men you've got..."

"There's too many ways Todd could give us the slip, too many places he could go. We can't risk losing him now. We might never have another chance like this."

Trying to understand his side, Laura stared down at the smudged toes of his sneakers, conscious of a burning in her chest. "I'm scared," she whispered.

Her words hung between them, a scarlet ribbon of pain. Then she heard him sigh and watched the sneakers advance across the three white tiles that separated them.

Corded arms wrapped around her, drawing her close. Pressed against the solid wall of his chest, she sought reassurance from the steady beat of his heart, but the sound only made her aware of the passing seconds and the short time left before he and Ben would leave.

"Please," she pleaded. "For me."

His hand rubbed across her shoulder blades and massaged the back of her neck, easing the knotted muscles.

"For us," she murmured.

He cupped her face to press his lips softly against hers. His kiss was a silent affirmation that sent hope surging through her. He did care for her. And caring, he wouldn't let anything bad happen to Ben.

Her smile of relief faded at the sound of his voice.

"I can't."

The words were like a death knell.

Ben's.

Disregarding the regret in his eyes, she wrenched free, propelled by bitter anger. "It was all a lie, wasn't it? The caring, the promises—everything. All lies." Her hands clenched in fists at her sides. "You think you can manipulate people's lives and avoid the consequences?"

"You don't understand."

"Oh, I understand, all right. You don't care who gets hurt, as long as you get what you want."

Eyes blazing at her accusation, he grabbed her. "Nothing's going to happen to Ben. I promise."

She winced as his fingers dug into her upper arm, but pain and the memory of other broken promises helped her maintain control. She met his glare with narrowed eyes. "Don't make promises you can't keep. You can't guarantee Ben's safety any more than my father could Jared's."

"It's not the same at all."

"Isn't it?"

Gazes clashed.

In the drawn-out silence, the sound of Connor's breathing scraped abrasively across Laura's nerves, but anger forced her to stand firm.

Connor released her and turned away, raking shaking fingers through his hair.

As she stared at his stiff back, frustration solidified into resolve. Before she could change her mind, she spoke. "I'm going with you."

"No, you're not."

The words, so reminiscent of her father's when faced with his children's attempts at independence, increased her determination. "I'm going along," she repeated.

Connor swung to confront her. "It's too dangerous."

"Not as dangerous as it is for Ben."

His expression was unyielding. "Forget it."

"If you refuse to take me," she announced with a flash of insight, "I'll go alone."

She meant it, and he knew it.

For once, he didn't hide his reaction. Laura watched disbelief, then horror, flicker over his face as he realized the possible effects of a blundering civilian on his plans.

"You'll be in the way."

Laura shook her head and craftily echoed his earlier instructions to Ben. "I'll stay with the car."

Connor's curse was short and crude.

Laura lifted her chin in challenge. If he insisted on going through with his plan, she'd be darned if she'd stay behind. The wait would drive her crazy.

With a growl of suppressed fury, he finally gave in. "Okay. You can come."

Her feeling of triumph was short-lived.

"But if you make the slightest move to disobey anything I say—anything—I'll haul you in for obstructing an officer. Clear?"

Intimidated by his threatening tone, she nodded.

He glanced at his watch. "Wait for me outside."

Laura watched from the car as Tom gave his son an awkward hug. The man's face reflected unspoken pride, a pride replaced all too quickly by slumped shoulders as Ben drove off.

She wished she could reassure Westing, but her own store of optimism was at low ebb. Connor, however, seemed to have enough for everyone. He took a moment to clasp the worried father's arm, and though Laura couldn't hear what he said, she saw Tom's shoulders straighten a little.

Connor hurried across the lawn and slid behind the wheel of the car, spearing Laura with a glance. "Put on your seat belt."

Compressing her lips, she did as instructed.

When he flipped on the portable receiver, rock music filtered into the car. Music, she realized with amazement, that originated in the car ahead.

Grabbing the radio mike, he thumbed a button and spoke. "We're heading out."

Laura stared out the side window, surprised that two pieces of electronic equipment could generate such a feeling of relief.

Maybe, just maybe, everything would be all right.

Turning north onto Broadway, Connor maintained a pace that set her teeth on edge, especially when several cars pulled into the open space between them and Ben. She peered anxiously at her watch, startled when Connor spoke.

"Just playing it safe. We know where he's going and Todd's not expecting him before noon."

She opened her mouth to thank him, grateful for his attempt to soothe her frayed nerves, but one look at his unyielding profile convinced her not to speak.

Parked down the street from Todd's apartment, they listened to his impatient demand for the backpack, followed an eternity later by his grunt of satisfaction at finding the money all there.

"You with me?" came Todd's voice.

Laura held her breath and mentally crossed her fingers, praying Ben would back out, but Ben must have nodded because Todd spoke again.

"Okay, let's go. We'll take my car."

Her sigh of frustration drew Connor's glance, and for an instant, before he looked away, understanding flashed in his eyes. Wishing for more—a word, a touch—she blinked back tears. Not since the awful weeks following Jared's death had she felt so isolated.

She tried to tell herself it didn't matter, she was strong enough to survive alone, but the lump in her throat only grew larger.

Connor had asked for her trust. She'd refused to give it. She had only herself to blame for ruining any chance for happiness with him. But accepting blame didn't lessen the ache in her heart.

"...Colorado license number Mary, Nora, X-ray, 446, heading south on 36 from Canyon. I've got a visual. Hold your positions."

As they crept past Crossroads Mall, Laura kept her gaze fixed on the red Camaro, three cars ahead. Todd evidently was a country-western fan because she caught the twang of a guitar from the radio in his car.

Connor drove with one hand, relaying each change of direction to the other Special Enforcement units. "West on Colorado Boulevard... North on Folsom... West on... Crap!"

Laura was thrown against the door as Connor stepped on the accelerator and swerved left onto Arapahoe.

"You ran a red light!" Probing cautiously at her throbbing shoulder, she decided it was only bruised.

"Next time, hang on."

She bristled at his curt response.

"Where're we going?" Ben's voice sliced over the receiver.

Todd laughed. "You confused? Good. Then so's the guy behind us."

Laura's eyes widened in shock. Connor uttered an expletive.

"What guy?"

Don't sound so nervous, Laura begged silently, but Todd apparently expected the question.

"The one who ran the red light back there."

She turned an accusing look on Connor.

He eased up on the gas pedal and shrugged. "It was that or risk losing them."

The receiver crackled.

"I don't see anybody. Are you sure we're being followed?" Ben asked.

"Pretty sure. We'll know in a minute," came Todd's grim reply.

This time, Laura anticipated Connor's command. Gripping the seat, she tensed her muscles. Connor hit the brakes and skidded onto a side street, sending dirty snow flying from beneath the car's wheels. She instinctively leaned away from the door as they passed within inches of a row of parked cars.

Through the receiver she heard the squeal of tires and then Ben's shaky voice.

"Hey, man, are you trying to kill us?"

"Shut up," Todd replied.

While Connor zigzagged up and down residential streets, Johnny Cash promised to walk the line and Laura squeezed her eyes shut, bracing herself with stiff arms against the dashboard.

Ben, apparently, was doing the same thing in the Camaro because she periodically heard his sharp intake of breath above the roar of Todd's engine.

Connor spoke rapidly into his mike. "I've been spotted near Arapahoe and Seventeenth. Suspect's taking evasive action. Request backup."

"Special Units five and six on the way, buddy."

Laura gasped as Connor stomped on the brakes. Her eyes flew open in time to see a car sail across the intersection in front of them. Seconds later, he hit the accelerator and they plunged on.

"How do you know we're going in the right direction?" Laura flexed her fingers and darted an apprehensive look at Connor.

He slowed the car a fraction while he checked along each cross street. "I don't."

Alarm stiffened her spine. "But the wire..."

"Is good as long as Ben keeps talking and we're in range."

Holding her breath, she listened to Loretta Lynn wail on the receiver. Was it her imagination, or did the music seem softer, more distant? Laura tried to tell herself that Todd had turned down the radio, but her anxiety rose in direct proportion to the lowered tones.

From far off, down a long tunnel, Todd spoke. "We lost 'em."

"Or they weren't after us."

Ben's words were scratchy and indistinct, like one of the old seventy-eights her father sometimes played on the antique phonograph in the basement. Over the hammering of her heart, Laura strained to make sense of Todd's reply.

"...probably right...play it safe...time to head for..."

A crackling filled the car.

While Laura watched in mounting horror, Connor slammed his hand against the machine. It popped loudly, then lapsed into static.

"We've lost them."

For an instant, before she spotted the mike in Connor's hand, Laura thought the hoarse words were directed at her. She gazed, uncomprehending, at his colorless face while he directed the Special Enforcement units to tighten the circle and begin a search, then called Dispatch to put out an All-Points Bulletin.

"Lost them. Lost them."

The words repeated themselves over and over like a broken record, gouging into the dark recesses of her brain. A wave of heat flooded her body.

"Lost...lost...lost."

In an ever-rising litany of despair, the words pounded through her, making her stomach churn.

"Laura!"

Connor's voice sliced through her stupor, drawing her back to reality, back to the nightmare.

"Put your head between your knees," he said. "You're as white as a sheet."

Hysterical laughter bubbled in her throat, but she lowered her head, propelled by his tone of command. While she drew in deep gulps of air, his fingers smoothed reassuringly along the back of her neck, then withdrew when she sat up.

"Do you feel all right?"

All right? Ben was trapped in a car with his lunatic of a cousin, racing God knew where to meet God knew whom, and Connor wanted to know if she felt all right? She stabbed him with an indignant glare. "Hell, no!"

"You will."

Laura welcomed the anger that scorched across the surface of her mind, embraced it in a desperate attempt to blot out her terror and the overwhelming desire to cower in Connor's arms.

"Another of your empty promises?"

His glance forgave her the insult. "Every cop in the city is looking for Ben. We'll find him."

"Where? Dumped in some ditch in the next county?"

Connor flinched. How had she known? It was an undercover cop's worst nightmare—losing his informer and finding the body days later...

It was hard to lose any informant, but Ben had become so much more than that. If only Laura hadn't forced them together, opened Connor's eyes and made him see the decent teenager behind the defiant mask.

His fingers clenched around the steering wheel as he fought to subdue his rising fear.

It couldn't happen.

Not to Ben.

He wouldn't let it.

Words of denial formed on his lips, but one look at Laura's stony face killed them before they could be spoken. She wouldn't listen.

Automatically, he continued to scan the cross streets as he drove north, knowing his chances of spotting the Camaro diminished with every passing minute. Knowing, too, that even if everything turned out all right, Laura might still refuse to forgive him the terror of this journey. Depression settled like a heavy weight in his chest.

He'd been a fool to succumb to her pleas and let her haunted look sway him. She had no business being here, distracting him with bitter accusations, when he needed to be clearheaded and sharp. It didn't matter that by bringing her he'd hoped to allay her fears, allow her to see how little danger there was for Ben.

He should have known better than to break rules—again—because now she was ten times as frightened as she would have been if she were waiting with Tom Westing. For a moment, he considered returning her to Westing's house, but he couldn't afford the delay. Besides, he was afraid the only way she'd go would be kicking and screaming. No, for better or for worse, they were stuck with each other for the duration.

Force of habit kept one part of his brain tuned to the radio. The other units continued to report in, but the news was not encouraging. At least five red Camaros had been sighted since the APB had gone out, but none was Todd's. With each report Laura's silence grew more condemning. By the time they reached the northern edge of the city and headed south back into town on Twenty-eighth Street, a dull ache had formed behind Connor's eyes.

He glanced down at the receiver, trying to raise Ben's voice by sheer force of will, but there was only silence. Not so much as a crackle disturbed the airway.

Where in the hell had they gone?

Waiting for a traffic light to turn green, he checked his watch. Fifteen minutes since they'd lost contact. He mentally reviewed a map of the city. Todd could have taken any of a dozen routes without being detected. He closed his eyes. A cold knife edge of fear settled between his shoulder blades as he pictured Ben, falsely secure in the belief that they had him in range. Would he panic when help failed to arrive or would he follow directions, stay with the car and out of harm's way?

The car behind him honked. Connor looked up and stepped on the gas, aware of Laura's curious stare.

"You've given up, haven't you?"

Connor shook his head, cloaking his uncertainty in vehement denial. "No." Then, in an attempt to drive the dull expression from her features, he reached out. "You can't think that way."

She ignored her words, her hand limp and lifeless in his grasp. Face averted, she mumbled just above a whisper, "What am I going to tell his father?"

Her tone alarmed him. He longed to pull her close and comfort her, but all he could offer right now was words. Inadequate words. "We're going to find them. No matter how far they run, no matter where they go—we'll get them. The police, the sheriff's department, CBI and the highway patrol are all on the lookout. Todd can't elude us forever."

"What if we don't?" She faltered over the question, the same one that haunted Connor's thoughts. "Or what if Todd discovers the wire before we get there?"

"Ben's a smart kid. He's not likely to give Todd any reason to be suspicious." Connor prayed he was speaking the truth. "Trust him, Laura."

Trust me.

He felt her tentative response in the slow movement of fingers beneath his, heard it in the shudder of breath she took into her lungs before she lifted her head.

She caught her lower lip between her teeth to still the quiver of her chin and nodded. "I'll try."

He smiled ruefully, acknowledging her reservations. Given the circumstances, he was a fool to expect her blind faith, no matter how much he wanted it. "Good enough."

"Dispatch to special units . . ."

Connor froze.

"Unconfirmed sighting of vehicle in question headed west on Mapleton near Fourth Street ten minutes ago."

Ten minutes ago! Swearing under his breath, Connor flicked on the microphone. "Special Unit One responding. Why wasn't it reported sooner?" he demanded as he whipped into the right lane and turned the corner.

"The officer was on a domestic dispute call and didn't hear the APB until a few minutes ago," answered the dispatcher.

"Do you think it's them?" Laura asked.

Connor, intent on crossing town in record time, merely grunted.

"But you can't be sure," she insisted.

"I'm sure."

"Why?"

"They haven't been seen anywhere else since we lost them, and if they wanted to get out of town unobserved . . ."

Her sudden intake of breath told him she'd pieced together the clues and arrived at the same conclusion he had.

West on Mapleton near Fourth.

Sunshine Canyon.

Chapter 14

The meeting place wasn't in town.

There was no other explanation for Todd's driving up Sunshine Canyon. Laura's heart sank as she wondered where he was heading. The twisting road led to the mountain community of Gold Hill, but she knew there were turnoffs along the way. Not many, but enough to confuse anyone following. And if he went on through Gold Hill...

One after another, the stately homes of Mapleton Hill slipped by while Laura eavesdropped on Connor's conversation with the other units. Unsurprisingly, they'd reached the same conclusion as he had—the Camaro spotted entering the canyon was probably Todd's. Why he'd chosen to leave town by that route was anybody's guess, but they agreed it was essential to follow.

Patterson, the agent in charge of the CBI units, warned Connor of the inevitability of losing radio contact, advising that they patch in to the State Patrol frequency's wider range. "If nothing else, we may be able to set up a relay through them."

While they sped toward the yawning mouth of the canyon, the Bureau deployed two cars north toward Lyons. Joe agreed to circle around and join up with Connor later outside the small town of Ward. "But if you're not there in thirty minutes," he warned, "I'm coming in after you."

Thirty minutes? If memory served her right, that was barely long enough to reach Gold Hill, let alone cover the distance to the state highway miles beyond. Before she could voice her puzzlement, the trees closed in around them.

Every speeding-car nightmare Laura had ever dreamed returned to haunt her as Connor stomped on the accelerator, sending them like a hurtling bullet up the canyon. Laura stared straight ahead, afraid to move. She clamped her fingers around the edge of the upholstered seat, unconcerned about the damage her nails might do to the nubby fabric.

Death loomed real and imminent. Each time they took a curve on the wrong side of the yellow line, she expected to meet an oncoming car head-on. Rocky cliffs blurred at the edges of her vision, and trees whipped by, their naked branches reaching out like bony fingers to futilely grasp at the car as it shot past. Her hope of finding Ben, her worries over his safety, vanished in the face of Connor's determination to kill them both.

Fiercely, she prayed that the previous week's warm temperatures had melted all the snow and ice from the road, while a portion of her brain thanked heaven that she'd not had time to put food in her churning stomach.

The canyon wall dropped away, providing a vista of mountains stretching into the distance, but Laura was unable to appreciate the view. They bore down on a blind curve with no noticeable lessening of speed. Throat dry, she squeezed her eyes tightly shut.

This was it. They were going to die. This was the point in her dreams where the car fought centrifugal force and lost, where it went sailing out into a cloudless sky before plunging thousands of feet to the treetops below.

She moaned as the car seemed to rise on its inside wheels, hang suspended and then, an eternity later, settle back on center. Laura's eyes snapped open. They were still on the road.

Before her pounding heart had a chance to accept the fact, she heard Connor's voice warn her, "Hang on. It's going to get a little rough."

The pavement ended abruptly. They hit the rutted dirt road with a spine-jarring bounce. Clenching her teeth, Laura managed to remain quiet. By the time they descended the final series of hairpin curves into Gold Hill, she'd gone beyond terror to stupefied numbness.

"You okay?" Connor lightly touched her hand.

Biting her lip to halt an eruption of hysterical laughter, she nodded. "But I'll never get on another roller coaster as long as I live."

Connor grinned grimly. "We have to make up time. Todd had a fifteen-, twenty-minute head start on us."

"Did you hear me complain?" She wiggled her cramped fingers, hoping they'd someday regain something close to normal flexibility. And then his words hit her like ice water splashed against the back of her neck. Gold Hill's storefronts were shuttered, the side streets empty of traffic with the exception of a couple of trucks and a battered vintage car. "He's not here."

"No. But I didn't expect him to be, with the weather so unpredictable this time of year. My guess is his contacts would pick a more easily accessible meeting site—up one of the more traveled canyons. I think Todd only came this way when he thought he was being followed."

Earlier, she'd heard Connor promise to meet Joe near Ward, but perhaps because not finding Ben was something she couldn't accept, she'd clung to the conviction that Gold Hill would be the end of their journey. The thought of continuing the search along miles of Colorado canyons sent her spirits plummeting. Tears stung the backs of her eyelids. She dug her nails into her palms until the urge to cry passed and stared out the side window as they slipped from town on yet another dirt road.

Much as she wanted to believe Connor's assurances, common sense told her not to grasp at straws. At some point in the next few hours, he'd have to admit they'd failed, but try as she might, she couldn't seem to prepare for the moment. Just the thought of his saying the words created a raw, curling ache in her chest that made breathing difficult.

Suddenly, it was all too much to think about: finding Ben with the money, the hurried preparations, the mad chase through town and the gut-twisting ride up the canyon, and now this—the certainty it was all for nothing.

An energy-sapping weariness settled over her, a fatigue even the jolting vibrations of the car didn't penetrate. Her head dropped back against the seat, and she closed her eyes, feeling smothered in the stifling heat of the closed car. It didn't matter.

Nothing mattered.

Connor rolled his window partway down, and cold air, mixed with the scent of damp earth and pine, brushed Laura's face, pulling her back from the well of despair. A tiny thought niggled at the edge of her mind, the product of a moment's insanity. Maybe she'd been looking at the whole thing wrong. Maybe instead of wishing they'd find Ben, she should be praying they didn't.

The idea had some merit. If Ben thought he was alone, he'd be less apt to act rashly, more likely to ride out the meeting with no one the wiser. Of course, if they never caught up with the Camaro, Connor wouldn't make his big bust. But what did she care about that? Ben would be safe.

Safe? Her mouth contorted. How could she delude herself that Ben could be anything close to safe?

The sound of static roused her from her morbid thoughts.

At her look of surprise, Connor explained, "We're getting near the highway."

The radio crackled again, and a faint voice spoke. While Laura tried to make sense of the words, Connor responded. "I read you."

Leaning forward, Laura peered ahead in anticipation as they rounded two more curves and at last caught sight of Joe's car parked on the shoulder of the main highway. They pulled to a stop behind the car, and Connor opened his door, leaving the engine idling.

"Wait here." Gravel crunched beneath his shoes as he walked away.

Resentment roiled through Laura. So far, she'd obeyed his every command, but this was beyond belief. How could he leave and expect her to meekly wait while he talked to Joe? She was as deeply involved in this as Connor was, and she deserved to know what was going on.

She opened her door and hesitated for an instant, studying the lean, hard lines of Connor's body as he braced himself against the roof of the car ahead and bent to talk with Joe through the open window.

Despite her fears, or perhaps because of them, she was gripped by a wave of longing. If only this were a dream. If only she could awaken in Connor's arms, feel the hypnotic magic of his mouth and forget everything.

A frigid gust of wind blew off the mountains, whipping her hair across her vision. She shivered. This wasn't a dream. It was a nightmare. And even Connor couldn't obliterate it no matter how hard she wished.

She moved forward, determined to hear what was being said, but before she covered half the distance, Connor nodded curtly at Joe and straightened.

His gaze raked over her. "I told you to wait."

"I—"

The pressure of his fingers on her upper arm halted her excuse, and before she could protest, he propelled her back to the car. Squashing her indignation at his high-handed treatment, she remained quiet only long enough for him to duck in behind the steering wheel and release the emergency brake.

"What did Joe say?"

"Nothing."

Joe pulled onto the highway; Connor followed. As their car picked up speed, Laura waited expectantly for Connor to continue, but he remained silent.

Was that all? No explanation, no words of bravado? She studied his profile, disturbed by a subtle shift in his demeanor. Lines of fatigue etched his face and a muscle jerked along his jawline, as though he were clenching his teeth. Laura suddenly wondered if he, too, was losing hope. The thought frightened her. It was one thing for her to give up, but if Connor abandoned the quest...

He stiffened at the touch of her hand on his thigh and released a drawn-out breath, darting a quick glance at her. His voice, when he spoke, was calm, leaving Laura unsure about what she'd seen an instant before.

"We're fairly certain he didn't head south. At least, the Highway Patrol reports no sightings around Nederland."

"Where are we going now?"

"North. Joe's going to Estes Park. We'll head down the South Saint Vrain Canyon—follow it to Lyons."

Cold that had nothing to do with the weather outside settled around her. She didn't ask what they'd do when they reached Lyons. She didn't need to. By the time they got there, the two CBI cars would have completed the circle from the east. There'd be nothing left to do but head back to Boulder.

When they reached the intersecting highway, Joe turned left, disappearing around a curve a moment before they swung right. As they followed the wandering river into the canyon, the far-off voice of a State Highway Patrol dispatcher faded from the radio, leaving behind only an abrasive crackling. Laura felt as though they'd lost their last link with civilization.

"I'm going to need your help."

Startled, she threw Connor a questioning glance. Not once since they'd left the Westing house had he indicated she was anything more than a stone around his neck.

"All the turnoffs and picnic areas are on your side of the highway, and most are well below road level. You'll be able to check them out better than I can."

So little, but the request made Laura feel useful, needed. She nodded and proceeded to scout around, craning to see through the undergrowth that clung to the steep slope, concentrating intently on the rest stops they passed every few miles. Her eyes began to sting, but knowing that success in tracking down their quarry might well rest on her powers of observation, she resolutely ignored the irritation. In spite of her best efforts, she saw no sign of the Camaro. Discouraged, Laura rubbed her eyes and flexed her shoulder muscles as Connor negotiated a descending series of curves without once touching the brake.

The massive rock walls closed in as the canyon narrowed, and even the weather contrived to add to the gloom with a light snow that shrouded everything in shades of gray and white. The car raced on down the highway, engine humming, tires whining, the radio spouting its nerve-racking static. Laura found herself longing for Connor to speak, to say anything. Even a repeat of his worn-out assurances would be better than the grim silence that hung between them.

The highway rounded a final outcropping of rocks and straightened. Ahead, Laura spotted another blue rest area marker.

A familiar voice reverberated through the car. "...care if you freeze your butt off, but *I'm* kinda attached to mine."

Ben? Laura stared at the radio. What was Ben doing on the State Patrol frequency?

"Look!"

Galvanized to action by Connor's sharp command, she swung to the window, finally comprehending that Ben's voice was being transmitted over the portable receiver, not the police radio. She scanned the visible portion of the turnoff, tense with anticipation. The close-crowded trees whipped past, blurring her vision.

"Slow down," Laura exclaimed in irritation. "I can't see a thing."

"Just try. If I put on the brakes, it'll call attention to the car."

Tables. A clearing. Snow piled along the river.

"Okay, so I'll stay." Ben's words rang clear and petulant.

Where are they?

There—a glint of metal?

No. Only an outhouse.

When they reached the point where the road rejoined the highway, every nerve in her body tensed. Praying for one clear look before the rest area disappeared behind them, she twisted for a last glimpse out of the rear window and was rewarded with a flash of red.

"The Camaro!" Limp with relief at her success, she slumped against the seat as Connor braked into the next curve.

"Are you sure?"

"Positive."

The car rolled to a stop.

"Anything else?" Connor's gaze bored into her.

She hesitated. "Maybe another car." She concentrated on a jumble of impressions. "There was something white. Not snow—shiny." Like a freeze-frame shot, the image clicked into focus. Excitement tinged her words. "Yes! It was a car."

"Good." Connor snagged his jacket from the back seat, shoving his arms into the sleeves and tugging the hem down to cover the 9-millimeter gun at the small of his back. He'd already weighed his options and knew he couldn't wait to go in until his backup got there. Ben sounded all right—for now—but the longer he remained with Todd, the greater the odds he'd be found out. Connor couldn't risk it, and neither could he take a chance on letting the others get away. Somehow he'd manage to hold them till Patterson arrived. He just wished he knew how many he was up against.

"I don't hear them anymore." Laura's voice held a note of panic.

Reaching in front of her to flip open the glove compartment, he soothed her with a hasty explanation. "Canyon interference. The transmissions can't penetrate rock. Don't worry—they're there."

Only two sets of handcuffs. Well, they'd have to do. He dropped them, together with keys and a spare ammunition clip, into his jacket pocket.

"Laura..." One hand poised over the door handle, he faced her. "I'm going in alone." The stubborn set of her chin and her quick intake of breath told him she was about to argue. Before she could get the words out, he continued. "Patterson's bringing a backup unit from Lyons—Joe contacted them before we split up. I can't wait, but someone has to be here to direct them to the rest stop. You're it."

Indecision flickered across her face as she weighed his words, and he steeled himself to ignore the precious seconds slipping by. For her own good, it was crucial she follow orders. Even if she were able to keep up, he couldn't afford to divide his attention between her and the situation ahead, couldn't afford to worry about her safety.

She must have sensed his determination, for she finally nodded, albeit with reluctance.

Connor breathed a silent sigh of relief. Thank God, for once she was cooperating, he thought as he circled to the rear of the car, though he wasn't sure what he'd have done if she'd argued. He couldn't waste a pair of handcuffs on her.

Opening the trunk, he retrieved a shotgun and swiftly checked it to make sure it was loaded. Under normal circumstances, he preferred his semiautomatic because it left him with a free hand, but the pump-action shotgun was a formidable weapon, guaranteed to impress the opposition that he meant business. Cradling it in the crook of his arm, he slammed the trunk lid shut.

"Connor..."

Laura's voice, low and laced with apprehension, drew him back to the driver's window. Her eyes were dark wells of anxiety in the pinched white of her face.

"Be careful."

Without speaking, he traced the soft curve of her cheek and nodded. An instant later, he had crossed the highway.

* * *

By the time Connor reached the rest stop, snow feathered his face, the same snow that spread softly over the landscape like a veil of gauze, muting shape and sound alike. Brushing impatiently at his lashes, he studied the side road. To a casual glance it appeared deserted, but training and experience had fine-tuned Connor's eye. In spite of the tangled growth that obstructed his view, he picked out the red Camaro easily enough, and beyond it, the outline of a larger car.

A familiar tension curled in his stomach, the product of the adrenaline that pumped through his body and heightened his senses to an almost painful level of awareness. Nothing moved.

In a low crouch, he raced to the relative shelter of the trees. Exhaling slowly, he waited. The undisturbed silence reassured him. The cars' occupants had evidently chosen to retreat, out of sight of the road. With utmost care, he began a cautious advance, alert for the slightest noise.

After what seemed an eternity, but in reality was little more than a minute, his ears caught a sound, scarcely louder than a whisper of wind against stone. A few feet more, and the sound became a voice. Taking his bearings, he worked his way forward until he came to a gap in the trees. Now came the hard part—getting near enough to see and hear without risking exposure. An inch at a time, he edged in an ever-tightening arc toward the clearing.

A twig snapped beneath his shoe, and he flung himself against a ponderosa pine. The distinctive vanilla scent of the tree's rough bark clogged his nostrils while he waited in the ensuing silence for the hue and cry that would signal he'd been spotted.

It never came. At long last the voice resumed its monologue, and Connor risked a furtive glance.

Two men faced Ben and Todd across a picnic table. The younger, thin and bearded, had Ben's backpack slung over his shoulder. The larger man, one foot planted on the picnic table bench, a forearm draped casually across his knee, talked to Todd. Both men could have passed for moneyed skiers in their sleek jackets and winter tans. Todd clutched a briefcase in one hand, the other thrust deep in his pocket.

A nice friendly meeting. No guns in evidence. But Connor didn't rule out the possibility. His grip tightened on his shotgun.

The heavyset man gave Todd a number where he could be reached in the future, and without conscious effort Connor memorized it, at the same time turning his attention to Ben. The boy, in contrast to the others, looked cold and uncomfortable—highly unlikely to do anything foolish. If he had the sense Laura credited him with, he was thinking of nothing more than making it safely back to Boulder.

The heavyset man straightened and motioned to his companion. The party was about to break up.

It was now or never. In seconds they'd be too spread out for Connor to cover them easily. And his backup would be here any minute now. Drawing a steadying breath, he raised his shotgun. "Police! Freeze!"

The four figures froze. Four heads swung in Connor's direction.

"Keep your hands out where I can see them," he ordered as he stepped into the open. He carefully ignored the look of relief on Ben's face, hoping that it would go unnoticed by the others. "And put the case on the table."

Todd tossed the briefcase with a careless shrug of his shoulder.

As Connor reached out a hand to prevent it from sliding off the edge of the table, a flicker of movement on the periphery of his vision alerted him. Sliding his gaze to the right, he aimed the muzzle of the shotgun at the bearded man's belly, catching him with his hand partway into his unzipped jacket.

"I wouldn't if I were you."

Convinced by the menace in Connor's voice, the man carefully withdrew his empty hand.

Before anyone else could get any bright ideas, Connor dug into his pocket, weighing his choices. Todd was a slimy little weasel, but manageable. The other two were unknown quantities. He pitched the handcuffs to Todd. "Cuff them." He jerked his head toward the two strangers.

Todd eyed the shotgun and Connor's grim face, then sullenly did as ordered.

Neither man resisted, though the heavier man's look was disdainful as he addressed Connor. "You're making a big mistake, Officer."

Connor tested the restraints, refusing to respond. Satisfied, he patted them down, then did the same to Todd and Ben, netting three handguns and a lethal-looking knife as well as four wallets in the process. Todd's and Ben's he dropped next to the briefcase after a perfunctory glance. The other two identified the strangers as Rico Vargas and George Edmonds, both of Corpus Christi, Texas.

"Kind of far from home." Connor smiled blandly. "Did you come for the snow or a little hunting?"

Neither man returned the smile. Edmonds, whom Connor privately dubbed "Big Shot" for his size as much as the air of authority he exuded, spoke in a bored tone. "I'd suggest you think twice before arresting us. I can't speak for Billings, but my friend and I have permits for the weapons."

"I'll bet you do," Connor answered agreeably. "Wanna kick that over here?" He indicated the blue backpack at Vargas's feet.

The bearded Vargas spat on the ground before complying with a jerk of his knee that sent the bag sailing through the air. Connor caught it in one hand, hefted it consideringly, then peered inside. "Didn't your travel agent advise you against carrying large sums of cash?" he drawled with raised eyebrows. He dropped the bag with a thud on the picnic table and flicked open the catches on the briefcase.

Inside, wrapped in plastic bags, lay what Connor estimated to be about four kilos of cocaine. Elation shot through him. It was a big haul. Not the biggest ever made in the county, but big enough. And unless he missed his guess, the two grim-faced bandits in front of him were no small potatoes.

"You're all under arrest for possession and sale of a controlled substance."

Edmonds and Vargas regarded Connor with indifference.

"You have the right to remain silent. If you give up that right, anything you say can and will be used against you in a court of law. You have the right to an attorney . . ."

Unease raised the hairs on the back of Connor's neck as he recited the rest of the Miranda rights. Todd was studying him through narrowed eyes. It didn't take much imagination to guess what was going on in his mind. Something had struck him as familiar, and it was only a matter of time before he made the connection between Connor and the man he'd seen in Central City. Connor had already considered this, and now could only pray that when the time came, Ben would have sense enough not to betray himself.

Recognition flared in Todd's eyes. "You're the boyfriend."

Connor maintained a look of indifference at the expected pronouncement, but Ben's muffled gasp made his mouth go dry.

"You're the P.O.'s boyfriend," Todd repeated, his face a mask of disbelief. He rounded on Ben. "*You* said he was a psychologist."

"I . . . I . . ."

As Ben groped unsuccessfully for a suitable response, Connor leaped into the breach. "You think I advertise the fact I'm a narc?" Scorn dripped from his voice. "I lied to the kid about who I was. I'm not stupid."

His bluff was rendered useless by the look of guilt on Ben's face, a look easily discernible to everyone in the clearing.

"You knew," Todd accused his cousin. "You set me up!"

Quailing in the face of his cousin's rage, Ben took a step backward, but not fast enough. Todd knocked him to the ground and straddled him, fists swinging. Ben raised his arms in a vain attempt to ward off the blows that rained down on him.

Todd, apparently intent on beating Ben to a bloody pulp, either didn't hear or ignored Connor's shout. Connor shot a harried glance at the handcuffed duo who stood alongside the snow-frosted stretch of tarmac, weighing what would happen if he stepped into the fracas. He decided not to take the chance.

He aimed his gun skyward and pulled the trigger. The blast of the shot bounced off the canyon walls, repeating itself in ever-diminishing waves. Startled by the sound, the fighters froze.

Connor pumped another round into the chamber of the shotgun. In menacing tones, he spoke to Todd. "Get off him, or the next one's for you."

With a nervous glance, Todd straightened.

"Help him up."

Angrily, Ben shoved aside the offered hand and stood, his back turned.

"Anything else?" Todd sneered in false bravado. "Like you want me to wipe his—"

"Shut up and move away," Connor interrupted, fighting to hold on to his temper. Damn it—where the hell was his backup?

Suddenly, in one swift motion, Todd pinned Ben to his chest and lunged toward the picnic table, grabbing the knife with his free hand. He turned the blade against Ben's throat.

"Your turn," Todd said. "Drop the shotgun."

Connor's fingers convulsively clutched the stock. Silence congealed around him.

"Drop it," Todd repeated, "or he's dead meat." To emphasize his point, he pressed on the knife, all the time staring deep into Connor's eyes. Ben blanched, and he uttered a strangled yelp. A drop of blood appeared on his neck just above the blade.

"Never give up your weapon." The words rang through Connor's head, as sharp and distinct as though the police instructor were shouting them in his ear instead of across a gap of eleven years.

Ben's frightened eyes pleaded with him.

"Without your gun, you're defenseless, and so is the hostage."

But he wasn't defenseless. He still had his handgun. He felt its solid weight fitted into the small of his back, out of sight. Ready.

With exaggerated care, Connor bent and laid the shotgun on the ground.

"Now the keys for the handcuffs," said Edmonds, giving Todd a nod of approval.

"I don't have them. They're in my car—on the highway."

"Then I guess we head for the highway," Todd replied.

"All of us?" Connor scoffed, playing on the slight hesitation he heard in Todd's voice. He curled his knuckles against his right hip, inches from the butt of his concealed gun.

"You, me and Ben." Todd darted a glance down at the picnic table, as though considering trading the knife for one of the handguns.

To pick up a gun, Todd would have to let go of Ben or lower the knife. Connor felt his muscles tense as he waited for Todd to make up his mind. A split second was all Connor would have. It would have to be enough.

Todd relaxed his hold, and time seemed to slow like a stream of molasses poured from a jar.

Ben grabbed the hand holding the knife and jerked free.

And in one smooth motion, Connor pulled his gun and fired at the exposed target.

Chapter 15

Connor stood at the side of the highway and watched the ambulance disappear. Almost an hour had passed since CBI had arrived and began to tie up loose ends. Patterson had taken charge of Vargas and Edmonds while his partner made the fifteen-minute drive to Lyons to notify authorities of the shooting. Patterson had left when the sheriff's department finished their examination of the area.

Thrusting his hands into his pockets, Connor stared out over the treetops through the mist of snow. He needed to get back to Boulder and write up an official report. Instead, he turned and trudged down the side road.

The clearing lay peaceful and still, snow beginning to fill in the now-hardening ruts and ridges where countless feet had churned up mud and gravel. Future picnickers would come and go, unaware of the tragedy that had played itself out in this idyllic setting. But Connor would remember.

He shivered and turned up the collar of his jacket, his gaze drawn to the spot where Todd's blood had pooled on the ground. It already lay hidden beneath a light blanket of snow. By spring, there'd be nothing left to prove a man had died here today.

Dark images flashed across his mind, memories he was afraid he'd never forget. Ben cradling Todd's body in his arms. Laura running down the hill and then kneeling in the dirt. Himself bent over Todd, hands bathed in blood.

In the fading light he examined his hands. He'd tried to scrub them clean at the river's edge, but a stain remained, crusted dark beneath his nails. Even while he'd tried to stanch the flow of blood, he'd knows it was hopeless. He didn't need the paramedics to tell him so half an hour later. He'd seen chest wounds before. Maybe if medical help had been closer...

Abruptly, he jammed his hands out of sight, remembering the horror on Laura's face as she stared at them. She blamed him. Hell, he blamed himself. There should have been something else he could have done. Tackled Todd. Anything. But he'd reacted. Swiftly and uncompromisingly. The way he'd been trained. And now, he had to live with the guilt.

Todd was dead.

Connor had seen death before, lived with its threat every day since he'd joined the police force. But this was the first time he'd caused it.

No, he thought, suddenly tired of the lie. He had caused a death before. Sam's. For years Connor had rationalized what had happened to the old man in a vain attempt to ease his conscience. But now he had to face facts. If he hadn't ignored Sam's call, the old man might be alive today. Connor's own irresponsibility had killed Sam as surely as his bullet had struck down Todd.

Sam and Todd.

His fault.

And if fate hadn't intervened, Ben, too, could have been added to the list. Unable to face the ghosts that haunted the clearing any longer, he headed for the highway. The walk to his car sapped his last bit of energy, and he sank wearily behind the steering wheel, letting his head drop against the headrest.

Snow spattered against the windshield, its sound a haunting echo of the pebbles that had heralded Laura's appearance in the clearing.

Laura.

He drew a ragged breath as realization hit him. To do his job, he couldn't allow his heart to be ruled by anything other than the law.

He'd turned his back on the rules.

Keep your own counsel.

Never get involved.

Expect the unexpected.

Because he didn't want to lose her, he'd fooled himself into believing he could separate his feelings from what he had to do. He should have known better.

And he'd lost her, anyway. After that final, condemning glance, she'd turned her back on him. He'd felt as though his heart had been ripped out.

He'd wanted to shout that he'd kept his promise; Ben was safe. Bruised and battered from Todd's attack, hands slashed by the knife he'd wrestled away from his throat—but alive nevertheless.

To save a life, Connor had taken one. The two should have balanced out, but oddly they didn't.

Laura had left in the ambulance with Ben. Without a backward glance. He couldn't fault her. He'd turned into a killer before her eyes. Each time she looked at him she would see his finger on the trigger.

It was no way to build a lasting relationship. No, he had to accept the fact that when he'd killed Todd, he'd killed any chance he and Laura might have had.

Connor turned the key in the ignition and put on the windshield wipers. Back and forth, the blades beat a hypnotic rhythm that suited his somber mood. He sucked air into his lungs and let it out to a count of six, in an attempt to ease the black mood that hung over him. It helped. A little.

Checking his sideview mirror, he pulled onto the highway and headed for Boulder.

Laura phoned Tom Westing from the hospital while she and Ben waited in the emergency room. Looking ten years older than he had that morning, Tom arrived in time to watch the doctor put the last stitches in his son's hands.

"No tendon damage," the doctor assured Westing. "He was lucky."

You don't know the half of it, Laura thought. She shuddered, remembering Ben's account of the struggle over the knife. If Connor hadn't fired his gun, she had no doubt Ben would have died instead of Todd.

On the ride back to the house to pick up her car, she and Ben filled Westing in on the events of the afternoon. His face grew grim when Ben recounted being held at knifepoint; his glance flickered to the spot of dried blood on Ben's throat and his eyes flashed with rage. In that instant, Laura knew that if Connor hadn't killed Todd, Tom Westing would have.

Any doubts she had about his feelings for his son were dispelled when he laid a hand on Ben's knee in an awkward gesture of comfort and met her eyes over Ben's bowed head. His gaze shone with quiet gratitude and something else—determination, maybe. It seemed as if Tom Westing, confronted with the reality of almost losing his son, had discovered what was truly important in his life.

It was a lot to read into a look, Laura decided, but somehow, she felt reassured. With his father's help, Ben was going to come through this all right. The boy's words, as she was leaving, bore her out.

"Thanks, Laura." Ben toed the grass. "I guess I've kinda been a jerk."

She squeezed his forearm. "Not too bad. Besides, at sixteen it goes with the territory."

With deep absorption, he studied the divot he'd raised. "You know, I don't think Todd wanted to..." He choked on what he was going to say, then cleared his throat and lifted tear-glazed eyes. "Tell Detective McCormack I don't blame him. I know he was just trying to protect me."

Laura reacted to the pain in his voice. She gave him a quick hug of sympathy before climbing into her car. "I'll do that, Ben."

Back in her apartment, she turned on her shower, stripped and stepped beneath the stinging spray, trying to scrub away the awful memories of the afternoon with soap and water.

Ben's words echoed in her mind.

Tell Detective McCormack I don't blame him.

Waiting on the highway, she'd been filled with foreboding as the minutes dragged by, until she thought she'd go nuts. She didn't know what insanity had pulled her from the car and started her down the road—some crazy notion that she might be able to help, or maybe just the need to know what was going on. Whatever the cause, she'd gone, and when that single, ominous shot had rung out, she'd waited, scared stiff. Strangely, it wasn't Ben's lifeless body she'd expected to find; it was Connor's.

She'd panicked, and, like a mindless fool, taken the shortest route to the picnic area—straight down. She still remembered the scene that met her eyes: two handcuffed men and Connor and Ben bent over Todd's lifeless body. All the while they worked over Todd, she knew it was hopeless.

She couldn't face Connor when he turned to her, couldn't bear to see the condemnation in his eyes. He hadn't wanted to get emotionally involved with her and Ben, but she'd forced him to.

The soapy washcloth fell from Laura's hand as she surrendered to searing pain that threatened to rip her apart. Hugging her arms around her upper body, she leaned her forehead against the wet tiles. Water sluiced off her shaking back and pooled around her feet, mixing with bitter tears.

How could Connor ever forgive her for insisting he do his job by her rules?

How could she forgive herself?

By the time she turned off the tap, the water ran cold. Her movements were sluggish and her skin felt numb. She stepped from the shower, but even pulling on a thick terry-cloth robe didn't help. Iciness invaded her every pore, reaching deep inside. Shivering, she wrapped a towel around her dripping hair and plodded to the living room to wait.

Surely he'd let her explain.

The minutes ticked slowly, painfully by.

Laura curled into the corner of the couch, drawing her legs beneath her, and groped in the deep pocket of her robe. Down in the corner, her fingers encountered the smooth object she sought, and she pulled it out. The stone's polished surface caught the waning light and glimmered softly in her palm. Magic. Laura wrapped it in her fingers and closed her eyes.

Call. Call.

The words became a litany that swirled in the air, bouncing against the silent walls of the room until they fell like petals in a summer storm. The amber resting in the nest of her hand slowly warmed. Lulled by its feather-light weight, Laura slipped into a cocoon of sleep.

Connor still hadn't called three hours later when she awoke on the couch. Dragging the gaping edges of her robe together, she dropped the worry stone into her pocket and made her way to the kitchen. Without turning on a light, she lifted the phone and punched in numbers on the luminous dial. A man answered on the third ring.

"Boulder Police Department."

"Detective McCormack, please. Laura Douglass calling." She rubbed at her throbbing temples.

"He's not here. Can I take a message?"

"No message." She returned the receiver to its cradle and flipped the light switch, wincing as the sudden glare triggered a corresponding flash of pain behind her eyes. It felt as if she'd used her head to batter down a stone wall.

Taking care not to make any abrupt moves, she washed down two aspirin with a glass of water, then opened the refrigerator. Although she hadn't eaten since breakfast, nothing looked good. She closed the door, filled the kettle with water and waited for it to boil, her glance straying to the stove clock. Nine-thirty.

Where was he?

The question refused to be ignored. Again, she reached for the telephone, this time punching in Connor's home phone number. Her relief at the sound of his voice was followed by disappointment an instant later when she realized she was listening to a recording. She spoke briefly into the phone, assuring herself he'd return her call when he finally made it home.

After all this time, she knew Connor wasn't quite the rigid, play-by-the rules cop he appeared. He'd shown her another side, a compassionate, caring side, that would forever alter her image of him. And that other Connor, hidden behind the controlled, public face he showed the world, was hurting. She wanted to lock him in her arms, take his pain into herself and soothe him with words of love.

Because love him she did.

The admission stunned her. They'd spent so much time together fighting over Ben that she'd given no thought to how deeply she really felt about Connor. Until now. And now, she faced the truth: that in spite of his infuriatingly overbearing manner, in spite of his tendency to believe he knew what was best for everyone else, she loved him. She loved his strength, his gentleness, even his rigid adherence to duty.

She loved everything about him.

A dozen times her hand hovered near the phone, but fear prevented her from dialing again.

The rejection she'd felt in the mountain clearing, spread like a cancer through her, feeding on the silence. She tried to convince herself she was overreacting. She told herself he needed time—time to accept what had happened, time to heal. But excuses didn't stop the ache in her heart. An hour and a half and three cups of coffee later, she conceded defeat. He wasn't going to call tonight.

Shortly after midnight, she fell into a restless sleep, her dreams punctuated with blood and despair, and didn't awaken until the harsh jangle of the phone sent her leaping from the couch.

"Connor?" She squinted through the gray gloom into the kitchen. Seven o'clock.

"No, dear. It's Mother."

Laura rubbed at the throbbing shin she'd knocked into the coffee table, conscious of bitter disappointment.

"What have you gotten yourself involved in, Laura Christine?"

There was no mistaking the accusatory tone in her mother's voice, but try as she might, Laura could think of no reason for her mother's disapproval.

"I always seem to be the last to know anything," Rose complained. "You could at least have called and warned me. Here I sat, drinking my cup of tea, without the slightest inkling—"

"Mother, what are you talking about!"

"Why, the morning paper, of course."

Dropping the receiver, Laura dashed to the front door. She scooped the newspaper from the hall floor and opened it to the front page. The headline leaped out at her: "Suspect Killed in Canyon Drug Bust."

Laura groaned. She slammed the door and returned to the phone, skimming the first paragraph of the article as her mother rattled on. It stated that after a heated gun battle during which one man was killed, Boulder drug enforcement officers, in a joint venture with the Colorado Bureau of Investigation, had taken three other suspected drug dealers into custody. Four kilos of high-grade cocaine had been confiscated at the scene. Someone had evidently done some careful digging because not only did they have a quote from Detective Connor McCormack "—The department has been working for months to cut off this major pipeline for drug distribution in the area—" but she was mentioned by name as having accompanied the police. Ben, she noticed with relief, was listed only as a juvenile suspect, thanks to the prohibitions against revealing the names of minors in the press.

"... but I must say *he* took it rather well."

"Daddy saw this?" Her heart pitched. His opinions might not influence the course of her life any longer, but they still had the power to hurt. Steeling herself, she asked, "What did he say?"

"Oh, you know your father. He just made a sarcastic remark about how it appeared you were changing professions again."

Laura laughed with relief, aware of what it must have cost her father to refrain from lecturing. "You don't need to worry, Mom. Yesterday was more than enough for me."

"I'm glad to hear it. Not that we'd try to tell you what to do."

Laura smiled wryly at the thought of these particular leopards changing their spots, but her mother's next announcement left her speechless. Rose and Henry had applied to become foster parents.

The more Laura thought about the idea, the more excited she became. The decision marked a turning point in her parents' lives, a willingness to learn from the mistakes of the past and a desire to make a difference in the lives of others on a personal level.

"We know we can't bring Jared back, but we want to try to help teenagers who are struggling with similar problems." Rose's voice was hesitant as she groped to explain. "We want a chance to get it right."

Her mother's parting words echoed in Laura's mind long after she hung up. A chance to get things right. It was what Laura wanted, too.

If only Connor would grant her that chance.

This time, when she called the Special Enforcement number, she got a familiar voice.

"I'm a father," Joe announced after she identified herself. "While I was chasing all over kingdom come, Brenda gave birth to twins. That woman never does anything by halves. You should have seen the smug look on her face when I got there."

At his insistence, Laura promised to stop by the hospital to see the newborns. Then she asked to speak to Connor.

"He's not here," Joe told her. "He's on leave until the inquiry."

She swallowed her disappointment. "Inquiry?"

"Into the shooting. It's customary when a cop's involved in a death. You'll probably be notified to make a statement even though you weren't a witness. Didn't Connor warn you?"

"No." How could he warn her, when he hadn't even called? The knot in her throat grew larger.

"Well, he will. And, Laura—don't worry. It's just a formality."

A formality. That wasn't what it felt like when Laura faced the investigating panel two days later. Oh, they smiled gravely at her, tried to make her feel at ease, but by the time she finished telling all that she knew, she felt like a rag shoved through the rinse cycle of a washing machine and hung out to dry.

Connor wasn't there, and his absence caused her sagging spirits to drop even lower.

Days and nights had dragged by while she prayed for him to return her calls. She'd tried to rationalize that given time, he'd allow her the chance to apologize for making a mess of things. But it wasn't until she entered the room that she realized how much she'd counted on the inquiry to bring them face-to-face.

One man—the chief of police, she thought—misinterpreted her crestfallen expression for apprehension and assured her she wouldn't have to face any of the other witnesses. In answer to her hesitant question at the end of the interview, she was informed that Connor had made his statement earlier that day.

Numb with disappointment, Laura managed to leave the room without giving in to the tears that prickled behind her eyelids, but it took every bit of control she possessed to paste on a smile when she spied Ben and his father waiting in the hall.

"Ben's next," Tom Westing informed her.

Ben's gaze darted toward the closed door.

"No need to be nervous." Tom patted his son's shoulder. "You'll do fine. They just want to hear what happened." He turned to Laura. "Detective McCormack explained the proceedings quite clearly yesterday."

An unseen hand clutched at Laura's heart. Connor had gone to see Ben and Tom, but not her.

"He commended Ben on the way he kept his head through the whole ordeal and said how much he regretted the circumstances that forced him to shoot Todd."

Tom was still speaking. She knew because she could see his lips move, but his voice was faint and far away. As she strained to focus, his expression changed.

"Laura, are you all right?" Concern laced his words. "You look as white as a sheet."

"I'm fine. Just a little tired." She peered at her watch. "Look, I have an appointment in a few minutes, but you can tell me how your interview went on Friday, Ben. Good luck." Her face, when she tried to smile, felt as though it might crack like old plastic, but it must have reassured them because they let her go.

Once she exited the building, her brisk pace slowed and her shoulders slumped. She'd lied. She didn't have an appointment. She'd cleared everything from her calendar in the hope of spending time with Connor, and now she didn't know what to do. Laura unlocked her car and slid behind the wheel, but instead of turning on the ignition, she stared sightlessly out the window.

She had to quit deluding herself. Connor would not call, and they wouldn't run into each other by accident. At least not anytime soon.

The easy way out.

For both of them.

Given time, the hurt would ease until, one day, they would meet on the street, smile politely and edge away, nagged by disquieting memories of once-shared intimacy.

Maybe it was for the best.

Laura drew a shuddering breath to loosen the sudden tightness in her chest and tried to insert the key in the ignition. Her shaking hand made it nearly impossible. Tears of frustration glazed her vision, and she gave in to them, resting her forehead against the steering wheel.

Crying did not cleanse soul, she decided when the tears finally dried. Her head ached, her eyes felt as though someone was sticking pins in them, and she was so stuffed up she had to breathe through her mouth. She pulled a tissue from her purse and wiped her nose.

Okay, she told herself, so maybe it's not for the best. What do you really want?

Connor. The answer was immediate and decisive. And so, too, was the realization that by doing nothing, by waiting, she had once again let someone else control what happened to her. Maybe Connor didn't want her, but she would have to hear the words from his own lips. Anything less was taking the coward's way out.

But first she had to find him.

Chapter 16

I come here when I want to get away. Connor's words echoed through her mind, providing the answer she should have thought of days ago. She'd find him at the cabin.

The drive up Boulder Canyon seemed to take forever, though more than once, she had to caution herself to slow down or risk never arriving at all. By the time she headed north out of Nederland, her nerves were stretched taut.

Just past a familiar mileage marker, she spotted the turn-off and rolled to a stop for a better look. Snow from the storm three nights ago still crusted the narrow dirt road, and a single set of tire tracks ran down the middle. Until this moment, Laura's only concern had been whether she would find Connor or not. Now that she saw proof he was here, other worries jostled for attention. What if he refused to see her, refused to listen? Her stomach knotted.

Quickly, she pushed the treacherous thoughts to the back of her mind. Before more doubts could rear their heads, she nosed the car beneath the overhanging tree branches, trying to remember how far Connor had said it was to the cabin. Two miles? Three?

It might have been three hundred for all the progress she made. Her focus centered on the battle to keep the car's tires in the ruts while still maintaining forward momentum. When she finally risked a glance at the odometer, she groaned in frustration. It had taken fifteen minutes to come just over a mile. At this rate, it would be nearly dark before she arrived. She increased pressure on the gas pedal . . . and felt the rear tires slip.

Her mouth went dry.

But before she could react, the tires found some traction and the car straightened out. Satisfied she could go a little faster, she held her breath and pushed the pedal down another fraction of an inch.

The road curved right.

Her car refused to.

In the next instant, it spun in a circle, slid sideways, and came to rest, front bumper planted solidly against a tree trunk. Her head snapped forward, connecting with the steering wheel, then bounced back.

Shock immobilized her, held her upright for the few precious seconds it took for adrenaline to wash through her system. Exhaustion and a stab of pain hit her at the same moment. She slumped against the seat and raised a trembling hand to probe her forehead, wincing when she encountered a tender spot. Luckily, the rest of her body seemed to be in working order.

Unfortunately, the car wasn't. The gears shifted, the engine strained, but try as she might, she couldn't maneuver it back up onto the road. She was stuck.

Laura groaned. She'd have to walk the rest of the way to the cabin. There was no other choice. Connor might not drive out for days, and she certainly hadn't come this far to give up and head back for the highway. Grabbing a flashlight from the glove compartment, she pocketed her keys, tucked her purse under the front seat and climbed from the car.

Her feet sank in ankle-deep snow that slid inside her shoes and crept up her calves. By the time she'd picked her way to the crest of the road, her slacks were wet halfway to the knees, her feet squished inside her loafers and she was cursing her stupidity for not taking time to change into warmer clothes back in town.

Telling herself that a brisk pace would keep her toes from going numb, she set out into the gathering dusk. Trouble was, her pep talk was exactly that—talk. Reality was the biting chill that pierced her jacket, the deepening darkness and her aching head. Before long, her world narrowed to the stream of light from her flashlight and the mechanical repetition of placing one foot in front of the other.

Lift, swing, drop.

Lift, swing, drop.

Time after time.

When a faint glimmer appeared through the trees, it took several seconds for her brain to register the fact. And even then, her legs refused to move any faster. Doggedly, she plodded onward, until she stood in the shadow of the cabin door.

She rapped twice, then dropped her fist to her side.

Nothing stirred.

Again she knocked, this time louder. He had to be here. There was a light burning inside and his car was parked at the edge of the clearing.

A bubble of panic formed in her chest. Maybe he'd seen her from the window. Maybe he was pretending not to hear, hoping she'd go away.

The bubble expanded, pressing against her throat as she pounded the wood with both fists. Abruptly, the door swung inward, unbalancing her, and Connor caught her as she stumbled over the threshold.

"Laura!"

Horror or elation—it made no difference which emotion tinged his voice. Right now, all that mattered were his arms lifting her, his chest solid beneath her cheek and the warm, smoky scent of him. Laura inhaled, then released a lungful of air with a sigh. Never had anything felt more like a homecoming.

Connor lowered her to the couch and tucked a blanket around her. Efficiently. Silently.

"Thank you." Laura managed a raspy whisper and formed her lips around a weak smile, but Connor didn't notice. He had already turned to drop a log on the grate. The resulting flare of heat scorched Laura's cheeks, but did little to speed the spread of warmth through her body.

"I'm not surprised you knew where to find me," he said without turning.

Laura nodded, acknowledging as he did how close the two of them had become. Connor continued to stare down at the fire. She bit her lip to prevent the tears that sprang to her eyes from falling. What had she expected—to be welcomed with open arms? Of course not. But somehow, having her fears confirmed made her feel lost and alone. She lowered her attention to her feet and concentrated on peeling off soggy loafers and socks.

Give him time. Laura pushed away the echo of Joe's advice and tried to ignore the needlepricks of feeling that shot through her feet as she curled her toes into the blanket. Connor might not want her here, but here she was, and her intuition still assured her she'd made the right choice in coming. The problem was, how to convince him. She touched the stone in her pocket, seeking inspiration, but it remained cold and unresponsive, as unyielding as Connor's stiff back.

"Where's your car?"

"A couple of miles back. I slid off the road."

"You shouldn't have come."

No words of comfort, no sign that he cared. Just "you shouldn't have come." The knot in her stomach tightened. "I had to. To tell you...I'm sorry."

Abruptly, he swung around, his eyes hard chips of sapphire. "What do you have to be sorry about? I'm the one who killed Todd."

Even sensing his pain, Laura flinched from the cold words and huddled deeper within the folds of the blanket. Getting here had taken so much out of her that she wasn't sure she had enough fight left to stand up to him, but she had to try.

"I'm sorry I didn't trust you all along. I'm sorry I didn't believe that you'd protect Ben. I'm sorry how things turned out." She looked up, wordlessly pleading for understanding.

"Connor—"

Impatiently, he cut her off. "No, Laura. No more. The fault's mine, not yours. I let myself get too close."

"There's nothing wrong with getting close."

"There is when I can't do my job." His voice flared with sudden anger, then sank back into a controlled monotone. "I got too close. I felt Ben's fear. Yours too. I felt both your pain. I reacted emotionally."

"And saved Ben's life. Doesn't that mean anything?"

"Of course it does," Connor replied wearily. "Ben's special. He...means a lot to me. Too much. Caring about him—and you—is what got me into this mess in the first place. When I care I forget the rules."

Keep your own counsel.

Don't get emotionally involved.

Always expect the unexpected.

Unspoken, the words he'd solemnly intoned weeks earlier hung between them. Laura bit down on a silent obscenity and reasoned with him. "The case is over. It won't happen again—Ben being there, me being there to distract you."

He shook his head. "That's just the point. You won't have to be there. What happens the day I hesitate, afraid to take a chance, because you're waiting for me at home? Who else will die because of us?"

His allegations rankled, and for an instant Laura let irritation take charge. "That's hogwash, and you know it. If all cops thought that way, no one would ever get married. What about your mother? Did she affect your father's performance? Or Brenda—have you noticed Joe hesitating because his wife could become a widow and his twins could grow up without a father?"

"They're not me."

Despair flooded through her. She was pleading for her life, *their* life. Together. But he wasn't listening, and with every passing moment she could feel him slip further away from her, sealing off his emotions, distancing himself, until finally nothing would penetrate the wall he erected.

Not even her love.

Her heart twisted at the thought of never again feeling the touch of his hand or the pressure of his mouth caressing hers, never again hearing him whisper words that made her heart race.

The sense of loss was so overwhelming it muffled her remaining arguments, leaving her with nothing but the unadorned truth. "Connor, I love you."

Connor battled the rush of feeling let loose by her declaration, feelings he'd come here to exorcise. What had love ever gotten him but trouble?

"I need you."

"Need you... need you... need you."

Bitterness rose like bile in his throat. Need? What did she know of the emotion? Need was a raw, gaping wound in his chest, a poison that oozed into his blood and spread through his body, sapping his strength, crippling him, rendering him incapable of performing his job. Why wouldn't she listen to reason?

"And I think you need me."

On the mark. But he'd nearly let need destroy him once. Never again. Better to cut her out of his life forever.

"I don't need anyone." Slowly, carefully, he enunciated every word. And died a little when shock registered on her face. In the heavy silence that followed, he turned his back, afraid he would weaken. Lifting the poker from the hearth, he jabbed at the fire.

Why did she have to look so crushed, so forlorn, like a small animal delivered a mortal wound? Didn't she know how strong she was? Strong enough to lose a brother. Strong enough to support the strays that passed through her office. Strong enough to go on without him.

Stronger than he was.

"You're a liar."

Wrapped in his misery, he wasn't aware of her approach until her whisper brushed his ear and she moved to his side, royalty cloaked in a blanket of wool. His startled gaze moved from the obstinate set of her mouth to her outthrust chin, took in her dark-smudged eyes and tangled hair, and settled on her forehead where she sported a goose egg, shot through with purple.

She'd never looked so beautiful.

"It won't work, Laura. *We* won't work. As soon as you're ready, I'll take care of your car or drive you to Boulder, if nec—"

"Hush." Stretching on tiptoe, she laid one slender finger across his lips, and in the same instant let the blanket slide to the floor. A twist of her body and she leaned against him, arms locked around his neck. Her breasts, through the sheer fabric of her blouse, clung to his chest, and her sweetly curved hips—

Connor groaned with frustration as his body, in flagrant disobedience to his commands, responded. His arms encircled her of their own volition and dragged her close to press against his sudden hardness. For three days he'd ached with the loneliness of their separation, and now that ache assumed colossal proportions as he envisioned the future without her. Mindful of her injury, he gently cupped her face and dipped his head to allow himself one last taste of her honey-scented mouth.

A kiss of goodbye.

A kiss that threatened to go on forever.

Why was it so difficult to do what was best for both of them?

Though his senses protested, he finally released her lips and stepped away. He drew a steadying breath. Next, he retrieved the discarded blanket from the floor and offered it to her silently.

Laura shook her head. "I'm warm enough."

She took a step forward, the look in her eyes a serious threat to Connor's resolve. He yielded ground. She glided nearer, and again he retreated.

If he weren't so determined on what he had to do, he might have laughed. She was stalking him—a magnificent, primitive goddess bent on seduction. As it was, he felt closer to tears than laughter.

Wadding the rejected blanket between his fists to prevent himself from giving in again to temptation, he halted and glared. "Enough, Laura. It's time to quit playing."

Playing!

Rage churned in Laura's chest at his patronizing tone. After all she'd gone through, he was treating her like some vacuous teenager who only needed a firm hand to straighten up. "Do you think I walked heaven knows how far and nearly froze to death for the fun of it? Do you think staying here when you've made it perfectly clear that you want me gone is some kind of a game?" She tossed her head and gave him glare for glare. "Think again!"

As they stood there, nose to nose—or as close to it they could get separated by six inches of height—Laura could have sworn she saw a glint of admiration in his eyes. But she must have imagined it because an instant later, he sighed heavily, ceding her the point.

"Okay, it's not a game. But it's no use. Accept it."

As quickly as it had flared, her anger ebbed away, replaced by cold, icy certainty. He was giving up. Without a word of regret, without even a struggle, he was throwing away everything they'd shared. She squinted to make out his expression, but the fire was behind him, casting his face into shadow.

"I can't," she whispered.

With an oath Connor flung the blanket at the couch.

Laura felt the breeze of its passing and flinched at the gesture of violence but held her ground, afraid that a sign of weakness would lose her the battle.

Sliding one hand into her pants pocket, she touched the worry stone.

The fire crackled.

Outside, a tree branch scraped against the cabin.

Connor crossed to the kitchen and removed something from the backpack on the counter. "Here. Put these on."

Reflexively, she reached out and caught the soft bundle he tossed. Socks?

He rummaged beneath the sink and pulled out a pair of hiking boots. "They're a little big, but if you lace them tight..." When she made no move to take them from his outstretched hand, he set them on the kitchen table and turned to stare into the darkness outside the window.

It was over. Whether she loved him or not made no difference. He wouldn't budge. His blasted rules meant more to him than she did.

A notion, elusive and out of focus, nudged her. She strained to capture it, but it skittered away, just out of reach.

His rules?

No.

Sighing, she relaxed her concentration, and in that instant the thought sharpened and took form. This wasn't a battle over rules. In truth, it never had been. All along their struggle had been over something entirely different. Connor didn't dread losing his nerve; he feared the loss of control he associated with love and commitment. For him, loving meant giving someone the power to hurt him the way Meg had.

At any other time, Laura might have used sympathy and reason, but not now. Not when it was she Connor didn't trust. And not when his fears were destroying their chance for happiness.

For the second time that evening, Laura allowed rage to overcome her better judgment. Grabbing his sleeve, she demanded his attention. "You're lying. Not to me. To yourself. You're hiding behind your job, behind your blessed duty, because you're afraid I'll hurt you. Like Meg did."

Connor's lips thinned and his eyes went steel blue. Beneath the soft cotton of his shirtsleeve, she felt his muscles tense but was too angry to care. Recklessly, she plunged on. "I'm here to speak a hard truth, Mac." Her tone made his nickname an insult. "Meg didn't love you. If she had, she couldn't have done what she did. She didn't love you, but *I* do."

His jaw frozen in rigid lines, he stared at her—no, through her. As though she were some kind of lower life form, unworthy of his notice, Laura thought. Her anger faded. Connor's expression made her want to run, to find a place where she could curl up and nurse her bruised heart. She had failed, and defeat sat in her stomach like the aftermath of a greasy meal.

She sank onto a kitchen chair and reached for the socks, blinking hard to prevent tears from falling. Why couldn't Connor understand that to win love, you had to be willing to relinquish control, to trust enough to say, My future is in your hands.

Her fingers halted in the act of pulling the bootlaces taut, as the truth, like a streak of heat lightning on a summer afternoon, seared white-hot across her consciousness. She couldn't expect more of him than of herself. If she wanted him to trust, she had to also. She couldn't just mouth platitudes; she had to be willing to accept the consequences, whatever they might be.

Could she do it?

Fear clogged her lungs like a swirling blanket of moisture-laden air, making it difficult to breathe. What if he still turned away?

Trembling with indecision, she cut him a glance.

And knew she couldn't let it end without trying.

Whether he admitted it or not, he was hurting as badly as she. Maybe he would scorn her efforts, but if he did, she'd be no worse off than she was now.

Squaring her shoulders, she stood and slid her fingers deep in her pocket, praying that the amber would cast its spell and steady her erratic heartbeat. Instead, it lay cold and leaden within her grasp. She stepped closer to Connor and extended the talisman. "Here. Take it back. It's no good for me anymore."

Confusion flickered through Connor's brain as she returned his gift. He stared at it. For some reason, probably due to the heat of her hand, it burned in his open palm when it reflected the flickering firelight. Magic, she'd called it once, but Connor was afraid to believe in magic, just as he was afraid to believe in love.

"If you want me to go, look me in the eye and tell me you don't love me. I won't stay."

He lifted his gaze from the stone and struggled to mouth the words that would set her free—I don't love you. So simple.

A band of pain constricted his chest.

He couldn't do it.

Looking into her eyes was like looking in a mirror. From their depths, he saw the reflection of his own love shining back.

The band tightened.

Was she right? After all this time, was he still giving Meg the power to destroy him?

Glancing back at the glittering stone, he suddenly saw the long, empty years ahead—the way they would be if he sent Laura away—and he knew he wouldn't be able to endure them.

In the long run, maybe love, like magic, was a matter of faith. And maybe it was time to let himself believe.

Encircling her wrist, he turned her palm up and returned the amber, gently closing her fingers around it. "You keep it. You're all the magic I need."

He pulled her close and laid his cheek against the tangle of her hair, breathing in her scent, while her arms slipped around his waist. He stroked her back, felt her soften against him. Healing warmth stole through him as he realized that only with Laura was he complete.

The band around his chest loosened . . .

"I love you."

. . . and fell away.

Like magic.

Like love.

* * * * *

Take 4 bestselling love stories FREE

Plus get a FREE surprise gift!

Special Limited-time Offer

Mail to Silhouette Reader Service™

3010 Walden Avenue
P.O. Box 1867
Buffalo, N.Y. 14269-1867

YES! Please send me 4 free Silhouette Intimate Moments® novels and my free surprise gift. Then send me 6 brand-new novels every month, which I will receive months before they appear in bookstores. Bill me at the low price of $2.89 each plus 25¢ delivery and applicable sales tax, if any.* That's the complete price and—compared to the cover prices of $3.50 each—quite a bargain! I understand that accepting the books and gift places me under no obligation ever to buy any books. I can always return a shipment and cancel at any time. Even if I never buy another book from Silhouette, the 4 free books and the surprise gift are mine to keep forever.

245 BPA ANRR

Name	(PLEASE PRINT)	
Address	Apt. No.	
City	State	Zip

This offer is limited to one order per household and not valid to present Silhouette Intimate Moments® subscribers. *Terms and prices are subject to change without notice.
Sales tax applicable in N.Y.

UMOM-94R   ©1990 Harlequin Enterprises Limited

ROMANTIC
TRADITIONS

Barbara Faith heats up ROMANTIC TRADITIONS in July with DESERT MAN, IM #578, featuring the forever-sultry sheikh plot line.

Josie McCall knew better than to get involved with Sheikh Kumar Ben Ari. Worlds apart in thought and custom, both suspected their love was destined for failure. Then a tribal war began, and Josie faced the grim possibility of losing her desert lover—for good.

October 1994 will feature Justine Davis's LEFT AT THE ALTAR, her timely take on the classic story line of the same name. And remember, ROMANTIC TRADITIONS will continue to bring you the best-loved plot lines from your most-cherished authors, so don't miss any of them—only in INTIMATE MOMENTS®

Silhouette®